Laughter in the Canyon

October 2008

To Diane + Eddie:

Enjoy the Journey!

Laughter
in the Canyon

⁂

With Love!

Laura Thompson

LAUGHTER IN THE CANYON

Published by
South Street Press
8 Southern Court
South Street
Reading
RG1 4QS
UK

Copyright © Laura Thompson, 2007

All rights reserved.
No part of this book may be reproduced in any form or by
any electronic or mechanical means, including information
storage and retrieval systems, without permission in writing
from the publisher, except by a reviewer who may quote
brief passages in a review.

First Edition

ISBN-13: 978-1-85964-193-4

British Library Cataloguing-in-Publication Data
A catalogue record for this book is available from the British Library

Typeset by Samantha Barden
Jacket design by Claire Coxon

Printed by Biddles, UK

*For my late, beloved father, James R. Thompson,
who taught me to have a sense of humour*

*For my mother, Mary Ann, who brought me into this
interesting world that has been a journey of living and
learning with the spirit of adventure*

*For my dearest friend, Ali Ghandour, who encouraged me
and guided me to finish this story*

A River Flows

I have a dream.
One day,
The Tree of Knowledge,
Portraying evil from good,
Shall cease to exist.
Everything is neither good nor bad.
The serpent shall have crept back into the Earth,
Erasing rivalry, fear and terror from Mankind.
Earth becomes a place of plenty.
Trust unveils itself upon the lands.
People act in unity within diversity.
The Creed of Fraternity embraces Liberty.

Contents

ACKNOWLEDGMENTS ix

PROLOGUE
Flight of Fancy xi

PART I
BORN AGAIN

CHAPTER 1
Life's a Jungle 3

CHAPTER 2
City of Lights 9

CHAPTER 3
En route 25

CHAPTER 4
Changes 41

CHAPTER 5
Rhythms and Sounds 47

CHAPTER 6
Search for Enlightenment 65

Part II
Magic and Adventure

Chapter 7
Astrological Predictions — 87

Chapter 8
Meaningful Coincidences — 95

Chapter 9
Mythical Love — 109

Chapter 10
Rugged Adventure — 127

Chapter 11
Mystical Encounter — 153

Epilogue
Past-Life Regression — 167

Acknowledgments

I would like to acknowledge all those people who have helped me along in my literary pursuits. You know who you are.

I have been blessed with beautiful friends who have always believed in me even during my darkest moments in life. I thank them for their loving support.

To South Street Press, Emma Hawker, previous Editorial Manager, who accepted my manuscript, then passed over the project to the current Editorial Manager, Dan Nunn, who has completed this project. I appreciate his hard work and kindness, including all the effort from his team on all aspects of publishing this book. In addition, I'd like to thank Claire Coxon for the cover illustration and design.

For my close personal friend, Ali Ghandour, who believed in me from the very beginning. I couldn't have done it without him and am blessed with his loving presence in my life. Thank you for coming into my life and making it more meaningful for me.

Finally, I wish all of you the best.

Prologue
Flight of Fancy

Cambridge, Massachusetts

Two students, a man and a woman, sat together holding hands on a grassy bank next to the Charles River. Along with hundreds of other students, they watched the crewmen get into their starting positions. It was the annual Harvard v. Princeton regatta. The race was broadcast over loudspeakers. The young man, Adrian Johnson, wore a Harvard T-shirt, blue jeans, loafers and no socks. His girlfriend, Diana Brigham, was similarly clad but instead of a T-shirt wore a beige sweater with a crimson 'H' on the front.

As the students cheered, Adrian jumped up and took pictures of the regatta and some snaps of Diana as she posed in both serious and silly ways. Diana reached into her knapsack, pulled out a cassette and popped it into her portable stereo player – Edith Piaf's 'La Vie en Rose'. Adrian stopped taking photos, sat next to Diana and put his arm around her. They sang to each other along with the music.

Adrian looked into Diana's eyes, stopped singing and said in his charming South African accent, 'You've brought the sunshine into my life.'

He leaned over and kissed her on the lips while everyone around them celebrated Harvard's victory, waving miniature crimson flags and dancing arm in arm. Diana's best friend, Cecilia, walked by and told her companion that Diana and Adrian were the hottest item on campus. Diana, unaware of her friend's presence, continued kissing Adrian.

The crowd was shouting, 'Harvard, Harvard, Harvard.'

Adrian fumbled in his pocket and took out a small, red Cartier box. He handed it to Diana. She opened it and saw a three stone princess-cut ring made of emeralds, her favourite. A tear of happiness trickled down her cheek and her hands trembled.

Adrian helped slip the ring on her finger and said, 'The three stones represent our past, present and future.'

Diana, who had only lived in the States since she was a teenager and never truly lost her British accent, whispered, 'You're so beautiful.'

For these two butterfly lovers, a moment of silence reigned amidst the commotion of celebration.

Adrian cupped Diana's hands in his and said, 'Do you know, ever since I met you, my dream has always been to marry you at Eagle Rock.'

'Where, sweetheart?'

'It's in the Grand Canyon.'

'Darling, I don't know how my family will react to a non-traditional wedding. I'll have to see it.'

'Diana, we're living in different times now.'

'I know, OK. I'll ask my father if we can use his plane and go out there for a few days.'

He took her hand again and guided her up so she stood beside him. 'When we're at the top of the canyon, I want to hold you tightly and laugh.'

'Imagine the echo of our laughter.'

The couple left the festive atmosphere early. He drove her home in his white 1952 Austin Healey. During the ride, from the Harvard campus over the Charles Bridge towards Mount Vernon Street on Beacon Hill, their hair blew wildly around their faces. Through the thick strands of her wavy, chestnut hair, Diana admired her engagement ring.

* * *

As Diana and Adrian entered the living room, Diana's mother, Lady Brigham, was playing on the grand piano while her husband sat next to her singing, 'Fly Me to the Moon'.

Diana danced up to her mother and father and showed them the ring. Lady Brigham stopped playing and looked back and forth between her daughter and Adrian. She stood up from the piano and hugged Diana.

Sir Brigham, dressed in a maroon velvet smoking-jacket, walked slowly over to Adrian.

Adrian extended his hand. 'May I ask for your daughter's hand in marriage, sir?'

Sir Brigham raised an eyebrow and scratched his left cheek. 'It looks as if it's already been decided. But I do have one condition: you have to promise me that you and Diana will stop involving yourselves in those anti-apartheid demonstrations. Once you marry her, your revolutionary days are over.'

Adrian drew back his hand. 'How did you know?'

'It doesn't matter. Do I have your word?'

His shoulders slumped. 'You know how important freedom and justice are to us. We only believe . . .'

Sir Brigham took the cigar he was smoking out of his mouth and puffed rings of smoke right into Adrian's face.

Adrian coughed and said, 'Yes, sir. I promise.'

With that, Sir Brigham shook hands with Adrian and welcomed him into his new family. Lady Brigham rang a tiny golden bell. Shortly afterwards, the butler served champagne and toasts were made. Lady Brigham returned to the piano while her husband resumed his place next to her. Diana and Adrian sipped champagne, chatted quietly with one another and listened to the joyful music.

Harvard Commencement Exercises

Thousands of students, undergraduates and graduates, dressed in caps and gowns, were gathered in front of the university hall grouped according to their school. Diana and Adrian proceeded to their seats in the centre, right in front of the platform and sat next to each other. Parents, family and friends watched the academic parade from the back rows. Once the students were seated, the president's procession advanced to the platform.

The band played the traditional brass fanfare for Harvard's president, who sat in a Jacobean chair. After the invocation, the commencement choir intoned an anthem. By the end of the anthem the students had become restless and started waving small crimson flags. In addition, the business students fluttered fake dollar bills in their hands high up in the air, the law school students waved plastic sharks, the government students held small globes and the education students carried books. Adrian snapped a shot of Diana shaking her shark by its tail. They laughed and kissed each other.

The buzz continued until the commencement speeches began. First, an undergraduate who spoke about the leadership qualities necessary to bring the world out of the Cold War, then a speech by a graduate student who addressed the power of purpose. Afterwards, a trustee of Harvard University delivered his speech in Latin in accordance with the traditions of the honourable and ancient institution. The audience applauded at the end of his discourse when he expressed the hope that the great intellectual heritage of Harvard would help each graduate to contribute positively to society, both locally and globally. It was time to confer degrees. The president rose from his carved chair, stepped forward and delivered a different pronouncement for each school. Diana and Adrian rose with their law school colleagues. Adrian squeezed Diana's hand.

Nearly two hours later all degrees were bestowed. The audience stood and sang the Harvard hymn in Latin and the ceremony finished with a benediction by an African–American minister. The band played the recessional, and then the students stood, cheered and once again waved their various paraphernalia. Diana and Adrian hugged each other.

Later, the couple met up with their respective families. Sir Brigham, himself a distinguished graduate of Cambridge University, was immensely proud of his only child graduating from this prestigious university. He whispered to her that she could use his plane for a few days with Adrian to visit the Grand Canyon and choose a spot for her wedding. Diana buried her head in her father's big chest and wept tears of happiness.

Day of Departure

Both families were present and all bid their farewells on the tarmac to Diana and Adrian. The brand-new Gulfstream jet took off from Boston to

Flight of Fancy

fly to the Grand Canyon and land on its small, dirt runway. Sir Brigham had participated in the decision-making on the interior design of his plane with a top designer. There were eight spacious beige leather chairs for the passengers with a built-in bar made out of black and beige buffalo horn. At the rear of the aircraft was a leather couch which turned into a bed at the push of a button. A royal blue curtain separated this section of the plane from the forward cabin. Diana's father's tastes were impeccable. Diana and Adrian waved their final goodbyes through the tiny windows as the plane ascended into the deep blue sky.

Diana asked the cabin attendant, 'After take-off, would you open a bottle of Dom Perignon and bring us two glasses?'

The attendant conservatively dressed in a navy blue suit, nodded her head in agreement.

Twenty minutes into the flight, the champagne and glasses were brought to Diana and Adrian, who were now sitting on the couch. Diana said to the attendant, 'We'd like to relax now; we'll call you if we need anything.'

As the cabin attendant walked away to sit near the front, Diana stood up and closed the curtain. She pushed the button that turned the couch into a bed, it was not much bigger than the couch but large enough for two people to lie horizontally.

Adrian poured the light, golden, bubbling liquid into the crystal flutes and made a toast: 'To the woman of my dreams!'

They clinked glasses, took a sip then intertwined their arms to sip from each other's glass to form a bond. Diana murmured, 'To eternal love.'

The champagne quickly made the pair light headed – at 32,000 feet alcohol can hit you twice as hard.

After one glass, Diana unwrapped Adrian's white silk scarf from his neck while he took off his navy blazer. He often wore this scarf while flying to protect his sensitive throat from the air conditioning. The sleeve of his blazer caught the champagne flute and it fell to the floor, shattering in the aisle.

'That's good luck,' Diana said.

Adrian made the first move and embraced her tightly. She felt something hard as steel below his belt buckle. He trembled with love, kissed her passionately and gently bit the back of her neck under her soft, silky hair leaving tiny red marks. Moving downwards, he pulled her V-neck jersey to one side and suckled on her soft, pink nipple.

Diana's breasts tingled. Adrian's legs became weak and he pulled her down with him to sit on the soft leather bed. She manoeuvred herself to sit on Adrian's legs and unbuttoned his blue-and-white-striped Oxford shirt. They sipped more champagne from one glass. Adrian squirmed in his seat ready to explode like a volcano. She unzipped his trousers and nervously caressed him under his black underwear. New sensations rippled throughout her body. Adrian pushed up Diana's skirt and then pulled her silk pink panties to one side and guided her on top of him. He pumped his hips upwards and backwards a few times like a gentle, rolling wave. They both felt as though they were in heaven.

When he became conscious again after what seemed an endless minute, Diana whispered into his left ear, 'I hope we're together for ever.'

'For ever and ever.'

After making love, they fell asleep for a few hours in each other's arms.

Upon awakening, Adrian, the more experienced, realized Diana hadn't achieved any prolonged pleasure. He kissed her drowsy eyes and gently, glided deep into her warmth one more time. They were a perfect fit and this time Diana shivered as she gazed into Adrian's eyes and kissed his dark, rosy lips. Passion consumed their hearts and, with moderate turbulence shaking the plane, they held on to each other tighter than ever before. Droplets of perspiration clung to their bodies. Neither of them had imagined it could be this beautiful.

Adrian clasped his strong, lean arms around Diana's soft, voluptuous body and said, 'It's impossible not to love you.'

The Gulfstream jet was now flying over the West Rim of the Grand Canyon.

Captain Jones announced over the loudspeaker, 'Hey kids, look out of the window and see where you're getting married.'

Diana and Adrian stopped their lovemaking and turned their heads to see Eagle Rock. It was a magnificent eagle with a wing span of hundreds of feet carved into the cliffs of the Grand Canyon.

Diana exclaimed, 'Oh darling, it's amazing!' She kissed him on his forehead, then on his half-closed eyes. The plane shook and rattled. They both jolted upright on the bed and quickly dressed. The captain announced that they should fasten their seatbelts and Diana pushed the button to turn the bed back into a couch.

'I hate turbulence,' she said.

'Don't worry,' Adrian replied. 'The hot air rising always causes air pockets over the canyon in the afternoon.'

The attendant opened the curtain and warned them to keep their seatbelts fastened. Adrian took Diana's hand into his and wrapped his arm round her shoulders. She was just snuggling her head on his chest when the plane took a sudden dip to one side and slid diagonally through the air.

They heard Captain Jones screaming inside the cockpit, 'Mayday! Mayday! Right engine fire. Can't extinguish it. Fire spreading to cabin . . . Need immediate clearance for emergency landing. Losing altitude, losing altitude, losing altitude . . . Plane uncontrollable.'

Diana screamed hysterically, 'What's happening?'

'I don't know.' Adrian was gasping for breaths of air.

Suddenly, after a moment of panic, Diana felt internally calm. 'I'll always be the woman of your dreams,' she said.

Adrian, also in an altered state of mind, said, 'Remember my white silk scarf.'

'What—'

'Destiny shall reunite us.'

They gasped again for air. They kissed each other and wept until, with the loss of cabin pressure, they passed out.

Inside the cockpit, Captain Jones continued in a strained, crackling tone, 'We're crashing one mile south of the Grand Canyon airport. We're crashing, we're crashing, we're crashing . . .' And then, in a sobbing voice, he cried, '. . . Goodnight.'

King's Chapel

In downtown Boston, bells chimed. A joint Anglican memorial service honoured Diana Brigham and Adrian Johnson in the ancient, stone church. A few designated family members made loving tributes that at times brought a few smiles to those sitting in the pews. Diana's best friend, Cecilia, wrote a special poem about the angelic love that existed between the two forsaken souls.

Cecilia ended her poem: 'I'm not a poet, but I hear the hidden music in their souls. Diana and Adrian travelled many roads together and, hopefully, they have now found eternal love.'

A Higher Dimension

Spectacular clouds in bright orange, yellow, red and blue surrounded the spirits of Diana and Adrian. The spirits looked like two separate translucent, swirling white balls of energy. Diana and Adrian didn't understand what had happened. They were physically dead yet their spirits were alive and they could feel each other's presence much stronger than on Earth. Diana learned all the secrets of the universe in an instant of time.

What takes years on Earth to learn takes only seconds here, she thought.

The two white balls of energy fused and became one. They were soulmates who had been created from one universal essence, but to experience life on Earth their souls had had to split: one to represent masculine energy, the other feminine. It had been their divine choice. Peace and unconditional love embraced the essence of their hearts.

The sorrowful emotions of their families separated their souls and pulled them back to Earth. The two spirits gazed at the funeral rites that took place not only for themselves but also for the pilots and the cabin attendant with their respective families and friends. Despite the sadness and death that surrounded those on Earth, Adrian and Diana did not feel death, only the lightness of being of their spirits. Unexpectedly, another swirling, brilliant blue ball of energy appeared, assigned to guide these two souls through their new cycle of life. Beginnings and ends in the universe were never ending.

Remarkably, Diana and Adrian heard this blue ball of energy speak and realized they could also talk. The tones of their voices sounded like music coming from violins. The two spirits departed with their guardian spirit, an angel who called himself Michel, who liked being reincarnated in France. He joked with his new initiates and told them that after seven hundred lives in France he still couldn't get it right.

Michel greeted his little angels Diana and Adrian, 'Bonjour, mes petits anges, allons-y.'

Diana and Adrian asked in unison: 'Where are we going?'

Michel replied, 'Back to Earth to fulfil your destiny.'

Adrian said, 'My head's spinning. I'm here. I'm there. Diana and I are somewhere, floating in the cosmos with you, Michel, where everything seems timeless . . .'

Michel interrupted, 'Remember Einstein's Theory of Relativity? His theory correctly postulated that there's no such thing as absolute time ticking uniformly throughout the cosmos. The reason you're confused is because on Earth, gravity slows time. Here, there's no gravity. You can simultaneously be in the past, present and future, because of warped passages in time. Physicists and mathematicians on Earth are discovering these extra dimensions or passages, however, their theories are still missing a few components. Mes petits anges, you can't know everything about everything.'

Diana asked, 'But what's this got to do with us?'

'Everything, my dear one. You're alive now in our higher dimension but soon you will return to Earth and live in yet another dimensional reality. Life in the universe is never ending with constant change. On Earth, you have the cycle of birth, growth, decay, death and rebirth too. But be clear that although matter changes into another form, the essence of your soul remains.'

Adrian sighed, 'Where are we going?'

Bells chimed, signalling to Michel that his mission was nearly over.

Michel replied, 'Adrian, it's your turn to go. You're about to be reborn again. Your poetic, philosophical and revolutionary spirit will give meaning and light to millions of people in a region rampant with conflict and corruption.'

'What about me?' asked Diana.

'Ah! Why, of course, you'll be born in the City of Lights, considered a centre of Enlightenment and one of the happiest places on Earth. The French connection is the reason I was assigned to both you and Adrian. Mon petit ange, your life shall be calmer than Adrian's but your mission will be the search for truth, identifying simplicity as a clue. And, you'll be innately driven to find your soulmate who was Adrian in this past life of yours. Why do you think you felt so good when you were together? Because you have known each other since the beginning of time and have been with each other in various guises and forms all over the universe.'

'Why don't people on Earth remember these passages of existence?' Diana asked.

Michel replied, 'Some do. Others know it in their souls but then, when this knowledge isn't nurtured by the family or society, they forget. Most of you are too busy to take the time and reflect upon your true origins, thus, you forget about your spiritual roots. The Indian civilization is an exception that comes to mind. The Hindu religion, for example, maintains the belief in the cycle of reincarnation.'

Adrian interrupted, 'I'm not leaving without Diana. I don't want to be separated from her ever again.'

Michel replied, 'In spirit form, you're always together, whether it's through a thought, a dream or a vision. You'll meet again on Earth's physical plane. Meaningful, coincidental events shall lead both of you together in a very exotic place. Trust in the process of the universe.'

Adrian's rational brain still dominated his spiritual essence, and he was unable to fully understand the knowledge that Michel imparted to him.

'Adrian, rest assured that when Diana comes back into your life, you'll know that something special exists between you, even if you think it's irrational. Diana will help and guide you along the spiritual path because throughout most of her incarnations she has always been more open and tuned in to our angelic world. Or maybe it'll be you this time who is more intuitive, and you'll be the one to guide her, based on all of your acquired experience, wisdom and maturity. We'll see. Remember, you will be another human being, no longer Adrian, and Diana will be another person. You'll both look different in your new life form. That's the rule of the game. Now, your time is up.'

As Adrian departed, he cried out, 'I love you. I love you. I love you.'

'I love you, too,' said Diana, with a pang in her heart.

'For ever and ever,' trailed Adrian's voice, spiralling down into some kind of psychedelic tunnel.

Diana was sad to see her cherished friend leave, although she knew in her heart and soul that they would meet again under extraordinary circumstances.

'Diana, it's your turn to return to Earth. Remember, your quest is to seek the truth and share the fruits of your research with your fellow human beings. Oh, one more thing. Don't worry. You too, just like Adrian, will be protected throughout your entire life by your loving, spiritual guides throughout the good, the bad and the sad periods.'

Diana was upset. 'The bad, the sad . . . What do you mean?'

Michel cut her off abruptly. 'See the glass as half full. Be courageous and adventurous, even during the most difficult of times. Know that you are always protected by us. Au revoir, mon petit ange!'

'Goodbye, Michel.'

'Have faith!'

The bells tolled to celestial music.

Michel rejoiced, 'I've completed another mission. These two enlightened souls have embarked on their chosen path. They'll become a natural beacon of light to others.'

He took flight and looked like a little blue fairy flying through billions of bright stars. Strains of music danced on the wind under the dark, blue starlit sky. Diana and Adrian had been guided towards their mysterious destiny at the right time and in the right place.

PART ONE

BORN AGAIN

Chapter 1

Life's a Jungle

Damascus, 1991

A burst of machine gun bullets bombarded a metallic green Mercedes 500 SEL on the road to the airport. Inside there was a chauffeur and a man sitting in the back seat. The chauffeur was hit in the arm but instinctively swerved out of the gunmen's range; his boss miraculously escaped the shower of bullets. The car was full of bullet holes. The man the hired assassins were after was Sami Shami. Sami, short for Samir, was in his late-twenties, tall, slender, well-built, with beautiful chestnut-coloured hair and hazel eyes that complimented his fair complexion. The governmental authorities had been told that he was responsible for the failed coup d'état that had occurred a week before in Damascus.

At his alma mater, Stanford University, Sami was known to be a political activist, who often made speeches about freedom and democracy. In one speech, he had boldly denounced the dictatorial regime in Syria that had been in power throughout most of the latter half of the twentieth century. As a teenager growing up in Syria, Sami became part of a movement that led to the creation of a Democratic–Socialist Party that advocated secularism, freedom and democracy. He was seen as a poet and a philosopher, filled with dreams of changing the political regime in the Middle East to one modelled on Great Britain's monarchical governmental system. Yet, despite his youthful revolutionary reputation, Sami had not been active in the Party since his college days in the States. The Syrian authorities had failed to uncover this truth in their fact-finding mission and falsely accused him of orchestrating the failed coup d'état. The government wanted a fall guy and issued a warrant to capture him. Sami was in the wrong place at the wrong time. From the day the warrant was issued, Sami became the most wanted man in Syria, with the highest ransom ever to be paid if caught dead or alive.

Sami had taken a chance in returning to Damascus, still considered a heavy-handed police state, but his mother missed him and had insisted that he visit the family while on sabbatical from his assistant professorship at Princeton University. Sami was travelling around the Middle East to study and research the Phoenician civilization for his new book so that he could attain full professorship. He hadn't seen his mother since he left Damascus at the age of nineteen, nearly ten years earlier. He was very happy to have seen his mother, father, brother, sisters, cousins, and friends while back home. Sami had been on his way from his parent's home to the airport where a private plane was waiting for him to take him to Beirut, another important city for the study of phoenician history.

After the assault on Sami's car, the chauffeur sped to the airport. The pilots waited for Sami, unaware of the attempted assassination. The car's special licence plates allowed the chauffeur to drive onto the airport runway right up to the plane. Sami jumped out of the bullet-ridden vehicle. He ran across the tarmac and climbed up the steps three at a time to board the plane, then yelled to the pilot to take off. The flight attendant scrambled to close the door as the plane taxied down the runway. Sami thought fast and decided the best way to disappear would be to go to Africa. He instructed the pilot to take him to Sierra Leone. The captain protested until Sami said that he would take care of all the expenses: this was a life or death situation. The plane lifted off as the army tanks rolled on to the tarmac. No exchange of artillery fire took place. Little did Sami know that his ordeal would last another nine years.

Sierra Leone

After a few phone calls and many hours later, the French ambassador to Sierra Leone, along with his assistant, greeted Sami at the airport terminal. His Excellency had become friends with Sami's father years ago while attending the private, boarding school, Le Rosey, in Switzerland. Sami was grateful to see his father's friend and hugged him. The assistant cleared his throat and told Sami that he had to hide in the jungle until his identity papers, notably his name, address and nationality, could be changed. His real name could no longer be revealed, so as to neither endanger his family, nor alert the authorities in Damascus. Sami told them he had prepared for this eventuality while en route in the plane and had already selected a new name – Mounir Munir. The ambassador smiled, knowing that the name of Mounir meant 'the person who gives light'. The falsifying of his papers for his protection would take about three weeks.

For security reasons, the ambassador put him up with a trusted young man, John Townsend, who was the son of another dear friend from Le Rosey. The alumni of this school, no matter where one was in the world, always helped out when the need arose. Only a few months ago, the ambassador had arranged for John to come and study a hidden tribe in the forest for his Ph.D. thesis. During this time John had built a hut near the tribe and had become physically fit through living in the jungle.

The ambassador's assistant unthinkingly introduced Sami Shami to John. Sami stepped up to John and said, 'There's been a mistake. My name is Mounir Munir. Pleased to meet you.'

John subconsciously noted the name change but never questioned why the ambassador would send this man to live with him for a short time in this obscure habitat. He didn't really care about the reasons; he had become lonely observing this indigenous tribe and the prospect of having someone to chat with about everyday things thrilled him.

During the three weeks, with John's help, Mounir learned the ways of the native Africans. The natives lived primitively in the open air and, depending on the occasion, walked around nude or with a minimal amount of clothing. It was a self-sufficient tribe and practised polygamy as a means of procreation and survival. They were hunters and gatherers as well as farmers. Roots were one of the main staples of their diets. As a tribe, they would go together and play and swim in the streams like children. Everyone was nude while swimming, with no inhibitions. Mounir was shocked by some of their habits and customs. Likewise, the natives thought that the customs of the foreigners seemed strange. Furthermore, though Mounir and John were considered handsome in their own social circles, the tribe thought the contrary. Used to John, but still curious about the stranger, some of the young girls would make clicking sounds with their mouths whenever Mounir walked by, who by now sported a big, bushy beard and moustache that covered his whole face. Only his large, hazel, intelligent eyes could be clearly seen. Facial hair was not considered beautiful by the local tribe. In fact, the natives were hairless except for the artistically designed hair on their heads. Out of respect for the tribal chief and his clan, John asked Mounir to keep his distance from them and accept their ways of life as a natural means to survive in the jungle. Overall, they lived together in harmony.

One morning, Mounir was thinking deeply about his dilemma. He had to notify Princeton that he couldn't return because his life was under threat. He wrote a letter to the president explaining what had happened to him while on sabbatical, and that he hoped to return one day. After he sealed the envelope, he tried to figure out what to do to stay alive. He knew the United States would grant him political asylum with the right to stay under his real name but that avenue didn't guarantee any protection. On the contrary, there were many informers in the States and if he kept his real name he would be an open target: it would be easy to find him and assassinate him. He wouldn't be safe anywhere in the world as Samir Shami.

With all this in mind, Sami decided to stay on the run, under cover with his false identity 'Mounir Munir', until justice prevailed or the regime fell.

John walked by and asked, 'What's that?'

Mounir looked up. 'It's a very important letter. How can I get it mailed?'

'I'll find a way to get it to the ambassador for mailing.' Mounir handed over the letter to John who took it and put it safely in his pocket.

Mounir stood up and stretched, and then walked along the trails in the forest chatting with his new-found friend.

Mounir was a city boy and unused to the wilds, so John prepared the meals by picking fresh fruit, digging up roots and fishing in nearby streams. He cooked the food over an open fire. Sometimes, he drained syrup from a tree to make a drink that served as a natural form of alcohol for the natives. When anyone needed to feel happy, they drank this elixir.

Even in the jungle, man has figured out a way to get high, Mounir thought.

During one meal, John and Mounir talked about the differences between the natives and the civilized world. How could it be that man could be so different in his ways? While some, extremely primitive, didn't know what an aeroplane was, others, highly civilized, had landed on the moon. Mounir confided in John about what had happened in Damascus and emphasized his innocence.

'Do you think the Syrian regime will ever fall or be overthrown?' John asked.

'Right now, too much corruption, greed and lust for power exists in the hands of a few, who are backed by a strong military and police force. As soon as anyone speaks out against the regime, he's put in prison, disappears or is murdered. Many attempts have been made to overthrow the government but all have failed. The Syrian people want freedom of expression and democratic reform but are helpless. No one wants to help from the outside. Even the US wouldn't think of overthrowing the regime in its interest of promoting democracy because there's no oil.'

John patted Mounir lightly on the shoulder. 'Have hope. What your country needs is someone like Gandhi who can bring down an evil empire peacefully.'

'I hope you're right. What about you? What school are you preparing your thesis for?'

'Stanford.'

'No kidding. That's where I got mine in philosophy and mythology.'

Mounir started to reminisce about his student days and soon both were laughing, aided by a bit too much of the tree wine. Laughter was a temporary release from their serious conversation about world affairs.

A short distance away, the natives were performing a coming-of-age ritual for the young women. It was a female-dominated society. One fully-clothed adult woman wore a wooden mask that evoked beauty and prosperity for the newly initiated. This woman danced around as if she herself were hallucinating on secret potions until she was transformed into the spirit that would initiate these young women into womanhood and sexual maturity like the birthing of a beautiful butterfly. After the initiation was finished, she tripped and fell, damaging the mask. According to custom, she could not keep a cracked mask. It had to be either destroyed or given to a stranger. Then, the sorcerer leaped like a flame in close proximity to John and offered him the mask. He knew their rituals and accepted it graciously. Mounir felt as if he were dreaming.

John said, 'I'll give this to my sister. She's a great appreciator of art from around the world.'

Mounir was about to reply when they heard a jeep coming up the dirt trail that led to the village. It was the ambassador's assistant who came to interrupt John and Mounir's African paradise. He told them that Mounir's papers were in order and that he could now leave the country. Mounir was sad and happy at the same time but he knew that he couldn't hide in the jungle forever. He wished John success with his thesis and thanked him for his kind hospitality. 'I shall be forever grateful to you for the protection you have provided for me during this traumatic time in my life,' he continued.

'Thank the ambassador,' said John.

Mounir left with the ambassador's assistant down the bumpy dirt road as the rays of the sun glimmered through the trees.

Chapter 2
City of Lights

Paris, June 1996

Nicole and Marc-Antoine de Villiers waited in front of their house on Avenue de New York for their chauffeur to come and pick them up. Marc-Antoine's colleague was getting married and they were invited to the wedding reception at the Rodin Museum. Nicole was French–American. Her father was a self-made entrepreneur from Paris who had fallen in love with her American mother while studying at Stanford, both sides of the family having a long tradition of going to this university. Nicole's parents had settled in Paris and Marc-Antoine had adopted her family as his own when his Uncle Harry had passed away the previous year. Marc-Antoine had revealed a terrible secret to Nicole before asking her to marry him. He told her that his parents had committed suicide at the Hôtel Negresco in Nice. Nobody ever told him why. Uncle Harry, his mother's brother, and also a confirmed bachelor and playboy, raised him from the age of seven onwards. Nicole kept this secret to herself and told her family that his parents had died in a car crash. No further explanation was needed.

Nicole gazed at the massive, iron structure of the Eiffel Tower and watched the Bateaux Mouches glide up and down the Seine. The evening was warm and humid and the sun floated high in the sky. She loved these long summer days when the sun didn't set until eleven o'clock in the evening. She hummed the tune of 'I Love Paris in the Springtime' to herself until her thoughts were interrupted by the arrival of the car and they were whisked down the quai and over to the Rodin Museum by Invalides.

At the wedding reception, the many guests were greeting and congratulating the French groom with his six-foot Russian bride. A former model for the *haute couture* houses, she had long, blonde hair and blue eyes. In contrast, he was a short man with dark, olive-toned skin and black hair. He had made his fortune through the family's business in the luxury industry. After waiting in line for a few minutes, Nicole and Marc-Antoine had their picture taken with the bride and groom. Nicole looked small in comparison to the bride though she was actually about five foot seven inches with long, wavy, chestnut-coloured hair and big, beautiful amber eyes. Marc-Antoine resembled the groom except that he wore thin, round spectacles.

It was a black tie event and everyone was elegantly dressed. Nicole wore a strapless, pink taffeta dress designed by Ungaro, along with fine jewellery and her Judith Lieber clutch bag. Marc-Antoine sported the typical black tie attire with one exception: his buttons and cuff-links were made out of diamonds lined with black onyx – a fashionably chic statement in their social circle.

Before the formal dinner, guests roamed around the museum and admired Rodin's sculptures. Nicole subtly slipped away from Marc-Antoine, who was chatting with his business associates, and walked out of the building to meander through the gardens. It was still daylight. She sat on a concrete bench and admired *The Thinker* and the fragrant flowers before returning to the salons of the museum.

She entered the main salon through two enormous glass doors and turned left to walk into another large room. Her favourite sculpture, *The Kiss*, was located in the back of the room. She walked around it, examining it from all angles. Next, she viewed and admired *Eternal Springtime*, placed on the mantel. She moved to peer out through a large window overlooking the courtyard and garden. Her eyes followed a pathway that led from the house towards a circular path with a sculpture installed in the middle of a large round basin. To the right, the golden dome of Invalides glowed.

A blue-eyed blonde in her late-thirties came up from behind and tapped Nicole on the shoulder. Nicole jumped out of her reverie to greet one of her best friends, Celeste Magon, who was originally from Brittany but now lived with her husband, Arnauld, and their two children in Paris. The women kissed each other four times on the cheeks, starting with the left cheek, according to the Parisian greeting adopted years ago.

Celeste said, 'We're sitting at the same table.'

'Wonderful! We can catch up on each other's news.'

As the women walked back to the main salon, Celeste, who seemed abnormally jumpy, dropped her bag. As she picked it up, she asked Nicole, 'Have you seen Arnauld?'

'Look for Marc-Antoine. They always team up and chase beautiful women.'

Celeste left Nicole talking with other guests and eventually spied Arnauld putting his arm around a woman and kissing her on the cheek. The woman kissed Arnauld on the lips. Celeste walked boldly up to Arnauld and tugged on his arm. He pushed her away while the woman laughed. Distraught, Celeste ran crying into the nearby ladies' room.

Slowly, everyone gathered and went to their assigned tables, decorated with floral bouquets. Each guest found a little gift at their place setting to keep as a souvenir of the day. Nicole noticed that Celeste was missing from the table. When she did arrive, she greeted everyone with a kiss except Arnauld, who ignored her too. Celeste sat down, pushed her gift aside and hid her unhappiness throughout the festivities. This was supposed to be a happy occasion; it was not for her to ruin a beautiful party because of her bastard of a husband.

Meanwhile, Hungarian musicians walked around the tables and played gypsy music while the guests dined and raised their glasses to toast the bride and groom. When the musicians appeared at Nicole's table, they asked her what she'd like to hear them sing. Nicole blushed and asked for 'La Vie en Rose', one of her all-time favourite songs. The violinists played the song as she stared into space with a single tear rolling down her cheek. This song always moved her soul. She wiped her tear with her white linen napkin and smiled at the musicians. Everyone in the vicinity clapped and Marc-Antoine discreetly tipped the gypsies, who moved on to the next table. After several courses were served, it was time to cut the wedding cake. The waiters poured coffee and served the cake while some people started to trickle out quietly. Marc-Antoine leaned over, kissed Nicole and said, 'I'd like to go now. I have to get up early and fly to Monte Carlo.'

'I'm having such a good time. Can't we stay a bit longer?'

'I'm tired.'

Nicole kissed Celeste goodbye and noticed that she didn't seem to be her usual bright self but dismissed it thinking that she was probably preoccupied with her children. Nicole and Marc-Antoine headed out of the door. This was an evening that Nicole would remember.

Avenue Foch

In the salon of their lovely home, Arnauld was shouting at Celeste and accusing her of having an affair. Celeste stared at him in disbelief. Damn the nanny. Only once had she been with the gardener and the nanny had caught her, but what was one time compared to Arnauld's weekly affairs, each with a different woman? His actions were unbearable and at that time had driven her to satisfy a sexual need. She should have fired the nanny but she was so good with the kids. It must have been when the nanny slept with Arnauld that she had let out their secret. A rummaging sound in the side drawer of the Louis XVI desk aroused her. She walked towards Arnauld to calm him.

Arnauld pointed a pistol at her, his finger on the trigger. Celeste froze in her tracks. This act of jealousy bordered on insanity. A shot zinged through the silent air and grazed her head. A second shot hit her side below the stomach and she collapsed in a pool of blood. Arnauld screamed at her but to no avail. He put the pistol in his pocket, ran over to her and picked her up in his arms, before dropping her in horror. With blood dripping from his hands, he took out his pistol and pointed it at his temple.

Too late, the nanny arrived on the scene and dialled the emergency number. The children, David and Nathalie, who were six and four years old respectively, had been awakened by the gun shots and had run downstairs. David, not sure of what had happened, quickly covered his sister's eyes and brought her back to her sheltered, pink flowery bedroom. The nanny called Celeste's sister, Daniela, who lived nearby, and told her to go to the emergency room at the American hospital in Neuilly: Celeste and Arnauld had been in a terrible accident. A few more words were exchanged and the nanny agreed to stay at home with the children.

As Daniela arrived, she saw the medics cover Arnauld with a blue sheet and rush Celeste into the operating room. Hours later, nurses wheeled Celeste into the Intensive Care Unit. Daniela alternated between pacing up and down the corridors and sitting and praying until the surgeon, Dr Armstrong, came out with some news.

Dr Armstrong sat next to Daniela and told her that the operation had gone well. He had removed the bullet lodged near her stomach that had miraculously missed all of the major organs and the other bullet had only grazed her head. Celeste had miraculously survived physically. However, psychologically, she had experienced a near-fatal catastrophe and would no doubt need psychiatric treatment to make a full recovery.

Daniela cried and said, 'I knew something like this would happen one day. They were insanely jealous of one another.'

Dr Armstrong changed the subject, saying, 'She asked for you in German.'

'German? Celeste doesn't speak German. She's never even set foot in the country.'

The surgeon scratched his chin. 'It's a strange phenomenon, but we've documented many cases where patients speak other languages after having experienced acute trauma. We ask the family and they don't know how it's possible.'

'I certainly don't,' replied Daniela.

'One more thing – your sister spoke of medical procedures that only a surgeon would know about. Is she studying medicine?'

'She's a housewife, Dr Armstrong.'

'Why don't you go home and get some rest? You'll be able to see her tomorrow afternoon.'

Daniela called Nicole the following day and told her what had happened. Nicole went to the hospital that afternoon, by which time Celeste had been taken out of the ICU and could receive family and close friends. When Nicole entered the hospital room, Celeste was propped up, watching television. Nicole took her hand and held it the whole length of her visit.

Celeste looked at Nicole and said, 'I haven't told anyone this but when they were operating on me, I floated above my body and could see everything: the incisions the doctor made, the nurses chatting about one of their son's birthday party. Then, a translucent white angel came to me and said, "It's not your time yet. Your children need you . . ." and she floated away like a butterfly. I saw the flat line on the heart monitor and the doctor and nurses frantically trying to revive my heart. Somehow, I slipped back into my body and my heart started beating. That's all I can remember until waking up here.'

'Mon Dieu! That's incredible. I remember my mother telling me a similar story after her heart operation. Marc-Antoine and I were waiting outside her room and her heart stopped and the nurses and doctors ran into the room and wouldn't let us in while they revived her. She saw us sitting there, holding hands and wondering what was going on. She hadn't even known that we were there because we were early. When she told me the story, I shivered. I told Marc-Antoine months later and he sort of believed it.'

Celeste started sniffling.

Nicole kissed her on the forehead and said, 'The most important thing is that you're alive. I'm very sorry about Arnauld . . .'

The nurse came in and told them that visiting time was over. Nicole squeezed Celeste's hand as Celeste drifted off to sleep.

Small Chapel in Paris

About three days later, a memorial service was conducted by a priest. Many bouquets of flowers decorated the altar, along with a photo of Arnauld. Daniela gave a short eulogy because Celeste was too weak and had to sit in a wheelchair throughout the ceremony. The service lasted about an hour. Afterwards, family and friends followed the black hearse in their own cars to the cemetery. As the coffin was lowered into the ground the priest offered more prayers, while each willing person took a small shovel and scooped up earth to throw on top of the coffin in the grave.

Marc-Antoine had flown up from Monte Carlo for this solemn occasion and to support Nicole. Daniela had arranged for everyone to come over to Celeste's house for a light buffet dinner. It was the family's custom to always remember the good traits of the individual no matter how they had passed away. Some volunteered to tell stories with a humorous twist, which did lighten the dark mood. Nicole was gazing out the window and Marc-Antoine walked up to her and offered a glass of champagne that she gladly accepted.

Not looking at Marc-Antoine, she said, 'The more I live, the more I don't understand. Why do things like this happen?'

'Ma chérie, you shouldn't analyse life so much. Think of it as destiny. Fate intervened and cut his life short and saved Celeste. Why? I don't know. With hindsight, there's a reason for everything.'

Nicole insisted, 'But why are we all here and why do we exist? Is there life after death?'

Marc-Antoine replied sarcastically, 'Darling, I think you've drunk too much champagne. However, if I die first, I'll make a sign and you'll know it's me, and then your question will have been answered about life after death.'

'What kind of sign?'

'I'll come back as a chickadee!' he exclaimed.

Nicole laughed and Marc-Antoine shrugged his shoulders, shook his head and walked off to chat with the guests. She continued to gaze out of the window and heard light pellets of rain hit the foggy glass. When it was time to leave, Celeste told Nicole not to worry about her: her family would take care of her and the children until she could manage by herself. Nicole hugged Celeste, relieved to know that her family would be a source of strength, support and love.

Monte Carlo, Summer 1997

Nicole and Marc-Antoine divided their time between Paris, Monte Carlo and New York. In terms of her profession, people referred to Nicole as an angel investor and philanthropist. At the age of twenty-one, both she and her brother had inherited a fortune from their maternal grandfather, a successful inventor. Since then she had become an active board member for a foundation based in New York. As an angel investor, an activity that she shared with Marc-Antoine, she would provide seed capital to start up companies across all industries. Marc-Antoine was the financial genius in the family. Out of all their businesses, travel and tourism interested Nicole most and, as a result, they had invested in a couple of castles in France that eventually became part of the Relais and Châteaux chain – one in Normandy, one in the Loire Valley. The hospitality industry was a happy diversion for both of them but one where Nicole took the most responsibility for their portfolio.

It was fun decorating the castles and bringing in young creative chefs to establish fine restaurants. In the castle in Normandy, there was a room created for tasting Armagnac liqueur. At the castle in the Loire Valley, named Mont Joli, there was a magnificent wine cellar for sampling the wines of the region. Mont Joli itself was situated in the middle of a vineyard. In the summertime, Nicole loved to look at the luscious, leafy green vines. During the autumn harvest, she would walk and talk with the grape pickers down the narrow, dirt trails carved out between the cultivated vines. Peace and happiness reigned in her soul as she roamed this fertile land. Without a doubt, Nicole preferred the tranquil, rolling hills of the Loire Valley with its ancient history to the harsh weather of Normandy.

Marc-Antoine's own speciality was financing oil deals and bartering oil for sugar or other food products. For example, when Iran needed to sell its oil and South Africa needed to buy that particular type of crude oil but couldn't pay in hard currency, it supplied sugar as a means of payment. Marc-Antoine got a kick from dealing with rogue countries, such as Libya, Iraq, Iran and South Africa. The higher the risk, the sooner he arrived on the scene. Nicole wasn't really aware of the high risks her husband took, absorbed as she was with her own business activities, friends and lifestyle, until she received a call on her cell phone from Silvio Biscotti in Rome.

'Ciao, Nicole. I'm sending my plane to pick up you and Marc-Antoine at Nice Airport. There's an important dinner at my house and I want both of you to be there. Tell "il dottore" that the number two man to the President of Russia is going to be there, as well as the Finance Minister and the Minister of the Interior. It'll be an opportunity to discuss our refurbishment project with them. The Finance Minister's daughter, Katerina Pushkin, is also coming. I told her about you and she wants to meet you. I've invited a couple of my friends, too. We'll be about fifteen. Ciao, bella! Un bacione!'

'Ciao! Ciao! Un bacione,' was all Nicole could say before she heard the click of the phone.

A few hours later, she and Marc-Antoine were at the helipad in Monte Carlo. The seven-minute helicopter ride was always beautiful as they flew over the Mediterranean Sea around Cap d'Antibes towards Nice Airport. Once they arrived, they were privately escorted to Silvio's Gulfstream jet, named the *Pucci Gucci Girl*. The one-hour flight to Rome was uneventful. A preoccupied Marc-Antoine didn't say much, while Nicole flipped through the pages of *Paris-Match* reading about the royal family of Monaco and the movie stars partying in St Tropez.

Dinner at Silvio's

The butler greeted the guests and brought them to the garden to be served champagne, wine, vodka or whatever cocktail they desired. Silvio was a great host and loved being the social butterfly flitting from one person to another. He was good looking, dapper and sported a blond beard – his trademark. He greeted Nicole with a big kiss. She loved to flirt with Silvio because she knew he did everything in fun – a typical Italian – and that he was also madly in love with his exotic, mysterious, Chilean wife, who seemed to prefer travelling to being in Rome. Marc-Antoine didn't like the flirting but brushed it aside since the man was his business partner.

During the dinner, Nicole conversed with Katerina, the Finance Minister's daughter, who reminded her of the Russian bride at the wedding reception they had attended the previous year at the Rodin Museum. Katerina was also a tall, slender, blonde, blue-eyed beauty and very intelligent. She wanted to study in the States and of course Nicole recommended a few reputable universities. If she was interested in Stanford, Nicole could set up an informational interview with the dean because her father was a trustee of the university. Katerina beamed a gracious smile.

After dessert and coffee, Yuri Karpov, the Minister of the Interior, clinked his wine glass with a knife, stood up and sang. A velvety, tenor voice floated through the dining room. It was a traditional Russian folk song from his childhood. The dinner guests clapped as he finished and all stood up to make a toast with a shot of vodka.

'Nasdarovia!'

'Cheers!'

Fifteen rounds of vodka and toasts. Only the Russians could handle the shots of vodka; those who were smart exchanged theirs for water. Nicole and Katerina quietly excused themselves to have a decaf double espresso in the games room. It was adorned with a huge, grey stone fireplace, which Nicole immediately went over to inspect.

Katerina giggled when Nicole stood inside it. Needless to say, no fire roared there on that warm summer evening. Moments later, the two of them chatted on the oversized sofa and sipped their coffees. Katerina, young and full of hope for a bright future, only wanted to talk about schools and New York. That's why Silvio wanted me to come and entertain Katerina, Nicole thought. So much in life centred on connections.

Marc-Antoine came into the games room and sat next to Nicole. 'I'm sorry, but tomorrow I'll be flying to Moscow with Silvio and the others to follow up on this construction and rehabilitation project for the Kremlin,' he said. 'Silvio insists that we stay here for the night and his secretary will take care of your flight arrangements tomorrow.'

'When will you be back? We're supposed to go to Cannes together. I don't want to celebrate another birthday without you because of your damned impromptu business trips.'

'It's an opportunity to be seized. You never know when another one might come around,' replied Marc-Antoine.

Nicole sighed with exasperation, 'Well, I don't believe in missed opportunities. Couldn't you postpone the trip until after my birthday?'

'No,' he replied bluntly.

Katerina, a little embarrassed at witnessing a small dispute between husband and wife, left the room and joined her father who was still drinking shots of vodka, singing and crying with his fellow Russians.

The Dream

A few days later while at home in Monte Carlo, Nicole woke up and felt as though she were paralysed. She tried desperately to move her arms and legs. A sensation of heavy lead filled her listless body. She prayed to God for help and just lay there in the hope that some kind of sensation would return to her limbs. The phone rang and she couldn't answer it. She felt helpless and confused. As she quieted her thoughts, she remembered having a dream before waking up. It was a strange dream.

It was as if she were some kind of prostitute in Moscow, seducing Marc-Antoine. Why a prostitute? Marc-Antoine was sightseeing in Red Square while his partners were negotiating at the Kremlin. This woman, this prostitute, picked him up. It was so bizarre because Nicole felt and saw everything as if she were really there. What was worse was that the prostitute resembled Nicole, but with bleached blonde hair and haunting blue eyes, the colour of the deep Pacific Ocean. Of course, Marc-Antoine fell for this woman immediately because she looked like Nicole. He brought this Slavic woman back to his hotel room with lustful intentions. He poured whisky into two glasses. This Russian woman rubbed her body against his as he stood drinking his whisky. Suddenly, he dropped to his knees and passed out.

At that moment, Nicole changed from being the Russian prostitute to become embodied in the aura of Marc-Antoine. In this dreamlike dimension, Nicole felt lifeless, almost dead. Marc-Antoine screamed out for help but no one heard him. Only Nicole. His limbs too were heavy like lead. He saw his life flash before his eyes. She left his bodily aura and looked down at him from above in a detached way and wondered how she could help this man in pain. Something guided her to surround him with a loving, healing white light so that he would survive. An inner voice whispered to her to pray very hard for the angels to come and save him from whatever had happened.

After this dream, Nicole had woken up in a lifeless state, unable to move. However, once she had finally remembered her dream, she miraculously started moving her legs again and slowly climbed out of bed. She went to the kitchen and prepared chamomile tea.

That morning Silvio called on her cell phone. Nicole was reluctant to tell Silvio about her peculiar dream. Not only did it involve Marc-Antoine and a prostitute, but also the dream had disturbed her psyche. First, she was embarrassed about the prostitute part, then the drugged effect that Marc-Antoine's body suffered and finally, how she saw everything and experienced his pain. How to explain this out-of-body observation? She decided to focus on the health of Marc-Antoine?

With a nervous cough, she asked, 'Is Marc-Antoine all right?'

'Why do you ask?'

'Well, I had this strange dream about him. He lay on the ground lifeless, screaming out for help. There was no one there to help him. I heard his cry and came to him in spirit form and prayed that God would keep him alive. As I woke up, I couldn't move because I felt as though I were drugged. It was the worst feeling I've ever had in my life.'

Nicole could hear the fear in Silvio's voice as he confessed. 'Thank God we flew over in my plane, because Marc-Antoine became deathly ill and we had to fly him out of the country immediately so that he could seek medical help in the West. Right now, we're at home in Rome and the doctor has told us that he had been poisoned with Collyre, an eye liquid similar to Visine. Apparently, it's common for Russian women to seduce foreign men and slip Collyre into their drinks to make their victims drowsy. Many innocent victims have died from an overdose. Luckily for Marc-Antoine, he was in good physical condition and survived. The doctor said it would take a few days for him to recuperate. When we discovered him in his hotel room, his attaché case had been slashed and his money and watch stolen. It's scary that these women carry knives on them. I'm only telling you this because of your dream and because you're such a dear friend. By the way, you know Marc-Antoine's sense of humour. When he came out of his stupor, he said he had dreamt that he was seduced by a virgin.'

Silvio always knew how to lighten up harsh events for Nicole. But she was surprised at how accurate her dream had been and that Silvio had been honest with her about the incident. He could have easily covered up this story. She'd remember both this unusual experience and Silvio's sincerity.

Cannes: Celebration of Nicole's Birthday

Nightingales sang a sweet lullaby in the lush gardens of Villa Esperanza, adorned with the tallest palm trees in Cannes. One came and sang for Nicole to wake her up on this special day. She opened the windows to a glorious sun and clear blue sky. Descending the nineteenth-century marble staircase, through the salon and dining room that opened out onto a terrace, she sat down at the table prepared for a sumptuous breakfast. The table was filled with rustic bread, labneh, mint leaves, greens, tomatoes, cheese and fresh fruit. The household servant served tea, coffee and freshly squeezed orange juice. Every morning, a generous breakfast was served, Lebanese style.

It was the home of Sir Jeffrey Love III and his wife, Lily, who both happened to love Lebanese food. Sir Jeffrey Love III preferred to be called Jeff, insisting that titles were used only on official occasions. His passion in life was Mesopotamian poetry and Sumerian mythology while his wife's was entertainment. Lily was a film producer who spent most of her time travelling between London and Los Angeles. They enlivened parties with their presence and, at the same time, they enjoyed fiercely intellectual and philosophical conversations. Jeff had often recounted the Sumerian myths to Nicole and she felt she had become an expert on the epic tale of Gilgamesh that encompassed man's eternal struggle with the limitations of human nature, and Inanna, the goddess-heroine who tried to bring eternal life to mankind. Why Jeff could capture Nicole's imagination with these myths was a mystery but she enjoyed his storytelling.

Lily bounced in and kissed Nicole on the cheeks. 'Are you ready for tonight?' she asked.

'Can't wait. I love the fireworks here; some of the best in the world. But Lily, I need to talk to you. Would you like to take a walk with me before lunch?'

'Love to, darling.'

On the Croisette, Nicole looked at the yachts scattered on the shimmering blue bay, anchored in place waiting for the dazzling display of Italian pyrotechnics scheduled for that evening. As she walked with Lily, she told her what had happened in Moscow to Marc-Antoine and not to tell a soul. Lily promised to keep her mouth shut.

Nicole continued with tears in her eyes, 'I'm not happy with him any more. He openly flirts with women right in front of me without a care. Now, I think he's been having one-night stands and going to bed with prostitutes. Thank God, we haven't been making love for the past couple of years.'

'Have you tried to repair your relationship?' Lily asked.

'Everything, I've even gone to psychologists. The last one told me if Marc-Antoine was unwilling to seek therapy as a couple, our relationship was doomed. Well, he adamantly refused to go to the psychologist with me.'

'Why?'

'I think he's content with the status quo, but I'm tired of life with him. We don't even hold hands any more. My mother asked me if there was any affection left between us and I told her no.'

'That's tough. I can't believe you haven't made love in years. I need it every day!'

The ladies laughed.

In a more serious tone, Lily put her arm around Nicole and asked, 'What are you going to do?'

'Probably file for a divorce.'

'Darling, there are many eligible bachelors in this world. When I meet one that I think you'll like, I'll let you know,' said Lily.

'Tonight, I'm going to forget all my worries and have fun.'

'That's the spirit, darling.'

Hours later, the twinkling stars lit up the dark, blue sky as the guests arrived for Nicole's birthday party on the beach in front of the Carlton Hotel. First, she greeted Kerala and Rajiv Misra, who had flown in from New York. They were world-renowned Indian folk musicians. Next, Mohan Singh, a producer and director in Bollywood, arrived from Bombay via London. Mohan gave Nicole a bear hug that lifted her off her feet. Kerala, Rajiv, and Mohan were very clear to Nicole. They met at a charity function in New York and had since become good friends.

Once, at one of the many dinner parties the Misras hosted in New York, Mohan had told Nicole about a film he had produced and directed in the Sixties that paid homage to the beloved Prime Minister Nehru and his love for children, and how it had touched the heart of his daughter, Mrs Indira Gandhi. Coincidentally, the film was featured the same year Mrs Gandhi became Prime Minister and the government of India decided to give him the National Award for Best Children's Film. Nicole marvelled at the way Mohan managed to humbly tell his story while being innately proud of his accomplishment. Years later, he had bagged the best director prize at an international film festival in Italy for his film *Victory of Love*. He was in his sixties now but he looked as though he were only forty-five. Nicole enjoyed his company, even though he continually tried to convince her to believe in the concept of reincarnation. One of his future films was to be based on the theory. Deep down, Mohan was a hopeless romantic and in love with a famous Bollywood actress whose face was seen on posters, magazines and books everywhere in India. He explained that she couldn't come this time because she was on a photo shoot. Finally, Lily and Jeff arrived, after organizing a surprise cake for Nicole. Four more mutual friends from Lausanne were present and, in all, they added up to ten. Nicole apologized for Marc-Antoine's absence, due to his ill health.

She looked at the greyish-white half moon glowing over the Bay of Cannes. Appetizers were served, then the main course of lobster followed by the birthday cake and singing. Lily had hired a professional photographer to take pictures of the party. Smiles and laughter were contagious. A band played music nearby and Nicole took off her sandals and started dancing with Jeff and Mohan on the beach. The sand felt cold beneath her feet but she continued shaking her body rhythmically to the fast and furious beat of the Brazilian samba. Later, the dazzling display of Italian pyrotechnics accompanied by music illuminated the sky in colours of red, green, orange, white and gold.

The beauty of the fireworks stunned Nicole and she wished she had someone to share this romantic moment. The Mediterranean Sea pulled her deep into a reverie and an image of her future beloved came to her as if sent on a thought wave. Was it the champagne or a dream? Maybe there was some truth in Mohan's beliefs about reincarnation and the role fate plays in one's destiny.

The celebrations ended and Nicole graciously thanked Lily and Jeff for a glorious birthday amongst dear friends.

Chapter 3

En route

Rome to Riyadh to Athens, 1999

Despite the improvement in the political climate in Syria, Mounir was still on the run, moving from country to country. One night during his long absence he dreamt that his mother was anxious. He called her.

'Mama? Mama?'

'Mounir, is that you?'

'Mama . . . Mama is everything all right?'

With a shaky voice she said, 'I wish you could be with me at home. Your father is dying.'

Mounir's eyes filled with tears when he heard this depressing news. But what could he do? He felt helpless. He was still wanted dead or alive in Syria. He asked to talk with his father.

In a weakened state, his father insisted, 'Stay where you are until the government overturns your death sentence. I want you to live. I love you.'

'Papa, I love you, too.'

Mounir put down the phone with tears running down his cheeks. He had no choice but to follow his father's advice and never return to Damascus until his innocence was proclaimed. Although after further thought, he rationalized that no one could trace him because he had changed his name. The situation frustrated him because he wanted to be with his father. Why did destiny have him constantly on the move to escape death?

What he didn't realize was that his absence had made his father stronger. He was fighting courageously to hang on to life until those around him came to terms with his dying and eventual death. He secretly prayed to God to speak with his son before his soul left his body and his wish was granted. During the last eight years, he had become an emotional rock for his wife, knowing that her son's precarious life and death situation made her psychologically fragile. His beloved wife could rely on him during the worst of times. Mounir's absence had helped his parents grow spiritually together. Without even knowing it, Mounir had given them the best gift possible.

After eight years of running, Mounir was still miraculously alive. Although he avoided Syria, he occasionally travelled back to the Middle East from Europe. While in Rome, he arranged a trip to Riyadh where he planned to meet his cousin, Salim Shami, who had previously set up a business years ago under the fiefdom of King Fahd. It was time to board Alitalia. En route, he dreamed of a woman. A woman he had never seen before in his travels, studies or professional life. Or was it a vision? The details of this dream were ingrained into his memory for ever. He would always remember her big, beautiful, amber eyes.

The plane landed on Saudi territory. Those women who were dressed in Western style took off all their make-up and put silk scarves over their heads to respect the laws of the state. Mounir smiled at the women. First, they took advantage of the open, Western culture while outside their country and then conformed to the laws of the country once on its soil. Was it the hypocrisy of man-made laws or simply respect for each country's inherent social customs?

As Mounir disembarked from the plane, a recurring question streamed through his consciousness: who was the woman in my dream? Absorbed in his own thoughts, he walked through passport control, collected his luggage and found his way out of the terminal. Moments later, his cousin came forward and welcomed him.

Mounir wondered, 'How long this time?'

Salim noticed Mounir's sadness so he brought him home and showed him to his guest room. Mounir was grateful to have some peace and solitude in the safety of his cousin's home. He sat down on his bed, took out a pad of paper and wrote page upon page. His emotions, fears and hopes filled the blank paper. Writing was his therapy. He externalized all his experiences by writing about them. It helped him overcome his tumultuous past, to let it go and leave all of his baggage behind. Somehow, the process of purging himself on paper made him feel spiritually closer to his distant family. He prayed for his dying father and for his friends and colleagues who had been jailed or killed because of the regional unrest. The stress of living on the run had taken its toll on him. He would usually sleep three or four hours only during daylight since, he was informed, most successful assassinations occurred at night. Anxiety had given him the beginning of an ulcer and the smallest of noises rattled him.

Tomorrow, he would talk to Salim about his business plan. Tonight, he just wanted to rest; it was the first time in a long time that he had felt comfort and safety within the confines of his extended family.

When they're caring and loving, family is the best place to be healed, thought Mounir.

And his cousins adored him. A cup of gunpowder tea with finger sandwiches, fruit and salad was brought up to his bedroom. He ate everything with pleasure. There is nothing like home-made food. He drifted into a daydream, dwelling again upon this mysterious woman until, with a full belly, he fell into a deep slumber.

Early the next morning, Salim played a bugle in front of Mounir's bedroom door. Mounir almost sailed out of the window but quickly realized that this was one of Salim's pranks – his cousin had never lost his youthful spirits. Mounir opened the door and laughed.

After breakfast, Salim told Mounir, 'I have bad news for you, my brother. Someone recognized you at the airport and reported you to the authorities. We have arranged a private jet for you to go to Athens. You must leave now.'

Mounir, shaken with disbelief, asked, 'Is this possible? Even with this bushy beard?'

Salim embraced his tender-hearted cousin and said, 'I'm afraid so, my brother. May God be with you. Know that we love you and if you need anything, call me. Hurry now.'

'But I have business I want to discuss with you.'

Salim lit up a cigarette and puffed on it nervously. 'When you return, we'll talk about it. Right now, it's not safe here. You have to get out of here, my brother.'

Mounir sighed. His life kept him running. How long was this unjust manhunt going to last? He put his head into his hands and wept silently. 'My God, Athens. What shall I do there?'

* * *

Streams of thoughts entered Mounir's mind as the plane approached Athens. It's a beautiful summer day. Sometimes things don't go your way and that brings you down. Daydreaming gives hope. Cycles of coming and going. Activity followed by inactivity. Don't think so much about everything. What do you need in life? Change.

Thoughts changed to desires. Mounir had always wanted to come to this land of ancient myths. He decided that he would explore as much as possible of this country with its myriad islands – and Turkey, too, if the gods permitted it.

Don't let these events break your spirit, a little voice reminded him. You're going to come out of this safely. You'll have a successful future. Your life resembles the bright light of a full moon on a very clear evening.

These messages comforted Mounir, although with the more rational part of his mind he wondered if it was just wishful thinking.

The cabin attendant, a pretty woman, dressed in a navy blue suit, seated herself in the front of the cabin, directly in front of Mounir. She turned and looked into the eyes of this young man, the only passenger on Salim's private jet, who appeared fidgety and anxious. 'You must be a very special person to have this type of service,' she said. 'I hope you overcome whatever is troubling you and wish you a beautiful journey through life.'

Mounir's face lit up with a moment of happiness and he smiled a big, beautiful smile at this kind woman. Later, he would remember how important it was to treat others with acts of kindness rather than with words of meanness.

The plane landed, and he was greeted at Ellinikon Airport by a friend of his cousin Salim. 'Welcome to Athens my friend,' said Mikis Papadopoulos.

'Hello, Mikis, how are you? It's so kind of you to meet me at the airport and to take me around your country. Salim has mentioned many great things about you,' replied Mounir.

'Yeah, Salim and I studied at Cambridge University together to get our doctorate in economics. Those were the fun days. He told me that you got your Ph.D. at Stanford. Lucky you to have studied in sunny California. Tell me, my friend, where would you like to go first?'

'Please, call me Mounir. I don't want to stay in Athens, let's go straight to Mykonos and then sail to Santorini, Rhodes and Crete.'

'Good. We'll start our journey towards Mykonos with my family's sailboat. It'll take about four hours from the mainland,' said Mikis as they stepped into the car.

'Fine,' said Mounir, as the exhaustion of his life on the run began to overcome him. He stared out of the window and drifted off into deep thought while Mikis drove.

Mounir was determined to rebut this unjust accusation legally through the courts and prove his innocence. Thereafter, his death sentence would be lifted by the government and the Minister of Communications would announce to the national, regional and international press that it had been proven that he was innocent of all charges. All the people would know that truth and justice would prevail. This was his vision of the future. Meanwhile, each day he woke up alive, he thanked God for one more day to live. Life had become precious. He tried to live in the present and not to worry about the future or regret the past. Fate had dealt him a difficult hand of cards to play; however, with his youth, intelligence, perseverance and hope, he believed he'd overcome this tremendous obstacle in his life.

Mikis woke Mounir from his reverie. 'Mounir, we've arrived at the yacht club.'

Mounir blinked and rubbed his eyes. Mikis introduced Mounir to the captain of the ship, whom they all called Theo. Off they went, on a luxurious, ultra-modern, thirty-metre sailboat, through the choppy waters to Mykonos. It was moderately windy, as was often the case during August. Mounir's mind was overworked and he dozed on a plush, royal blue sofa in the lounge while Mikis conversed happily with Theo in their native Greek language. Mikis was worried for his friend. Salim had told him what had happened to Mounir and how he was now constantly on the run in fear of his life. He would do everything he could to help Mounir because Salim was like a brother; therefore, a cousin or friend of Salim's was also his friend.

A Brief Interlude in Mykonos

The captain announced their arrival at Mykonos. They moored near Elia beach, one of the most beautiful beaches on the island. The sea rippled in a blue turquoise pattern; a slight breeze cooled off the intense heat of the sun. Mikis and Mounir dived off the boat and swam, while Captain Theo cast his line to catch a fish. After their late lunch, the two young men took a small, motorboat to shore to watch the beautiful rose and gold sunset over the bay anchored with yachts and small fishing boats. Back on the boat Theo puffed on his cigar encircled by the silence of the sea.

Mikis and Mounir strolled around the tiny village admiring the charming simplicity of the architecture. Most of the houses were painted in white with royal blue trim to reflect the colour of the sea. Surrounding the homes were voluptuous vines of fuchsia-coloured flowers, emitting a divine aroma that intoxicated one's soul.

'It's so charming here. Let's stay for a few days,' suggested Mounir.

'Sure,' said Mikis. Just as Mikis spoke, Mounir was greeted by an old schoolfriend.

'Habibi, what are you doing here? It's been years since I last saw you. You're still as handsome as I remember you from our college days, and I love your dashing beard,' said Sofia Capucilli.

Mounir blushed. He remembered that she was from an Italian diplomat's family; her father had been ambassador to Lebanon. They had met at a private school in Beirut. Mounir's parents had sent him to school there, like many other families from Damascus, because the quality of education was considered better, more liberal and consistent with international standards. Although Mounir had been accepted to go to his father's alma mater in Switzerland, he had preferred to be closer to home.

'Hello, Sofia. It's wonderful to see you again. Meet my friend, Mikis Papadopoulos,' said Mounir.

They politely acknowledged one another.

'Would you like to come over for dinner?' Sofia asked. 'I'm having a casual dinner party with live Greek music.'

Mounir and Mikis looked at each other, then at their shorts and T-shirts.

Sofia laughed, reading their minds, 'Don't worry. You can borrow a couple of shirts from my husband. He's about your size.'

They all laughed. Mikis and Mounir joined Sofia and they walked together up a hill to reach her beautiful villa, nestled in the mountain with a spectacular view of the town of Mykonos, overlooking the Mediterranean Sea.

As they entered her house, Sofia kissed her husband, Michael.

'Honey, meet an old classmate of mine. We went to the same high school in Beirut. He's with his friend, Mikis Papadopoulos.'

Mounir introduced himself. 'I'm delighted to meet you. Your wife's sweet to invite us to your dinner party.'

'She loves having a large crowd. I didn't catch your name . . .'

'Mounir Munir.'

Michael couldn't remember Sofia ever mentioning this name. Sofia's eyes popped out of her head and Mounir shot a cool glance at her, signalling silence.

Michael sensed some uneasiness in the room and patted Mounir on the shoulder. 'A friend of my wife's is also my friend. Welcome, and please make yourselves at home. You can freshen up with a change of clothing in one of our guest suites.'

'You're most gracious,' said Mounir, and Mikis nodded his head in agreement.

Sofia hurriedly rang for one of the household staff to show Mounir and Mikis to their individual suites.

Michael reflected that he would have to ask Sofia more about her friend later.

After Mounir had showered and put on some fresh clothes, Sofia knocked on his door and asked if everything was all right. He opened the door and let her in.

She twirled her long blonde hair with her index finger and said, 'So, it's true. I heard about your death sentence and how you're on the run, that you'd changed your name and appearance. But you can't fool an old classmate, my dear. Don't worry, I'll keep your secret and introduce you to my dinner guests as Mounir.'

Mounir stepped forward to hug Sofia but she stepped backwards.

She continued, 'I'd advise that you and Mikis depart during the festivities and set sail for another island. One never knows who may be lurking about. Mykonos is a small island and word gets around quite quickly about who has been at our parties. You know how they gossip in our social circle.'

Mounir chuckled at that comment. His easy-going demeanour lessened the tension in the room. He replied, 'I hope to return your hospitality one day when I wake up from this nightmare.' He stepped forward one more time to hug her in gratitude and she accepted. Mounir realized how much he desired the warm embrace of a loving and kind woman; however, his insane life hadn't yet allowed true love to blossom.

The festivities began. There was a beautiful buffet of exquisite and delectable food. Sofia knew how to entertain. Mounir looked hungrily at the assortment of appetizers that included stuffed vine leaves, baked spinach with different cheeses, grilled octopus and squid, cheese pastries, and cucumber with feta cheese and mint. Mikis was more interested in the main dishes. There were mussels in white wine sauce, baked shrimp with feta, grilled lamb on skewers, and chicken with lemon. Mounir prepared himself a plate of the different salads while Mikis ate the souvlakia.

Sounds of traditional Greek music permeated the air. The musicians played 'Siko Horepse Syrtaki', 'Zorbas' and then, the Syrtaki dance. Everyone held hands, formed a serpentine line, and then began dancing the traditional Greek dance. Mounir thought this would be the opportune moment to leave the party inconspicuously. He tapped Mikis on the shoulder and together they said goodbye to Sofia and wished her all the best. Mounir kissed her on the cheek and thanked her once again for her gracious hospitality.

Sofia said to both of them, 'May God be with you.'

Mounir replied, 'Inshallah.'

Sofia's chauffeur dropped them off at Elia beach, where the moon was shining brightly across the bay.

Mikis noticed two beautiful women walking arm in arm along the water's edge. He said to Mounir, 'Let's invite them to the boat.'

'OK.'

The girls agreed. They were scantily clad in mini-skirts and summer tank tops, which aroused Mikis. Mounir's mind was elsewhere as he navigated the little, motorboat towards the sailboat.

Once aboard, Mikis offered the women some champagne. The four of them finished off a few bottles of Veuve Clicquot and became somewhat drunk. Mikis tried kissing one of the girls, whose name was Anna. She was a pretty blonde blue-eyed Swedish girl from Stockholm. The other, Helen, was a brunette with green eyes from Athens. They always vacationed together in Mykonos. When Mikis attempted to kiss

Anna, she turned her cheek and kissed her girlfriend. Mounir watched Mikis trying in vain to pick up Anna. His vision was becoming blurred from too much alcohol but he kept gazing at the potential *ménage à trois.*

Helen put her arms round Anna's waist and kissed her tenderly on the eyes, then moved to her soft cherry lips. Anna caressed Helen's breasts until her nipples became erect. The girls aroused Mikis beyond belief and he tried to kiss Anna again but she pushed him away. His Greek temper mounted while Mounir observed the three with curiosity, interested in how women made love to one another and whether his friend would triumph or not. Mikis shouldn't have been so vexed: Mykonos was famed for its gay tourists. The girls stood up and danced together, holding each other closely until Mikis screamed something in Greek. Helen, who understood Mikis, told Anna it was time to go and the girls politely thanked Mikis for the champagne bubbles. He stomped around the deck and wouldn't go near them. The girls trusted Mounir and asked him to take them back to shore.

The girls kissed Mounir goodbye on the cheek and once again, walked arm in arm on the cool sand giggling with happiness under the full moon. Back on the boat, Mounir looked at Mikis and shrugged his shoulders.

Afterwards, Mikis went to wake up Captain Theo to tell him that they had been advised to depart from the island as soon as possible. The captain lifted the anchor and set sail for Crete, which was a much bigger island than Mykonos. With thousands of inhabitants Mounir would be able to walk around without being recognized by anyone. The chances of him meeting a dear friend, as in Mykonos, would be remote.

Mikis showed Mounir to his bedroom. 'Sleep, my friend. You need the rest. Tomorrow morning we'll have breakfast on the deck and plenty of time for chatting because it's a long sail to Crete from here.'

Mounir thanked Mikis, 'You're like a brother to me.'

'Goodnight,' said Mikis.

'Goodnight.'

Setting Sail for Crete

When Mounir emerged on the deck the next morning, Mikis asked him if he'd had a good night's sleep.

'Wonderful,' said Mounir.

As they ate their breakfast, Mikis told Mounir how, since he was a young boy, he had been fascinated by mythological tales. Mounir humbly admitted that as a result of his academic research he knew quite a few of the Greek and Phoenician myths.

Mounir began with the story of Europa and the creation of Europe.

'Europa,' he told Mikis, 'was the beautiful daughter of Agenor, the King of Phoenicia. As you know, ancient Phoenicia is now Syria and Lebanon, a region of the world where my heart and soul dwell.'

Mikis acknowledged his friend's nostalgia with a grown-up smile, then changed his countenance to that of a delighted child, eager to hear more of the story.

Mounir continued, 'Zeus was the father of gods and men. He was recognized by the ancient Greeks as the lord of the heavens. When Zeus first saw Europa in Phoenicia, he immediately desired her and thought the best way to be noticed by her was by changing himself into a beautiful white bull, since she loved nature and wildlife. He noticed that she gathered wild flowers with her friends in a lush green meadow by the sea. His idea was that he'd walk by as a bull through this field when she was there. The day he did, she was awed by the beauty of this beast and went over to adorn his horns with freshly picked flowers. The bull was so gentle that she decided to climb up on his back with the help of her friends. Zeus, disguised as the bull, ran off with Europa and flew across the Mediterranean Sea and brought her to the island of Crete.'

'As we too set sail for Crete.'

Mounir chuckled and picked up where he left off. 'Europa's friends were astonished by this feat, which they believed only a god could have devised. When their stupefaction subsided, they ran to tell Europa's father what had happened. King Agenor decided that his son Cadmus, Europa's brother, must find his sister and bring her back to her homeland. Cadmus consulted the Oracle of Delphi and was told to abandon his search for Europa. Instead, he was to roam the lands until he found a cow with the distinguishing mark of a white circle, similar to a full moon, on each of its sides. He was to follow this cow until she knelt down to rest, whereupon he was to build a city.'

Mikis exclaimed, 'According to Greek legend this city was Thebes.'

'Precisely. Cadmus became the King of Thebes and taught the inhabitants the alphabet and the art of writing. As you know, the

Phoenicians invented the alphabet. And Cadmus is still one of our heroes in Lebanon,' said Mounir, proud of his ancestral origins.

'But what happened to Europa?'

'Ah! When Zeus landed on the island of Crete, he made love to Europa. The love he had for Europa was so strong that he gave her name to an entire continent, the mythological origin of Europe that we know today. Europa bore Zeus three sons, one of whom became King Minos, King of Crete.'

'Wow! Legends of princesses and gods. You're a good storyteller, my friend.'

'It's part of our culture,' said Mounir.

In the background, Theo hummed and sang songs from all over the world. The wind was perfect for sailing and it was a beautiful sunny day. Once again, it was time to fish. Mounir caught a sea bass big enough to feed all three of them. Mikis prepared and grilled the fish, which they ate with olive oil, lemon, dark brown olives and fresh rosemary, and drank ouzo, a strong white alcohol that had been produced by Theo's family for many centuries. Mounir enjoyed talking to Mikis in the same way as he had enjoyed his conversations with John in Africa. That time with John and the hidden African tribe seemed like centuries ago. He wondered what had become of him, another good man who had helped him along his path to freedom and justice. Mikis interrupted Mounir's daydreaming and urged him to continue his retelling of the myths of Crete.

The Mysterious Labyrinth

The history of Crete was relevant for Mounir because of its relation to the story of Europa. The Minoan civilization, one of the world's earliest civilizations, was named after King Minos, her son.

Mikis tried to impress Mounir. 'Knossos was the capital of Crete during King Minos' reign. It was at the Great Palace there that a labyrinth was constructed. This labyrinth was used only by the gods, goddesses, priests and priestesses who were initiated into the rites of divine wisdom and compassion.'

Although Mounir knew the legend of the Minotaur, he didn't want to hurt Mikis's feelings. 'Well, what did they do at the site of the labyrinth?' he asked.

Mikis replied, 'There are different versions of its origin. There's the legend of the gods and goddesses performing sacred rites at this site, which has been passed down orally through many generations. Then, there's the Greek myth.'

'It's man's inherent nature to create stories as a means to pass on a nation's history, culture and knowledge.'

Mikis nodded his head in agreement and continued, 'According to the Greek myth, King Minos failed to sacrifice a beautiful white bull to Poseidon, the God of the Sea. Poseidon put a spell on the king's wife, Pasiphaë, so that she fell in love with a bull and gave birth to the Minotaur, a monster with the head of a bull and the body of a man.'

Mounir wryly interrupted, 'You can see many minotaurs in the paintings of Picasso, some of them erotic.'

Mikis laughed and resumed, 'King Minos hired Daedalus, the draughtsman, to construct the labyrinth at the Great Palace so that the monster could be confined. As fate would have it, King Aegeus of Athens killed one of King Minos' sons, Androgeus. With this event, King Minos sought revenge by forcing the King of Athens to pay him an annual tribute of seven maidens and seven youths. These youths and maidens were sacrificed to the Minotaur in the labyrinth. It was his way of showing his power and avenging the fate of his son. Then, one day, Theseus, a great hero and the son of Poseidon, joined the annual tribute of victims and slew the Minotaur. The gods were finally appeased and rewarded King Minos with prosperity through seafaring trade across the Mediterranean Sea. King Minos became renowned not only for founding the Minoan civilization, but also for his benevolence, justice and power. This, my friend, is the Greek myth of the labyrinth. However, from a metaphysical point of view, I find the other legend far more intriguing.'

As Mikis paused, Mounir stood up, stretched his lean, muscular body towards the sun and sat back down again on the sofa to listen to this man who had an intellect to match his own.

Divine Healing Energy

Mikis was distracted for a few moments by a book on Reiki that he found lying on the coffee table. Theo must have left it there. Reiki was a healing system whereby a practitioner placed his hands on the body or slightly above the body to rebalance the energies of the individual. Reiki healed physical disease, the mind and emotional disturbance.

Reiki, as far as Mikis knew, had its origins in India. Somehow, over the centuries, this system of healing had been lost until the mid-nineteenth century, when it was rediscovered by a Japanese Christian minister, based in Kyoto, named Mikao Usui. During one of his lectures, a student had asked him how Jesus healed the sick. Dr Usui didn't have the answer and felt challenged to research this profound question. After years of research, Buddhism gave him clarity and insight. He found striking similarities between the lives of Buddha and Jesus. He derived from the Sanskrit texts an ancient healing system that he believed both Buddha and Jesus used to heal others physically and spiritually. Since he was Japanese, he called this healing system Reiki. Ki represented universal energy, like the Chinese Chi. Reiki was defined as the universal life force energy. The masters, such as Buddha and Jesus, tapped into this universal energy to heal the sick.

Mounir looked at his friend reading the book, 'Come on, man, do you believe in Reiki?'

'You know about Reiki?' asked Mikis incredulously.

'Having lived in California, one is bound to learn about alternative healing practices.' Mounir chanted, 'OM MANI PADME HUM!'

Mikis laughed, 'Hey, Mounir, let me try and explain how one of the healing symbols of Reiki is believed to have already been used by the gods, goddesses, priests, priestesses and their initiates at the Great Palace of Knossos. Remember that this would be before 1500 BC, almost a thousand years before Buddha. The question is, how did this knowledge of healing travel from India to Crete, or vice versa?'

'I agree,' said Mounir.

'At a temple in the grounds of Knossos Palace, there was an initiation space that had the same design as one of the Reiki symbols. You know, use of symbols was part of the Reiki process of healing back then as it is today.'

'Maybe it's coincidental, or maybe the design was a popular architectural symbolic form during that period of history.'

'I beg to differ with you. I believe the gods, priests and so on were knowledgeable about this ancient healing system and that they used this symbol to heal the people. You see, the symbol increases the holistic energy of Reiki in a precise area of the body. The practitioner then calls upon a god, goddess, angel or spiritual helper to help him be a conduit of the universal life force energy to heal the person in need. This healing process was done with divine love.'

Mikis sighed, 'I don't really know why I'm discussing this ancient healing system with you, but maybe this information will be important to you one day.'

Mounir, the scholar and pragmatist, replied, 'There's no evidence that this ancient healing system used in Knossos is the same one practised today under the name of Reiki. Furthermore, your legend relates to the mysterious labyrinth, that has no factual foundation . . .'

'OK, Mounir. Theo can explain it better. He's a Reiki master.'

Mounir teased Mikis and said, 'Let's not forget that the path to enlightenment is compassion for all beings great and small; the process of karma, reincarnation and rebirth is a paradox to resolve; and . . .'

Mikis interrupted, 'Stop it.' Then winked at his friend and said, 'One day your spirit and mind will open up to these esoteric mysteries. It'll have to be a special person to show someone as obstinate as you the way.'

Mounir cried out, 'It'll be the love of my life. Oh no! Now I have a headache. Captain Theo, help!'

Theo had Mikis take over the helm. Mounir looked at Theo while he placed his hands about an inch from the top of his head. He felt burning heat then nothing. His headache was miraculously cured.

Theo said to the boys, 'You've been thinking and talking too much. Cool yourselves off in the water.' He dropped the sails until the boat became idle. The young men jumped into the refreshing deep blue sea and frolicked and played like young dolphins until Theo reeled them back in to set sail once again.

Crete

Captain Theo spotted the land mass of Crete getting nearer. Simultaneously, the three men saw a black helicopter with a red stripe flying towards them. They immediately sensed they were in danger.

Mikis said to his companions, 'Quick, put on your scuba gear.'

Theo radioed the coastguard for help and asked for an armed speedboat. All of a sudden, men in black suits and red skullcaps started shooting at the boat. Mikis threw Theo his scuba equipment and steered the boat until the captain was ready.

Fuelled by adrenaline, the three men grasped each others hands and leapt into the water.

Moments later, the boat exploded. The three men were rocked violently below the surface from the impact of the explosion and watched bullets whipping harmlessly past them through the water. The helicopter flew away with the men in black suits pumping their fists in the air, sure that if the explosion hadn't killed them, then the machine guns had. They didn't see a patrol boat speeding in their direction. The lieutenant aboard the coastguard ship thought his good friend and colleague, Captain Theo, had been murdered by these fanatics. He was angry and wanted revenge. Going against his training, Lieutenant Sorbo gave the order for the patrol boat to open fire on the helicopter. Moments later, a direct hit on the fuel tank blasted the black helicopter and its notorious red stripe out of the sky. Bits and pieces of the helicopter slowly floated down to the sea.

The lieutenant shouted, 'That was for Captain Theo.'

Meanwhile, Theo was employing an underwater mini-computer device that he could use to encode messages with his finger. He sent a note to his buddy, Lieutenant Sorbo: 'We're fine. Located two miles north-west of Crete. We'll surface and fire a warning shot when you give us the thumbs up.'

Lieutenant Sorbo cried with relief, 'That man has more than forty lives. He's luckier than a cat.'

He sent back a message to Theo, 'We've blasted the bastards out of the sky. All is clear.'

After about thirty minutes the three men were found and brought aboard. All was safe for now. Both Mikis and Mounir were shaken up by the event and Lieutenant Sorbo gave them a shot of ouzo to calm their spirits. Mounir now learnt that Theo acted as a professional bodyguard for Mikis's family.

Theo advised Mounir to leave Greece, 'Whoever is chasing you, they came very close to killing you this time.'

There must be an angel protecting me because every time I get into trouble, he saves me, thought Mounir. This was his second escape from an attempted assassination.

Mikis looked at Mounir and said, 'Salim certainly has interesting cousins.'

Mounir gazed towards the horizon and wept silently. 'When is the running going to stop?'

Moments later, again, the beautiful woman reappeared, as if in a dream, wearing a long, flowing, white gown and offered him a red rose. This loving gesture comforted his soul and confirmed his belief in guardian spirits.

Chapter 4
Changes

The Alhambra, Summer 1999

Nicole and Celeste arrived at Malaga Airport and met Celeste's new husband, Edouard D'Orsay, who had flown in from London. Together, they drove to the Hotel Barceló La Bobadilla, set in the foothills of Andalusia, north of Malaga, where they would meet Nicole's brother, John, and his latest girlfriend. Marc-Antoine had refused to join them. The incident in Moscow had created permanent emotional tension between him and Nicole. A short break apart would hopefully do both of them some good. Nicole felt unloved and betrayed. What ever had happened to trust and fidelity in their relationship? She had sensed the warnings but ignored them. During this brief interlude in Spain she would try to talk it over with her brother.

A few days later, before their excursion to Granada, Nicole and Celeste found themselves alone in the lobby. Celeste was looking radiant and healthy and Nicole realized that she hadn't seen her for a while. Her marriage to Edouard had brought positive change to her life. Celeste told Nicole how she now lived between London, Paris and Geneva and also spent time in a winter chalet in Mégève and a summer villa in St Tropez. Her children, husband and travels kept her busy. She had become a lady of leisure. Nicole was happy for the turnaround in Celeste's life. She shuddered at the memory of Celeste's husband's horrific suicide. Plastic surgery concealed the mark on Celeste's temple from the bullet that grazed her head and no one could see the scars on her stomach. Although Celeste had recovered physically, psychologically she still had trouble being alone. Nicole thought how noble Edouard was to have fallen in love with Celeste and her two children.

Finally, John and his girlfriend, Sarah de Fleur, a former model for Madame Carven and also an actress who had once starred in a Bond film, walked into the lobby. They all wanted to visit the Islamic gardens of the Alhambra in Granada. Alhambra, or 'Qal'at al Hamra' in Arabic, meant 'red fort', the name deriving from the red clay found in the nearby mountains that was used to build the fortress around AD 1000. The Alhambra was one of the best conserved Arabian palaces of its epoch. It was well-situated on a hill overlooking Granada. John volunteered to be their scholarly guide, much to the girls' delight. His knowledge of Arabic culture was vast and he had a passion for oriental art and architecture, in addition to his curiosity about native tribes in Africa and throughout the world.

John started the tour and recounted how a Jewish vizier had built the original palace in AD 1052, then how, in the fourteenth century, later successors, Yusuf I and Muhammed V, added on their own architectural splendours and landscape designs.

He led the girls to the Court of the Lions and said, 'This section is the highlight of Muhammed V's palace, with a fountain in the centre of the courtyard surrounded by twelve marble lions. The lions are a curiosity in Arabian art because the Koran forbids the figurative representation of animals as well as humans. That's why some scholars attribute this fountain to the Jewish vizier rather than Muhammed V.'

Sarah said with awe, 'It's the most beautiful courtyard I've ever seen. Celeste take a picture of me under the portico.'

Celeste took a photo of Sarah alone, then with Nicole and John in front of the magnificent Court of the Lions.

They meandered through the halls, arcades and patios that led one into the other until they came upon the summer garden called Generalife, or 'Jinan al-Arif' in Arabic, that bordered on the Alhambra palace.

John remarked, 'Look at the central canal with the fountains shooting water over it from each end and the lotus flowers sitting on the top of the waterbed.'

It was a marvellous sight. 'What a beautiful oasis to have survived across the centuries!' Nicole remarked.

After their tour of the magnificent gardens, the four of them ate lunch in a nearby restaurant. The lunch lasted for three hours and John became exceptionally open about his ex-wife. He declared, 'I'm now emotionally recovered from my divorce. It has taken ten years to straighten out our affairs.'

Celeste teased, 'It's about time. Ten years is a long time.'

Sarah said, 'We've been thinking about getting married and starting a family.'

'That would be lovely,' replied Nicole, though she felt confused. His last marriage had been to a Hollywood actress who eventually divorced him to live permanently in LA while he was diligently working on his Ph.D. at Stanford. Why would he want to marry another self-centred actress, although Sarah was great fun to have around?

A few silent minutes passed and the waiter brought the bill. John paid and they left the beautiful gardens of Alhambra.

The next day, the friends went shopping, horse riding, played tennis or lazed like lizards by the pool. Fortunately for Nicole, only John was by the pool when her cell phone rang. She was walking nearby in the vibrant green gardens under the shadows of the palm trees, trying to cool off from the intense heat.

John yelled out to her, 'Do you want me to answer your phone?'

'Please.'

John heard a man's voice, handed her the phone and in a low tone joked, 'It's your secret lover that no one has known about for the past five years.'

Nicole laughed at his comment. He knew damn well she believed in monogamy, even if she did have a few fantasies from time to time. She answered as she walked a few metres away from John to have some privacy. It was her psychologist from Paris. She was glad the others were not around and started talking to him. He teased her saying he wished he were in Spain with her, looking at the aqua-blue Mediterranean Sea.

'Can I come over?' he asked. 'I'll book a hotel and we can meet secretly in my room. No one would know that I'm there.' He knew Marc-Antoine wouldn't be there.

'Are you crazy? I'm seeing you to help me mend my relationship with Marc-Antoine, not to have an affair.'

He insisted, 'I'm going to London in two weeks for the weekend; would you like to join me?'

Exasperated, Nicole said, 'Please don't ever call me again and I'm terminating our sessions. You're supposed to help me.'

The psychologist hung up, knowing he was in the wrong.

When she hung up, John commented, 'Ah! How is your lover?'

Nicole said, 'Sometimes, I wish I did have a lover.'

Sensing the sadness in his sister's heart, John asked, 'What's wrong?'

'I didn't want to say anything in front of everyone, but now seems like a good time to talk to you. There's no love anymore between Marc-Antoine and myself. We haven't been affectionate for the past couple of years. Nor have we held hands. Look at you and Sarah, you're always walking arm-in-arm, kissing each other and laughing. I don't even want to be around Marc-Antoine.'

Celeste, Edouard and Sarah interrupted Nicole's conversation with her brother, with pina coladas. A few seconds later, Marc-Antoine breezed in. He greeted everyone else before saying hello to Nicole. She looked at him with eyes like glacial daggers. Everyone instantly felt the animosity that existed between the two of them. There went Nicole's vacation of peace and relaxation.

That bastard! she thought. He promised he wouldn't come here.

She decided not to let Marc-Antoine's presence ruin her short break. She would still enjoy the last evening with her brother and friends, for which a big party had been planned.

Last Evening in Spain

The festivities commenced. At the beginning of the gala dinner, there was a show of flamenco dancers to honour the traditional Spanish style of dancing. It was beautiful and emotional. During the entertainment, dinner was served. Nicole sat at the opposite end of the table to be as far away as possible from her soon to be ex-husband. To her delight, John sat directly across from her.

While Marc-Antoine recounted the story of his most recent trip to Moscow, John spoke to Nicole. Nicole tried to be attentive to both of them. To be more precise, she looked at John's facial expressions but couldn't resist listening to Marc-Antoine. However, John persisted with a raised voice, and got Nicole's attention. As they briefly spoke, he relayed a message of hope to her by recounting an experience in Cairo when he'd visited the Pyramids about a year ago.

He told her, 'I met this wise old man there who asked me if I had a sister. When I said yes, he said, tell her everything will be all right. She'll lose a loved one but meet another, who will say these words to her: "Ana Bahibbik".'

John knew that Nicole understood the words: their Egyptian uncle had said the same thing to his beloved wife, their father's sister. She understood John's message and gave him a shy, wry smile.

At the other end of the table, Marc-Antoine was describing how he had been working on a deal to get approval from the Russian President's top aide to refurbish the Kremlin using the skills of renowned Italian architects and experts. He and his colleagues were waiting for an answer from their partner, who was in the last round of negotiations at the highest governmental level. Marc-Antoine had carried an attaché case that contained $300 million in promissory notes underwritten by a prestigious London investment bank. They had walked from the Kremlin to Red Square and looked at all the stands where the vendors sold military paraphernalia, babushka dolls and fake Russian icons.

Marc-Antoine recounted what he had said to his colleagues. ' "If our deal doesn't go through, let's set up a stand and sell our promissory notes to the Russians and the tourists" . . . and my colleagues looked at me with bafflement.'

Marc-Antoine finished his story, 'I cried out to the people walking around Red Square, "Hey, everybody, come over here. We have authentic promissory notes worth $300 million. Buy one note for only ten roubles." '

With this last detail, his audience burst out laughing – even Nicole giggled. Only John and Sarah didn't respond; they were looking deeply into each other's eyes and clinking their wine glasses.

Why am I here and why do I have a crazy husband? Nicole silently asked herself. Maybe it's me who's crazy? She remembered a quote from the Russian author Gogol: 'Le fou est normal.' The crazy are normal.

Life was certainly colourful when you were surrounded by a dynamic crowd. Everyone's unique personality contributed to the interesting conversations, revelations and activities. The evening wound down with dancing to a marengè band. All night long, Nicole danced, her worries blown out to sea by the strong brass horns. Tomorrow would be another day, when she would have to return to reality.

Chapter 5
Rhythms and Sounds

Singita, Late Summer 1999

Africa, Africa, Africa – Singita, Singita, Singita. The rhythms and sounds, and smells of Africa. Singita meant 'miracle' in the South African local Shangaan language. Nicole hoped for a miracle to occur in her life. Marc-Antoine knew that their relationship was on the rocks so, shortly after their mini-vacation in Spain, he had invited Nicole to accompany him on his business trip to South Africa. His company had offices in Johannesburg and Cape Town. It was an exciting time to invest in the infrastructure of the new South African economy: the South Africans envisioned that they would become the next shining example of success, following in the footsteps of the Hong Kong miracle. Then, the rest of the African continent could follow its lead. President Thabo Mbeki, inaugurated in Pretoria earlier that year, had said in a televised speech before parliament that South Africa was a country full of potential and opportunity. All one needed was vision. He had announced that the twenty-first century would be the African century.

To pass some idle time while Marc-Antoine attended business meetings, Nicole strolled around one of the newly built shopping malls in Jo'burg, as the natives called Johannesburg. She entered a record shop and listened to various African artists, eventually buying a Johnny Clegg CD. His music was dynamic and reflected the fight against Apartheid and the spirit of the native African tribes. Upon reflection, Nicole felt something familiar about the country and its people. The music, their way of life, even their accent struck a faraway note in her heart that she didn't quite understand.

When Marc-Antoine had finished his first business mission in Johannesburg, Nicole suggested they go on a photo safari for a few days and stay at one of the lodges at the Singita Private Game Reserve. He hesitated but then agreed. First, they flew from Jo'burg to Skukuza Airport where they were escorted to a small four-seater aeroplane, scheduled to land on Singita's private airstrip about fifteen minutes later. Singita was considered one of the finest game reserves in Africa. It was an exclusive wildlife sanctuary in the Sabi Sand area beside the Kruger National Park, bordering both Mozambique and Zimbabwe. Nicole looked forward to an adventure in the real animal kingdom where one felt the raw power of nature, in contrast to the shams, trickery and political manoeuvres that existed in the corporate jungle that she had experienced first-hand and through Marc-Antoine's business adventures.

During the eleven-minute bumpy flight from Skukuza to Singita, Nicole turned white. She soaked her beige, short-sleeved safari shirt with perspiration and kept her dark sunglasses on to hide her fear. Images of a plane crashing pierced her imagination like lightning bolts. Her hands gripped the seat underneath her legs. Once the plane landed on the private dirt airstrip, Marc-Antoine helped her climb down the two-step ladder.

The park ranger greeted the passengers and said to Nicole, as he helped her into the open Land Rover, 'Hope you're not going to get sick in my jeep.'

She felt nauseous and almost fainted in the arms of the cute ranger. The rangers had a reputation for being ladies' men. Although quite weak from the turbulent plane ride, Nicole observed that the ranger eyed a few single women aboard as he drove away, before announcing that he'd be married in a couple of weeks.

All the guests wished him happiness except for a couple of ladies who whispered amongst themselves, 'What a pity!'

At the game reserve, Nicole was too sick to wait for Marc-Antoine to check in so the bellhop and a security man armed with a rifle escorted her directly to their bungalow. She passed out on a luxurious, king-sized, canopy bed for about an hour.

On waking, Nicole vaguely remembered what the host of the lodge had said when they arrived, 'Afternoon tea will be served at four o'clock. After, you'll go on a night safari from five to seven. Please don't leave your room until the porter comes and escorts you because there have been incidents with wild animals when guests have strayed on their own.'

A knock at the door meant it was time for tea and the night safari. Nicole felt better and wondered why her reaction to moderate turbulence was so strong. Why did the other passengers remain unaffected? Nicole left her thoughts to blow away on the mild breeze while walking to the lodge with Marc-Antoine and the armed escort. The ranger was relieved when he saw Nicole revived, in good spirits and happy. There was nothing worse than a sick or miserable guest on a photo safari, bouncing along in a Land Rover in rough terrain. Nicole met the other guests who were designated to be in the same vehicle for this late afternoon excursion. Everyone hoped to see the Big Five: elephant, lion, African buffalo, rhinoceros and leopard.

Once in the savanna, the guests were so consumed with finding the Big Five that they failed to notice a majestic purple and orange-hued sunset painted across the sky that the game ranger graciously pointed out to them. 'There's more than ferocious wildlife surrounding us,' he said. 'Across the vast savanna plains, you can see the light and shadows of nature in striking colours. Even an artist can't capture this beauty on canvas.'

Nicole loved sunsets. She realized the sunsets in South Africa were as magical as those in Egypt and Japan, countries she had visited. After marvelling at the sunset, it was time to track a leopard. At dusk, leopards usually lounged on a tree branch or somewhere on the ground protected by trees and bushes. Everyone aboard the Land Rover was eager to spot a leopard in the wild. Then the ranger and his tracker found a female resting under a tree on top of a five-foot termite mound. How lucky!

The ranger described the leopard as elegant, majestic and the most well-proportioned animal, compared to the lion or any other cat. 'There is something mysterious about her, look at the beauty of her curves, feel her power . . .'

Then one South African lady blurted out, 'You sound as if you're fantasizing about a woman.'

The fellow passengers burst into laughter. It was the same ranger who was to be married in a couple of weeks. Meanwhile, the leopard secretly basked in the attention of the onlookers with sublime grace. Certainly a feline to be admired.

After the sighting of the leopard, they drove off to a new destination. Lions had been spotted.

They must have eaten a good dinner, thought Nicole.

Four young male lions were lying on their backs with their legs stuck up in the air, showing off their big, fat bellies. One lady spotted a lioness peering through tall grass at the Land Rover. Then, one of the young males decided to give the group a show. He walked slowly over to a pond, yawned and then kneeled down with a bulging belly and lapped up some water. After hearing all about ferocious lions, this seemed faintly ridiculous: docile and content lions who were not at all interested in the humans looking at them.

After an hour of watching the svelte leopard with her dazzling topaz-coloured eyes, then observing the well-fed and contented lions, the group was in for a big shock. Night had fallen. The ranger asked the tracker to sit in the back seat of the Land Rover so that he could shine a floodlight on the surroundings – the headlights of the jeep were not strong enough in the pitch blackness of an African night. Little did the amateur safari hunters know that elephants are quite frightened by bright lights at night, and if they are with their young can become overly protective.

The ranger said to the tracker, 'If we come upon elephants, we'll have to dim the lights and use the infrared lights.' And then, a warning to the passengers, 'You'll have to remain still and be very quiet. If we scare them, they'll charge. One elephant could squash our Land Rover in one giant step – like Godzilla on the march.'

Although his comments made Nicole realize the enormity of this majestic beast, she still wanted to see an elephant in the wild. Animals in their natural habitat were very different from those in zoos. Out in the wilderness, they were ferocious, hence the need to tread with caution. Suddenly, the ranger stopped the car in its tracks and yelled at the tracker to extinguish the torchlight immediately. Seconds later, the infrared light shone upon a herd of elephants with their young. The Land Rover was literally three feet in front of a gigantic female. Her ears were flapping as she raised her trunk and trumpeted a fierce warning signal.

Nicole, who sat in the passenger seat next to the ranger, perceived that he was panicking.

Sensing danger, she asked the ranger in a low, calm voice, 'Don't you think we should take off and get out of here?'

In a flash, he revved up the engine and drove through thick brush until he found a trail where everyone would be safe. Driving through bush country with a minimum of lighting and not knowing whether or not the elephants were close behind was a frightful experience. In the distance, everyone heard the elephants trumpet.

What if we get stuck? Nicole wondered. Then, we're doomed.

The ranger hit a dirt road and the tracker once again illuminated his floodlight. There were seven tourists aboard and all let out a collective sigh of relief. The glaring trumpeting noise of that huge elephant with its long ivory tusks remained in their minds for the rest of the evening.

On the way back to the lodge, Nicole confided in the ranger that she was now scared of elephants. He tried to reassure her and explained that they were completely docile creatures during the daylight hours as they munched on tree leaves, dug for roots and ate grass. It was only from dusk until dawn that elephants could become ferocious because of their poor night vision. It was their instinct to protect their young as well as themselves from night predators. During the day, their eyesight was good and they actually were gentle creatures, rather curious of the people in Land Rovers who observed and admired their powerful beauty.

The ranger didn't convince Nicole. The once-treasured animal, that she had even ridden on the back of as a small child while on a vacation in India with her family, was no longer her favourite. All she could imagine was that with one big step or a charge, everyone would have been crushed. As a result of the trip, the leopard took on new meaning for her and became her preferred animal.

After her first eventful night safari, Nicole showered and relaxed in front of the burning fireplace in the bungalow. Nights in Africa could be cold. The crackling sounds of the fire moved her into a reverie where she was moved by the perfection in the world. She felt at one with God or what some called the Universal Force. Then, the wind from the chimney howled and awakened her with a swift realization that life was often imperfect as Marc-Antoine opened the door to their bungalow.

A heavy burden enveloped her heart as she looked at him. Something wasn't right but she couldn't figure it out and dismissed the physical sensation in her chest. He grunted a greeting at her and headed for the shower. Wasn't this supposed to be a trip to mend a broken relationship? Sometimes people reached a point in their lives and could no longer change, even if it would be for the better. Although accompanied by her husband, Nicole felt alone and lonely. She dreamed of having someone she loved by her side who shared her interests and passions in life, and who would put her first. Wasn't life all about love? Wasn't love important? Or was she being idealistic? She hoped not. Nicole scrutinized her life and wondered what the next steps would be on her journey in life.

There was a knock on the door, the porter was ready to escort Nicole and Marc-Antoine from their bungalow to the lodge for dinner in a beautifully-styled colonial dining-room. The walls had been decorated with the prize heads of various species of hunted animals. A roaring fireplace dominated the room, six foot high and six foot wide, with a shy lad stoking the fire to keep the guests cosy and warm.

The ritual was to have dinner with the people that you had been on safari with. In Nicole and Marc-Antoine's group, there were three South African women and a newly-wed French couple from the Normandy region. The South Africans were outlandish and funny. Nicole got the impression that they spent their time checking out all the game reserves in Africa. Flirting with the rangers was part of their game plan.

One of them said to Nicole, 'We're disappointed that our appointed ranger is in love and soon to be married.'

The ranger overheard the conversation, 'That's right, ladies. I'm unavailable. You should've come a year ago when I was still free.'

Jacques, the newly-wed, was full of their morning safari, 'We can't believe we saw lions mating.'

'You're lucky,' the ranger said, 'that only happens once every two or three years.'

'How appropriate for newlyweds!' said one of the South African ladies. 'Bravo!' Toasts were made, 'Chin-chin! To your health!'

Dinner continued with idle talk and went on until midnight. Afterwards, the guests returned to their bungalows to be rested and prepared for the next day's early morning safari with the same armed game ranger, who always brought along his trusted Shangaan tracker guide.

Nicole entered the suite to the sweet smell of wood burning in the fireplace. Someone must have come in earlier to rekindle the fire. A low, burning flame simmered in the fireplace and reminded her of the times she had occasionally stayed at Hotel de la Cigogne in Geneva during the winter when the night staff would prepare a lovely fire before she'd go to sleep. Fresh air, adventure and the crackle and sizzle of the fire put Nicole into dreamland from which she was awakened by another knock at 5.30 am. Marc-Antoine slept and lightly snored on a sofa in the adjoining room. Thus far, their interaction with one another had been minimal during this trip. Nothing had changed.

Nicole felt like sleeping some more but forced herself to roll out of bed; she didn't know when she would have the time for another wildlife safari. Africa was a long way away from both Paris and New York. During the morning safari, a couple from New York joined their group. Nicole liked New Yorkers but all these two talked about was how they couldn't wait to eat at McDonald's once they got home after a seventeen-hour flight. They were boisterous and complained that the South African cuisine was too fancy and complicated and, also, how they missed the hustle and bustle of New York. Nicole cringed at the thought of fast food but agreed that New York was one of the most vibrant cities in the world.

Her mind drifted from the Americans: I want to bring a bit of Singita back with me to Paris and New York. Nicole felt this adventure was the start of many more and represented something else. Her life was in the process of a miraculous transformation like a butterfly emerging from its silk-spun cocoon. Visions of fluttering white wings danced before her eyes.

The Land Rover drove quietly towards a herd of over two hundred African savanna buffalo while the Shangaan tracker on foot followed four young male lions who were stalking the buffalo. The lions were very patient. They advanced a few feet at a time, camouflaging themselves in the tall blond grass. The guests wondered why the lions were not perturbed by the subdued engine noise of the Land Rover following their cautious steps. The buffalo herd continued to graze, unaware of the lions.

The ranger said, 'The wind is blowing in a favourable direction for the lions so that the buffalo can't pick up their scent.'

The lions laid low in the bush and were only feet away from the herd. Still the buffalo didn't sense their presence. The wind continued to cooperate with the lions.

All of sudden, the lions pounced on the buffalo. They found their victim, hopefully, their next meal. One lion jumped on top of the buffalo and gripped him with his claws, simultaneously biting his neck, while another attached himself to the buffalo's belly. They held on with their sharp claws that dug deep into their prey's thick black skin. The other two lions circled around the same buffalo. The only reason that the lions were in with a chance was because it was getting dark. A big thunder and lightning storm was rolling across the savanna, making the morning dawn seem like dusk, their usual time of hunting.

Once the buffalo herd realized one of their own was being attacked, they charged and attacked the lions with their curved horns. They were fierce and chased the lions fifty feet away. The lions' hunting mission had failed and the maimed buffalo ran away with the protective herd. The safari group observed this surreal scene for an hour. Neither the buffalo nor the lions were fazed by the Land Rover with its passengers snapping pictures and filming the action.

This stuff is on National Geographic, thought Nicole. How cool to see it live!

Almost no one wanted to see a real live killing by the lions and, subsequently, were all pleased to witness such a spectacular hunt.

After the hunt, the sky darkened further and a freak storm appeared not far off in the distance. The ranger sped away, fast and furious, trying to get to the lodge before the storm struck. He advised everyone to put on their rain gear, hats and sunglasses to protect themselves. The storm was faster than the driver. Hail the size of half a golf ball pelted their heads and bodies. It hurt but, as far as Nicole was concerned, it added spice to their escapade. She witnessed enormous lightning bolts strike the ground and heard rolling thunder across the sky but mostly she shielded her head with her arms from the hail. Everyone was soaking wet despite the rain gear.

Back at their bungalow, Marc-Antoine took a hot shower and Nicole jumped into a hot jacuzzi to get the morning chill out. The storm lasted for about an hour and then the sun shone brightly – everything dried within five minutes. It was time for lunch. Nicole walked to the lodge without an escort, knowing she was taking a chance. But she arrived safely under the warm heat of the sun. Fifteen minutes later, Marc-Antoine, accompanied by an escort with a rifle, arrived at the outdoor restaurant.

The wooden chairs and tables on the main deck of the lodge, where a buffet lunch had been planned, had also dried out. The outdoor restaurant overlooked Sand River, which drought had reduced to a stream in a parched river bed. Freak hail storms didn't replenish the water supply. A herd of elephants down below decided to join the guests for lunch. Some munched on the long grass bordering the river and some drank from the stream. Nicole remarked how truly peaceful they were during the day, as the ranger had explained, and how majestic they appeared to her now. In the fields behind the elephants, a herd of impala could be seen grazing. Periodically Nicole peered through her binoculars to gaze at the animals while she ate lunch with the other members of the party. Marc-Antoine, true to nature, flirted with one of the South African ladies right in front of her. Nicole didn't care any more: she knew their marriage was nearly over.

During lunch, the director of the hotel announced a walking safari but Nicole was too tired and decided to take a siesta. Marc-Antoine and the South African ladies decided to go. Nicole walked back to her bungalow and sunbathed in the nude on the deck next to the private pool. It was pure bliss. While watching the animals in the savanna below her, she noticed a sketch pad, paintbrushes and watercolours set aside on a low wooden table. Although it had been years since she last sketched or painted, she decided to try to paint the animals. Actually, it was eight years ago when she decided on a whim to take drawing classes at the Art Student's League in New York City. Those were her bohemian days. Her conservative French–American parents were not thrilled at all when she left her post at the World Bank in London to study art in New York for a year. At that time, Nicole rationalized that she was only twenty-five, with a long life ahead of her, so why not? She discovered she wasn't at all talented but she was imaginative and got lots of laughs from her fellow students and art teachers. Having a good sense of humour, she was able to laugh at her own paintings; sometimes her human figures looked like aliens. One day, one of her art teachers asked her if she would like to pose in the nude for his painting project. She decided to take this as a compliment but refused out of modesty. At Singita, Nicole painted an imaginary hippo swimming amongst the tall reeds in the Sand River. She giggled at her creation.

After relaxing and painting for an hour, she met Marc-Antoine and the ladies at the lodge and had afternoon tea with them. It was time for a late afternoon safari. Nicole was hoping to see hippos and rhinos this time. Along the way, her group encountered a family of wart-hogs.

Three babies followed their mother in line formation, their little tails sticking straight up into the sky. After a feast of termites, one of their delicacies, the wart-hogs went over to a pond and drank. It was an adorable scene right out of a Disney film.

Meanwhile, the tracker, looking for the faecal matter of rhinos, spotted some mounds and pointed out the piles to the tourists. It looked different from that of the elephants, a bit smaller and darker. As the sun slowly faded into the horizon, rhinos were finally tracked down. It was a beautiful family of three. The mother and her baby were frightened by the noise of the Land Rover and ran towards the bush while the father stayed behind to defend his family. The rhinos ran slightly sideways with a little hop or kick with their heavy feet. Nicole called it 'the rhino hip-hop'. The ranger followed the family as silently as possible so as not to make them nervous. 'Rhinos are usually calmer,' he said. 'Something must have happened earlier to cause their jumpiness.'

The tracker found another big white rhino that ran and hid in the bush. Nicole could see his tiny round eyes as he peered out of the branches and wondered what he might be thinking. She loved the rhinos and the wart-hogs. Each species had its own distinct personality, but her favourite of the Big Five remained the leopard: sleek, mysterious and clever.

After the rhino hunt, the ranger pulled up next to a big pond inhabited by a family of hippos. Again, a family of three. The mother hippo, whose instinct was to protect her baby, decided to test the visitors. She moved close to the edge of the pond and opened her mouth wide open to show her large teeth, tongue and tonsils. A ferocious *grande dame*! The father hippo swam in circles near the middle of the water and the baby sometimes followed him, but mostly stayed near its mother. Round, brown eyes stared at the guests. Mama hippo was a show girl. Again, she approached the edge of the watering hole and showed half of her voluptuous body. A moment later, she whipped her body in a half circle with her jaws wide open, crashed back into the water and swam away with a smirk on her face. It was quite an act. For the third time, she came increasingly close to the tourists but never left the water.

The ranger explained her actions, 'It's their feeding time. She's warning us with her deep roaring grunts and snorts that she and her family are hungry, and want to come out of the water and graze on the grass.' The setting sun was the signal that dinner time had arrived for the hippos.

Nicole was amused and intrigued by the mother hippo's show of bravado. The experienced South African women were nervous though, because hippos were considered the most dangerous of all the mammals and the number-one killer of naïve tourists. One of the jittery South Africans jumped into the Land Rover while the other two crouched behind its big tyres. The ranger and the tracker stood in front of the vehicle with their rifles ready. Nicole and Marc-Antoine were off to the left of the ranger. Motionless, Nicole observed the scene.

The hippo had an impressive array of tusk-like canines and incisors. If it were provoked when a calf was nearby, or if its way to the water was blocked, then the hippo would be aroused to attack, which invariably led to death. What Nicole was learning on this safari was the golden rule: 'Respect the role of wild animals in their natural habitat and, in return, they will leave you alone.'

Finally, the mother hippo left the water's edge and swam to the middle of the pond to rejoin her family. Then, the ranger communicated to all the guests that it was now safe to have cocktails.

Since cocktail hour was part of the safari excursion at dusk, it was not really considered too dangerous as long as the golden rule was respected. Everyone felt at ease and started socializing while the ranger and the tracker put their rifles down and set up a table with a white tablecloth. Bottles of red and white South African wine, beer and gin and tonic were served, along with some small bites. The cook at the lodge, in a devilish mood, had secretly spiked the hors-d'oeuvres with small amounts of hashish. Anyone who dipped into the food and sipped the wine was soon high from the hashish and semi-drunk from the wine.

After a few glasses of white wine and a couple of bites one South African woman yelled out to the hippos, 'Replay.'

Nicole, also affected, said, 'Wow, look at that mama hippo dancing, twirling and splashing in the water.'

Another South African remarked, like a radio commentator, 'There goes the papa hippo. He's submerged himself and is now running on the bottom of the lake.'

The male hippo did indeed disappear to reappear on the other side of the lake. How she had seen the hippo running underwater was beyond Nicole. Everyone imagined the raid of the hippos and they all laughed, danced and imitated the movements of the show-off mama.

Reality struck this surreal cocktail hour when the female hippo became impatient with these noisy people and gave one more round of grunting and snorting, showing the power of her body. In that instant, everyone jumped for cover into the Land Rover while the ranger and tracker hurriedly picked up their rifles, ready to fire if necessary. When the female hippo turned her back and disappeared under the water, they quickly repacked the picnic basket and threw it into the boot. The ranger revved up the engine and sped away, the tracker sitting on a special seat at the back, on the lookout. The tourists were silent, happy that they left this hippo family in peace.

For Nicole, the photo safari adventure was a great success. A wide variety of animals had been tracked and she had seen the Big Five. The only animal not spotted was the cheetah but apparently it was the wrong season. Oh well, Nicole could look forward to another safari in another country where a cheetah sighting would be more probable.

A lovely fire roared in the central fireplace at the lodge and the safari travellers consumed more cocktails before dinner near the warmth of the hearth. Nicole's cold body shivered and her teeth silently chattered. She walked over to the fireplace and stood in front of the blazing fire hoping to warm herself up. There were three stools near the fire, all occupied. An Italian man, a famous Formula 1 driver, and his son were sitting there, conversing with a woman who was probably their private safari guide. The Italian gentleman offered Nicole his seat. She didn't mind standing after riding in a Land Rover all afternoon but he insisted.

She was flattered and sat down and spoke Italian with them. She found out that the man's son lived in New York with his mother and that school vacation had just begun. The boy wanted to go on a safari to see bush-babies. The thirteen-year-old was obsessed with these creatures. Throughout the conversation he kept insisting, 'I want to see the bush-babies. I want to see the bush-babies, Papa!'

They must have arrived that evening: the teenager was so adamant and excited about starting his safari adventure as soon as possible and it was true that one could only see the adorable bush-babies at night. They were nocturnal and foraged mainly in the trees. At night, with a floodlight, one could see the bush-babies jumping wildly amongst the branches of the trees in search of food or sometimes calmly looking down at the tourists with their big, black-ringed eyes. Nicole understood the young boy's impatience but the father and guide preferred to put it off until tomorrow night and eat dinner – typical adults.

Dinner was announced. The guests went to their respective tables with their fellow safari travellers. Nicole and Marc-Antoine's group was in a jovial mood since cocktails had already begun with the late afternoon show of the hippos. Dinner and wine were served. Nicole asked the three women if they had always gone on safari together.

One lady said, 'Oh no, I'm just a "rent-a-friend".'

Marc-Antoine said, 'And, I'm just a "rent-a-husband".'

Everyone laughed while Nicole rolled her eyes.

Apparently, two of the South African women were sisters, who had been on many safaris together, while the other was a dear friend. This was the first time the sisters had been able to convince their 'rent-a-friend' to come along with them and she finally admitted that she was having a good time.

Out of the blue, Marc-Antoine changed the topic to politics and criticized the South Africans for their past political and economic discrimination against non-whites. The South African women felt uneasy and tried to defend themselves.

'Rent-a-friend' said, 'I know you foreigners think we're horrible people.'

'Not really,' Nicole replied. 'We're aware that some of the whites helped abolish apartheid and that change came from within as well as from external factors.'

The elder sister, with the other two women nodding in agreement, commented, 'What you may not know is that the whites too suffered from the oppression of the government and the lack of freedom of expression. It was a police state even for us. Today, it's much better, with freedom of the press and freedom of movement for us, the blacks, and the minorities. It'll probably take several years with serious steps toward socio-political reforms to overcome the damage done by apartheid.'

'Rent-a-friend' interrupted, 'President Mbeki asked all of his people to take responsibility for themselves and then the nation shall evolve into a prosperous and free country. We have hope because the leaders of the past and present have had vision and foresight.'

Nicole expressed her view that the situation in South Africa was analogous to sailing around the Cape of Good Hope, where ships either triumphed or perished. The captain of the ship navigated his crew as best as possible to journey around this dangerous peninsula. In the case of a freak and treacherous storm, he'd be called upon to inspire faith and courage in his crew so that they could get through the tumultuous seas to eventually see the light at the end of the tunnel and reach their final destination. The simile represented hope for the peaceful integration of the multitude of nations that comprised South Africa and for renewed prosperity. South Africa could become the beacon of light for the rest of the continent of Africa. As many people knew, this was the dream of former President Mandela and of his successor President Mbeki.

The conversation moved on. 'Rent-a-friend' remarked, 'Blacks think that Aids is a white man's disease, that's why they won't wear condoms. Such a belief is especially true among the tribes. And, a black man is rich by the number of wives and daughters he has, because when he marries off his daughters he is compensated in riches. He doesn't take into consideration whether he can feed, clothe and educate his huge family. He also thinks that the white man was blessed by the sky or God. Everything fell out of the sky and was given to the white man. That was why the white race was rich.'

The ranger perked up and commented, 'Remember the film called *The Gods must be Crazy*. It was filmed in South Africa. A Coke bottle dropped out of the sky, a tribal man found it and wondered what it was and what it represented.'

The conversation became lighter and lighter and the ladies traded jokes with the ranger.

Nicole excused herself from the table, pondering on the crazy world we all live in. She wished everyone well since she and Marc-Antoine would be leaving in the morning. Marc-Antoine lingered on with the dinner guests. The night porter, fully armed, walked Nicole back to the bungalow.

Cape Town

Singita. Singita. Singita. How Nicole had loved her trip to Singita. She and Marc-Antoine made the return journey to Johannesburg. Again, she had a terrible reaction in the four-seater plane but they landed without mishap. Marc-Antoine had one more trip to make. He had planned to go to the Democratic Republic of Congo to meet President Kabila at the Marble Palace to discuss diamond and gold projects. Nicole had a sickening feeling about this trip in her gut and pleaded with Marc-Antoine not to go, to postpone it for another time, but Marc-Antoine insisted that when an opportunity arose it must be seized. Nicole acquiesced and visited some friends in Cape Town until Marc-Antoine returned.

Cecil and Corné Clifton greeted Nicole at the airport and brought her to their home overlooking Table Bay. Their household servant served tea on the terrace as a high noon sun streamed down on her cheeks. The sun's warmth comforted Nicole's soul. As she conversed with Cecil and Corné, she marvelled at the glorious view of the royal blue bay filled with sailboats adorned with brightly coloured spinnakers. Off to the right, she had a partial view of the majestic Table Mountain. Nicole and Corné chatted for a couple of hours because they hadn't seen each other for a year and a half. Then Nicole, overcome with fatigue from travelling, asked if she could take a nap. Corné rang for Nadia, the head of the household staff, and told her to show Nicole to her room as well as bring some fresh fruit and mineral water. Nicole thanked Corné and they kissed each other on the cheeks four times as was the Parisian custom.

A few hours later, Nicole received a call on her cell phone from Michelle Delamare, the executive assistant to Marc-Antoine at the company's office in Johannesburg. Michelle hesitated but told Nicole what had happened.

'Marc-Antoine was to meet with President Kabila at the presidential residence when rebels came out of nowhere and started shooting at everyone near the palace. Your husband was caught in the crossfire and hit in the chest . . .' Weeping, she continued, 'He was such a good boss. The CEO sent a private plane to pick him up and fly him back to Jo'burg to be operated on at one of our hospitals. There was no way they were going to let Marc-Antoine be treated in a country wracked by civil war and with poor medical facilities . . .' She sniffled, 'Marc-Antoine died aboard the aircraft. His last words were that he wanted to see you before he died. He requested to have his funeral in Cape Town because he thought it was the most beautiful place on Earth.'

At this point, exhaustion filled Nicole's body. She couldn't believe what she had heard. Was she dreaming? She knew he did business in rogue countries because the challenge and danger thrilled him and probably because he thought he was invincible. Nicole started shaking and crying. For Marc-Antoine to have been killed in the crossfire of a civil war in the darkness of Africa. How could this happen? It didn't make sense. A pain recurred in her chest and triggered the memory of the pain she experienced while in Singita, and then again when she had wanted Marc-Antoine to postpone his trip to the Congo. Somehow her intuition had forewarned her of these tragic events but she hadn't understood the warnings. Guilt seeped into her mind for not being able to prevent his death. Now she was helpless.

Sometimes the events in her life were too much for her to handle and sleep was her remedy for physical, emotional or mental fatigue. Nicole slept until Corné knocked on the door. When there was no reply she opened the door and walked over to sit on Nicole's bed. Overcome with grief, Nicole sobbed in her arms.

Riddled with mixed emotions, Nicole said, 'You know Marc-Antoine and I had a special connection but there was no affection between us and I was thinking of getting a divorce. Now this, how can I live with this guilt?'

Corné held Nicole's hand. 'It's not your fault. He was in the wrong place at the wrong time.'

'His assistant, Michelle, said he wanted to be buried here.'

'I know. She called me too. Don't worry. Cecil and I will take care of the arrangements.'

Nicole, still weeping, said, 'I hope to return your kindness one day.'

Memorial Service

Three days later, the service was held at a small chapel in Cape Town. Nicole prepared a short address and spoke to the circle of family, friends, colleagues and acquaintances. Finally, gazing at the ceiling of the chapel, she said, 'Marc-Antoine, we want you to be happy. Unleash your chains from earthly possessions. Free your soul. Take flight. Understand the meaning of love until happiness reigns in your spirit. We wish that you cross over to the other side in peace. May God be with you.'

Then she walked over to the coffin and placed forty-seven white, long-stemmed roses across the mahogany casket, one for each year of his life. She prayed silently for him and slowly inched herself towards the entrance of the church. Her diaphragm constricted and her breathing became heavy; grief and sadness overwhelmed her spirit. She desperately needed fresh air. Out of the corner of her eye, she saw her parents and her brother. When the service ended, they came over and hugged her, reminding her that they would always be there for her during the best of times and the most difficult of times. Her eyes filled with tears. A thought flickered in her mind that in a former life John must have been an enlightened monk. Why this strange thought all of a sudden? Was stress making her irrational?

As Nicole kept up with the protocol of the events, more thoughts raced through her mind: things happen for a reason, although I don't know what it is at the moment. Mon Dieu! I don't understand the timing of Marc-Antoine's death. Why did he die so young?

Many people gave their condolences to Nicole. Finally, Corné rescued her from the crowd and they quietly left the family, friends, colleagues and acquaintances to mourn Marc-Antoine. Nicole desired to fly to New York as soon as possible, to get lost in the crowds. Run away. Escape from reality. What better place than Manhattan?

Corné took Nicole to Table Mountain to breathe in the pure air rolling in off the bay and gaze at the red sunset. Nicole practised some Chi Gong that she had learned in New York. The relaxing physical movements of Chi Gong helped her to relieve stress from her mind and body. She breathed the mountain air in deeply, then exhaled about ten times while moving in a figure of eight and swaying her arms like tree branches in harmony with the wind while Corné sat in silence, watching the sunset.

After the sun set, they were both in better spirits and ready to go back. Corné telephoned Cecil to say they'd soon be home. He understood that Nicole needed his wife's friendship and comfort during this traumatic time. As planned, Cecil had followed Marc-Antoine's wishes with a party overflowing with Iranian beluga caviar, Russian vodka and Dom Perignon champagne. For those who didn't like those delicacies, the cook had also prepared grilled fish, chicken and vegetables. Also requested was a group of *gitanes* – gypsies – who would play bohemian music with violins, accordion and guitar.

Marc-Antoine had always said that when he eventually passed away everyone was to remember and talk about the good times and enjoy themselves at his farewell party but when Nicole and Corné arrived they found everyone sad. Nicole walked around the house pleading with them all, 'Please, remember the good times. Marc-Antoine wanted a party for all of you to get together and enjoy one another, reminisce about the old times. Enjoy! Eat the caviar, drink the vodka. You know he was a gourmet and a gourmand!'

Little by little, the guests relaxed, recounted their stories and some even started laughing. An hour or so later, Cecil, a very warm-hearted South African, stood up and made a toast in honour of Nicole. Champagne was poured and everyone raised their glasses.

'Chin-chin!'

Nicole, in turn, made a toast thanking Cecil and Corné for organizing this beautiful party that Marc-Antoine would have heartily approved of and then went over to her mother, father and brother and hugged them individually, exchanging a few private words.

* * *

The next morning, John accompanied his emotionally distraught sister to the airport, for her flight to New York, in a chauffeur-driven car.

During the journey, John told her, 'Tomorrow, I'm going to Pretoria to try and work out a grant to study the bush people.'

Nicole, who still had her wits about her, said, 'You'd be better off making documentaries on the African tribes rather than undertaking scholarly research that very few people read.'

'Even in times of stress you can come up with good ideas.'

They both smiled and then John asked, 'Why was Marc-Antoine supposed to meet with Kabila? Didn't you find it odd when he mentioned this trip?'

'I did have a strange feeling about it and asked him to postpone it but he insisted on going.'

John replied, 'Perhaps he was a spy working for the French government.'

'Oh! You've been reading too many novels!' Nicole exclaimed.

'At least you're smiling now,' teased John.

'May I change the topic?' asked Nicole. 'Where's Sarah?'

'She left me for Hollywood,' said John, glancing down at his shiny, black shoes.'

'I'm sorry.'

'I'd rather not talk about it.'

Finally, the chauffeur arrived at the international terminal and arranged for a porter to take care of Nicole's luggage. Meanwhile, Nicole gave John a big, comforting hug and jumped out of the car.

He rolled down the window and said, 'I'll always be there for you.'

Nicole replied, 'You're my favourite brother.'

She stood and waved goodbye until the car turned a corner.

As Nicole sat in the passenger seat on the plane, she closed her eyes and a tear trickled down her left cheek. Minutes later, a flight attendant tapped her on the shoulder and said, 'Madam, fasten your seatbelt. We're about to take off.'

Chapter 6
Search for Enlightenment

Departure from New York, Autumn 1999

Some months after her arrival in New York, Celeste sent Nicole an email: 'When you lose hope, there's nothing more to do than to move on and move forward with your life.' This was good advice and prompted Nicole to take a trip. She loved Paulo Coelho's *The Alchemist*, about a young man learning how to follow his heart and becoming transformed in the process. Nicole thought it was her time to embark on a journey and discover the hidden treasures of her soul. Since the death of Marc-Antoine she had turned into a cocoon but during the past few days she had felt little wings trying to flap on her shoulders and the last time she walked through Central Park she had seen a hawk circling over her head. These were signs from her heart, nature and one of her best friends that life goes on.

While in New York, Nicole had experienced pain and grief. It was normal to be emotionally upset and she sought psychotherapy. Her psychologist helped her immensely and told her to put aside some time every day to grieve. Supposedly, this speeded up the mourning process. Before dawn, Nicole would spend ten minutes allowing painful memories and thoughts of Marc-Antoine to flood her mind and heart. Soft instrumental music played in the background and scented candles flickered shadows on the walls. During this process, her heart felt heavy, almost as if she were having a heart attack, then tears streamed down her cheeks. Sometimes, she cried violently into a pillow. Other times, when filled with anger, she punched a pillow for a long minute. Once the ten minutes were up, she was counselled to stop and get on with her daily activities until the next scheduled grieving period the following morning. Afterwards, she always jumped into a hot shower to cleanse any negative emotions that had erupted during the process until she felt purified. Diligently, Nicole performed this ritual for forty days. Once the forty days were over, she occasionally practised these bereavement periods to purge any sadness from her heart. After a while, her psychologist thought she was coping well and Nicole realized that the tragic loss of Marc-Antoine need not ruin her happiness for ever. Time proved to be the natural healer and it was time to travel.

She decided that Egypt would be the first destination on her journey towards self-actualization. In her heart, she knew that other countries and people might play a role in helping her down the right path, but at the present moment the pyramids of Egypt beckoned to her and whispered in her ear to come and visit. Nicole had been to Egypt a few times to visit her Egyptian uncle's family and remembered one occasion when she found peace in the silence of the desert. She had been riding on a camel some distance from the Pyramids at Giza but still near enough to see the beauty and power of their geometric design. Her soul desired peace and happiness, and she knew something extraordinary would happen while on her trip through this magical and mystical country.

She called her uncle, Marwan Al-Saher, and asked if she could call his sister, Mouna Hanady, in Cairo while travelling in Egypt. Her uncle had recently moved from Cairo to New York because he had been appointed the Egyptian ambassador to the United Nations. 'What a coincidence!' Uncle Marwan said to Nicole over the telephone, 'I'll be going to Cairo next Friday. Book the same flight and at the check-in desk, we'll ask to be seated together.'

'That's great news! I'll see you at the airport.'

The next Friday, Kerala, Nicole's Indian friend from New York, drove her to JFK Airport to see her off to her exotic destination.

Search for Enlightenment

'What do you want to happen to you during your trip to Egypt?' she asked.

Nicole reflected for a moment, and answered with a smile, 'Enlightenment.'

Kerala said, 'That's deep. You're the only one I know who would say that. You know, your friendship to me is like a nugget of gold.'

She dropped Nicole off at the kerb. They hugged each other, and Nicole promised to call her when she returned to New York.

Nicole met her uncle as planned at the check-in desk, and they arranged to sit together in Business Class on their flight to Cairo. It was a pleasant trip for both of them, catching up with each other's news, watching movies and sleeping. When the plane landed at Cairo Airport, Nicole saw a huge bright yellow sun setting over the sandstone-coloured land.

This is a good omen, she thought.

As they departed from the airport, Uncle Marwan said to Nicole, 'Allah maak!'

Nicole gave Uncle Marwan a hug, and said, 'God be with you, too.'

He reminded her that if she needed anything to give him or his sister Mouna a call, and they would take care of her. She thanked him for his kind hospitality and his gracious welcome to Egypt.

Nicole had to change from the international airport to the domestic one, from where she flew to Aswan to be met by a chauffeur-driven Mercedes. When she arrived at the Old Cataract Hotel, built on the banks of the Nile, the manager of the hotel greeted her, 'Welcome, Your Highness.' Nicole was flattered and amused at the same time. It was the first time someone had addressed her as royalty. This sweet gesture would be retained in her memory. She arrived at 1.00 am and had to wake up early to catch a flight to Abu Simbel. The manager escorted her to the Agatha Christie suite. Agatha Christie had written *Death on the Nile* in this hotel and had stayed in the suite that was eventually named after her. Nicole was thrilled to stay in the same suite. In Christie's novel, the author described the opulent lifestyle of those who came and sojourned at the Old Cataract. It was the era of jazz, flappers and motorcars. In front of the hotel, felucca regattas took place on the Nile. Feluccas were sailing boats that zigzagged up and down the serpentine river. The Old Cataract was reputed for its quality of life as well as the celebrities who chose to vacation there. Nicole was enamoured by her suite, and with the authentic telephone from the Thirties that Agatha Christie had apparently actually used. The suite's original decoration had also been preserved – a mixture of art nouveau and art deco.

Amazing! thought Nicole.

All of a sudden, she felt exhausted from her trip and the excitement of being in Eygpt. She collapsed on the bed, phoned reception and asked for a wake-up call so that she could make her early flight to Abu Simbel near the border of Sudan, considered the jewel of the desert.

Abu Simbel

At 5.45 am the hotel operator called to wake her up. She answered the telephone.

'Good morning, Your Highness.'

Again she was flattered but wondered why everyone at the hotel insisted on calling her this. Nicole smiled because it felt wonderful to be treated like a princess. After she had showered and dressed, she descended the grand staircase and met the chauffeur in the lobby who drove her to the airport. She flew to Abu Simbel in an amphibious aircraft and landed on the serene blue water of Lake Nasser. From the seaplane she admired the temples that had been carved out of the sandstone-coloured rock. The majestic site took her breath away. Abu Simbel was located in the heart of Nubian territory, almost a stone's throw from Sudan and about 150 miles from Aswan. Ramses II, recognized as the greatest pharaoh in Egypt, had built these temples to honour Amon-Ra, Harmakhis and Ptah. Over the centuries, Abu Simbel became the monument that glorified Ramses the Great. Nicole stepped out of the seaplane onto land and walked towards the temple.

Marco, an Italian tour guide, spotted her all alone.

'Ciao bella!' he said.

She responded to him in Italian, 'Ciao, come stai?'

Italians were such flirts but so much fun.

'Since you understand Italian, why don't you join our group?' the guide asked her.

'I'd love to.'

'I'm Marco.'

'Pleased to meet you. I'm Nicole,' she said as she extended her hand. Marco pretended to kiss the back of her hand; Nicole blushed.

It was a tour group of about twenty people. Soon they were all at the entrance of the temple. Marco explained that the façade of this temple, represented by four gigantic statues, depicted the all-powerful ruler of his time, Ramses II. Nicole felt she was the size of an ant next to these enormous structures.

'These four colossal statues of Ramses II are twenty-metres high,' Marco said. 'From ear to ear, his head is four metres wide, and his smiling lips measure over a metre.' No wonder Nicole felt so small. Marco told the group to look at the signatures on the legs of Ramses II left by nineteenth-century tourists. 'The smaller statues sculpted near the legs of each colossus represent members of the royal family.'

The group continued and entered a sanctuary sixty-five metres from the entrance considered the most sacred place in the temple. There were another four statues seated in this space.

Marco continued, 'François Champollion, a French scholar, came to the conclusion that this temple was built for a reason. He called it the "miracle of the sun". Twice a year, at the solstices, the sun floods the temple and reaches this sanctuary, highlighting three of the four statues: Amon-Ra, Harmakhis and Ramses II. The fourth statue, Ptah, the god of darkness, is never struck by the rays of the sun.'

A member of the group remarked, 'What an extraordinary architectural feat.'

'That's why Monsieur Champollion called it the "miracle of the sun".'

The tour group left the Ramses II temple and walked over to the temple of Hathor, dedicated to Nefertari, the beloved queen and wife of Ramses II. Marco pointed out that the statues of Nefertari were as large as those of Ramses II.

He continued, 'It was the first time in pharoanic Egypt that a wife and husband were represented on a façade of a temple in equal proportions. Normally, the members of the royal family were shown next to the leg, no taller than from the foot to the knee, like you saw at the previous temple.'

A woman in the group said, 'Ramses II must have truly loved Nefertari to have had this temple erected for her.'

Nicole interjected, 'Maybe Shah Jahan was the reincarnation of Ramses II. He was the Mogul emperor who built the Taj Mahal for his beloved wife after her death.' Everyone nodded in agreement at the comparison of pharoanic Egyptian culture with that of seventeenth-century India. By this time the tour had ended. Nicole thanked Marco, left the group and strolled around the grounds near Lake Nasser.

She noticed a group of Sudanese people having a picnic. There was an incredibly beautiful woman sitting there dressed in black. What was striking about her was not only her beauty but also the henna painted in floral patterns on her hands. It was a work of art. Nicole remembered how her Indian friends had mentioned that Indian women painted their hands with henna before weddings. Perhaps this custom had come from Arabia. India or Arabia? It didn't matter but the mixture of cultures over the centuries proved interesting. In any event, the encounter with these people made Nicole curious to discover Sudanese cuisine at the hotel's Nubian restaurant.

The seaplane landed on Lake Nasser and picked up Nicole as arranged. Once aboard she waved goodbye to Abu Simbel. The flight was almost like a movie scene from *Out of Africa*, though Nicole was neither with a lover nor in a two-seater open bi-plane! Once more she dreamed that she could be with someone she loved to share all of these adventures. Oh well! At least she had her dreams and no one could take them away.

Aswan: Nubian Restaurant

Back at the hotel, Nicole showered, put on a terry-cloth bathrobe and tried to muster up the courage to dine alone at the cosy little Nubian restaurant. It would be her only chance on this trip. She overcame her anxiety about dining alone in a foreign country when she remembered what a friend from New York had said, 'Don't get stressed, get dressed!'

She repeated the mantra to herself, 'Don't get stressed, get dressed!' and put on a long, flowing, white summer dress, ornamented with artistic, turquoise jewellery and sandals to match. Before she went to the restaurant, she quickly surfed the Web on her laptop to learn more about Sudanese cuisine. It was influenced by the Arabs, the French, the English and the Italians; the last three due to colonialism. Sudan was composed of almost six hundred tribes whose common language was Arabic. Her computer battery died. She'd have to discover the food and drink through the palate rather than the Internet.

Search for Enlightenment

When she entered the restaurant, the *maître d'hotel* escorted her to a low table where she seated herself on comfortable pillows decorated with ostrich feathers. The waiter brought her a complementary glass of tabrihana, a slightly sweetened fruit drink, a traditional Sudanese welcome. She was given a warm towel scented with rose water on a copper platter to clean her hands. The waiter placed a large ivory cloth on her knees in place of the traditional Western napkin. Nicole tried to practise what little Arabic she knew but the waiter kindly responded in English.

'Surprise me with the specialities of the house,' Nicole said.

She had an open mind when it came to discovering the customs, culture and cuisine of different peoples.

First, the waiter brought her some shorba, a soup consisting of lamb flavoured with peanut butter and lemon.

The shorba prepared her tastebuds for the meal to follow. Next, the waiter brought her kisra, a pancake-like flat bread to eat with the main dish. The custom was to break off a piece of this bread, fold it and use it to scoop up the food, and then put it into your mouth. You ate the bread together with the food. Another waiter brought her a spectacular dish: a fish sculpted to look like a pyramid with green, dill-flavoured sauce poured over it.

Nicole exclaimed, 'What a clever idea!'

It was a white fish and very easy to eat with the kisra. To her delight, the fish pyramid was also accompanied with white rice, flavoured with raisins, almonds and coriander.

The waiter brought her a hand bowl to wash her hands after she had completed the main dish.

'Thank you,' she said. 'Your choices were superb and the fish was delicious.'

The dessert he brought was a crème caramel, a Sudanese caramel dessert.

'But this is a French dessert!'

The waiter replied, 'Yes, madam. Sudan was once a French colony and we fell in love with crème caramel. It is my favourite dessert, madam.' He flashed a smile and some teeth with golden caps reflected the light from the candle on Nicole's table.

Proud of her French heritage, Nicole said, 'You have good taste.'

After the crème caramel, she sipped a succulent clove-spiced tea. Her dining experience was accompanied by a Nubian musician dressed in a light-blue djellabah, playing the oud. As he sang and bounced on the balls of his feet while strumming his fingers on the oud, he easily charmed his audience. He was a cheerful fellow with a feminine voice. Nicole loved it when he sang 'Ana Bahibbik Ya Shocolata', trying to imitate the tune of 'Ya Mustafa'. He seemed to love chocolate, because his lips smiled and his eyes twinkled when he sang the word 'Shocolata'. He danced his way over to Nicole and asked her what song she would like to hear.

'"Ya Mustafa"', she replied, wanting to hear the real thing. It was a popular song in France during the Sixties, sung by Dalida, and still well known in French-speaking and Arabic countries.

All the French people in the restaurant sang or hummed along with Nicole and the Nubian musician, clapping their hands to the beat of the chorus. Nicole sang, laughed, and enjoyed the festive atmosphere. The only thing she missed was a loving companion with whom to share her life experiences. This seemed to be a recurrent theme, both when she was married and now she was widowed.

When she had finished her meal she returned to the Agatha Christie suite and waiting messages. One was from Lily Love who had invited her to see the opera *Aida* at the Pyramids just outside Cairo under the starlit skies. The invitation was for the day after tomorrow. Lily said she would be arriving with a couple of friends from London using her husband's private jet.

I'll rearrange my plans and fly to Cairo, Nicole thought. I'll call Mouna to see if I can stay with her. It'd be nicer to stay with family than at a hotel. Who could miss *Aida* when Verdi wrote it using Egypt and Sudan as a backdrop for the love story? How fortunate I am to receive this invitation!

After her extraordinary day of sightseeing, discovering a new culture and receiving the invitation to *Aida*, Nicole went to bed. These adventures were helping her to forget about Marc-Antoine.

Nicole hoped that one day she'd meet a successful man who was humble and secure within himself, who would become the love of her life. A psychic from New York had told her that she'd learn to trust men again, especially when a gallant white knight was destined to come along and sweep her off her feet in some exotic foreign land in the not too distant future. She managed a smile though profoundly immersed in her dreams, knowing that deep down she was a true romantic who believed in fairy tales.

Journey to Philae

Nicole woke up late the next morning. She had forgotten to ask for a wake-up call and missed her tour to Philae, a temple on a tiny island called Agilkia in the middle of the River Nile at the frontier of Upper Eygpt and Lower Nubia. The temple was consecrated to the Egyptian goddess Isis, one of the most important goddesses of ancient Eyptian history. According to one legend Isis was the devoted wife of Osiris. Isis and Osiris ruled over Eygpt until Seth, another god, became jealous and wanted to overthrow the throne. Seth tricked Osiris into climbing in a box that was instantly nailed shut, covered with melted lead, then thrown into the Nile. Isis grieved for her husband.

Then she heard Osiris had been found in Byblos. She went to Byblos and, with magical powers brought Osiris back to life long enough to conceive a child with him. She stayed in Byblos until she gave birth to Horus. Meanwhile, Seth found out that Isis had hidden the dead body of Osiris. He searched and found Osiris, cut him up into fourteen pieces and had his remains scattered throughout Eygpt. Once again Isis became forlorn and furious with Seth.

Once more, she looked for her beloved Osiris. She found all the body parts and, with the help of the gods, performed magic to rejoin his body. During the process Isis performed the Rite of Rebirth that gave Osiris eternal life. As she herself was a deity with wings, she flapped her wings to fill the nose and mouth of Osiris with air that gave him oxygen to live for ever in peace. The eternal resting place of Osiris on Earth was at the temple of Isis. These supernatural acts of love demonstrated the true devotion of Isis for her husband.

Followers worshipped Isis in Ancient Egypt and also revered her today. She had been called the Goddess of Magic, the Goddess of Love, the Giver of Life, the Queen of the Gods and the Goddess of Marriage and Protection. Isis had the ability to give the gift of immortality as she had done for her beloved husband. This was why she was often portrayed carrying the ankh, the Egyptian symbol for eternal life that looked like a cross with a looped top. Isis was also recognized as a divine healer. She shared her secrets of healing with her priestesses, who later passed on this information to priestesses in Crete, Byblos and Babylon – the lands and cities in proximity to Egypt. According to legend, whenever anyone felt the wind blowing gently on his face, Isis was at work trying to refresh his soul.

After waiting for an hour for breakfast, the waiter set up the table on the balcony overlooking the Nile. Nicole enjoyed watching the white-sailed feluccas zigzag slowly up and down the river. After breakfast, she dressed in beige Bermuda shorts, a short-sleeved white safari-style shirt and JP Tod loafers. She put on her Chanel sunglasses and slung her Prada knapsack containing her compact Canon camera over her shoulder. She left her room and walked down the grand, wooden, spiralling staircase to the main hall of the hotel. She told the concierge that she had missed her tour to Philae.

'Not to worry, madam,' he said. 'You can hire a taxi to the port of departure. We'll have a boat take you to the island, wait for you, and then take you back to the port. The taxi driver will wait for you, and bring you back to the hotel. You'll be safe. We'll arrange everything for you right now.'

Nicole felt relieved.

They drove for about twenty minutes before arriving at the port. Alongside the port were small hills with many goats grazing and walking around in freedom. At the entrance of the marina, the taxi driver told her he'd wait for her as planned. Nicole walked to the only boat that had a captain. It was a tiny, three-metre boat covered with a white canopy designed to protect passengers from the harsh sun. Slightly apprehensive about being alone with a strange man she jumped aboard, deciding to trust the arrangements of the five-star hotel, although, she murmured secretly to herself, 'Thank God for cell phones.'

The captain started the outboard engine. The boat put-putted very slowly down the calm quiet Nile. Many similar boats were still anchored in the small harbour as it was not yet tourist season. All of a sudden, the engine sputtered and though the captain pulled the cord back and forth many times to try to keep the engine alive, he had no luck. He threw his arms up in the air in exasperation. Nicole had a boat licence and asked the captain in Arabic if she could help him restart the engine. He nodded his head in agreement. It was a comical scene, each trying to pull the cord to jump start the engine. Impossible. Nicole looked around. The Nile was silent with no one in sight.

Merde! she thought. What do I do now? I don't want to be stranded on this boat with this guy in the middle of the Nile.

Nicole prayed to God for help. At that instant, another little boat appeared from around the corner, put-putting down the Nile in the same direction that they were going. Nicole started jumping up and down and frantically waving. The captain radioed over to the other captain. Help was on its way. The boat came over, and on it was a tourist group with a tour guide like the one Nicole should have been with this morning. Exchanging a few words with both captains, the tour guide telephoned for help and told Nicole that they were also going to see the Temples of Philae.

'You can join our group,' he said, 'but they're German so the tour will be in German.'

'I speak German,' Nicole said.

She felt her spiritual guides were truly protective. She profusely thanked the tour guide, who held out his hand to help her jump aboard. Nicole looked back and waved goodbye to the captain stranded in his boat until the summoned help arrived.

She sat at the stern of the boat, across from a young man in his late-twenties. She couldn't stop looking at him. He wore the most unusual outfit and didn't look like the rest of the group, who were speaking German amongst themselves. From time to time, the guide conversed with the Germans while the young man gazed off into the horizon, deep in his own world. The captain hummed as he navigated the tourists to the islet of Agilkia.

Nicole observed the young man and began by scrutinizing his feet. He wore French Mephisto sandals and each of his toenails was painted a different colour in dark tones. Two of his toes had silver rings, one decorated with an ankh, the other with a skull. It was the first time Nicole had seen a man with painted toenails and toe rings. He wore baggy black pants that descended only to his mid-calves, another novelty. Her eyes moved further up his body to observe a fluorescent orange tank top that covered his torso, along with many gold chains and leather strings embedded with different types of semi-precious stones hanging around his neck. He had four or five earrings attached to his right ear. His hair was jet black, styled in punk fashion, with a fluorescent blue stripe that sliced his head into two sections. Last but not least were his hands. His fingernails had been painted in dark green and black tones to match his toenails. He wore exotic rings on many of his fingers. What a character! She had never seen anyone like this before in her life.

The tour guide diverted Nicole's attention from this intriguing young man. They were about to arrive at the temple, which was beautiful to see, built on its own little island, surrounded by royal blue water. In the background, huge boulders lined the banks of the Nile. The boulders appeared to have different animal shapes, such as elephants and camels. Nicole thought she might have been hallucinating from the intense heat of the Egyptian sun. Finally, they all disembarked onto a dock and walked up a ramp that led towards the great temple of Isis.

In front of the temple, the young man approached Nicole and asked, 'Are you French?'

'Yes.'

'Me too, but I live in New York. My name is K.'

What a funny name! And he didn't look French. K videoed the temple while the tour guide recounted its history. The two stayed together while the Germans formed a larger group that followed the tour guide around the main temple.

'Why are you videotaping this temple?' Nicole asked K.

'I'm making a video about certain historic sites in the world and how they're linked to gods and goddesses and their sacred rites. This is the backdrop for my meditation and Reiki series.'

'Fascinating,' said Nicole. 'I had a Reiki massage once in New York at the Peninsula Hotel's Fitness and Spa Club. I didn't know what Reiki was but decided to try something new. What I thought was going to be a massage was this woman laying her hands about six inches above my body with warm heat emanating from them. The masseuse told me she was a Reiki practitioner, and she was healing me with this heat pouring out of her hands. I didn't understand what she did but it felt great, and at that moment in my life I needed to have a sense of peace and well-being.'

K continued videotaping the temple grounds while listening to Nicole's story. Engrossed in their own conversation, the two of them had lost the group. Finally, he opened up to Nicole, 'I'm a Reiki practitioner, and I'm here in the Middle East looking for a Master Reiki teacher to train me to become a Master Reiki healer. I found one in Cairo but he told me to come back when I was ready.'

'What exactly is Reiki?'

K, who was also a psychic, said, 'Are you having emotional problems?'

'Well . . .' Nicole was astounded that he could pick up on pieces of her life.

'Woman, you're thinking too much. It looks like flames are leaping out of your head.' Then K proceeded to ask her politely, 'May I place my hands near the top of your head?'

Out of curiosity, Nicole agreed.

He dropped his knapsack on the dusty stones, and placed his video equipment carefully on top of the bag. Nicole sat on a broken column, one of many that decorated the outer courtyard of the temple. K placed his hands over the top of her head. She didn't feel intense heat like her first encounter. On the contrary, she felt a coolness like an air conditioner blowing gently on her head. What a strange feeling! They were in the middle of the desert in the hot afternoon sun. The sensation turned glacial then back to normal.

'Your head was on fire. The energy was to cool down the intense heat. What did you feel?'

'A cool touch, which became glacial, then something like normal.'

'That's the healing process of Reiki. I'm only the conduit that channels the energy from a divine universal source. I hope you're feeling better and stop thinking so much.'

They both laughed.

When Nicole and K caught up with the tour group, the tour was already finished. They heard the guide suggest that they wander around the sacred grounds and he'd stay nearby to answer any questions. Nicole noticed some smaller temples next to the temple of Isis. On some of their ancient columns she discovered carvings of monkeys playing musical instruments. Were these chiselled art forms sculpted by the Romans, or influenced by Greek architecture or crafted by the Ancient Egyptians? Construction of the complex of temples at Philae spanned across many centuries and was probably a combination of many diverse cultures. Nicole and K walked on, each in their own reverie.

The myth of Isis and Osiris had lured Nicole to discover this place. She admired how the goddess Isis had been depicted as a deity full of compassion, tenderness, love and devotion. I'll come back here with a man I'm totally devoted to, and am in love with, she reflected, and the goddess Isis shall bless our relationship and be our protector in friendship, partnership and eventual marriage.

The tour guide announced to the group, 'It's time to leave. Please walk back down the ramp and get on the boat.'

While still near one of the temples, Nicole asked K for some insight before going back to the boat.

He snapped into a trance-like state and said very quickly, 'Soon you'll meet your soulmate but his life is tied to his country . . . You have a manuscript written in your heart; it's already a bestseller in the universe.'

After this wild and fast talking, his voice normalized and he looked at Nicole. 'Next time you're in New York give me a call when you're ready to receive Reiki. Here's my card.'

She rummaged through her bag but couldn't find any cards of her own.

K picked up on her predicament and said, 'I'll remember you.'

Nicole smiled and said, 'Thank you for your time and insight. I'm sorry I made you miss your tour.'

'That's OK. I don't even understand German. I really came here to video the temple.'

'Good luck!' Nicole wished him.

'You take care of yourself, honey.'

As promised, Nicole was dropped off at the pier from which she had embarked. She said goodbye to everyone in German, Arabic and French. The taxi driver was waiting for her unaware of all that had happened. First, being stranded on the Nile with the captain of the boat, and then rescued by another boat with a German tour group, accompanied by an eccentric French hippy with painted toenails who lived in New York. As her friends frequently commented, this kind of adventure only happened to Nicole. Strange things occurred to many people but somehow Nicole was the one who found herself in such surreal situations.

As she was being driven back to the hotel, she mused, there's a reason I met K. I'll know later. The universe made it happen. How curious that my boat broke down in the middle of the Nile with no one in sight until this other boat appeared out of nowhere. I'd better write down what K said before I forget . . . I hope the next man in my life is my soulmate. I don't know what he meant about a manuscript, he's way off target . . . Well, we'll see if anything he said comes true.

She jotted down some brief notes and let out a big sigh. The taxi driver cleared his throat to let her know they'd arrived at the hotel. Swiftly, she came back to reality, thanked him and gave him a large tip.

Search for Enlightenment

At the bar overlooking the Nile, she ordered a pomegranate juice to quench her thirst and smoked a hubble-bubble pipe flavoured with orange blossom to relax her mind. What a crazy and peculiar day! Perhaps this day was the beginning of her journey towards the Enlightenment that she had been seeking. After the smoke, feeling dizzy, she walked back to her suite and wrote for hours in her journal.

The next morning she received a wake-up call from the charming operator, 'Good morning, Your Highness. It's 7 o'clock.'

Nicole smiled and thanked him. She stretched, rolled out of the king-size bed, and opened the curtains to let the warm morning sunshine stream through the windows. The Nile was still sleepy and the feluccas were idle. She opened the glass doors and stepped onto the terrace. The sweet, soft, cool air wafted through her hair. The birds chirped with happiness in the nearby palm trees. After an hour of basking in the sun, her breakfast arrived and the waiter set up the table. She ate buttery croissants sprinkled with thyme and olive oil and drank freshly squeezed blood-orange juice. The colour of the juice reminded her of some of the sunsets that she had seen over the deep blue Nile. The crowds would gather on the cliffs, hundreds of feet above the river, to watch the sun's spectacular light show. After the sun hid behind the desert dunes, the spectators applauded. She finished her morning ceremony by sipping a cup of piping-hot black coffee. Nicole loved the dark rich taste of Egyptian coffee; it energized her. She broke up the remaining croissants into pieces for the birds to eat. It was a habit of hers to feed bread to the birds wherever she went. Once, near the lake in Geneva, a jealous swan bit her in the leg because she didn't have enough bread to feed them all. Thank God she had worn heavy-duty jeans that day. Although torn, they saved her leg from a nasty wound. Quick-thinking and fearless, Celeste chased away the old grumpy swan with a café chair that she had snatched from a nearby restaurant. Even the waiters from the restaurant started yelling and screaming at the swans to scram.

One dream leads to another in my never-ending dreaming. I must pack. It's time to go, thought Nicole. She would miss Aswan and the Old Cataract Hotel, a place where she had rediscovered peace and harmony within herself after experiencing so much sadness. Aswan was a great escape. She promised to return again. Before her departure, Nicole received a call from Lily.

'Are you coming to *Aida* with me?' Lily asked.

'Yes, it's an opportunity not to be missed. Events like this don't happen often in one's lifetime.'

'Fabulous, darling. Meet me at the bar at the Mena House Oberoi Hotel near the Pyramids at Giza around seven in the evening.'

'Ciao! Ciao!'

On the way out, Nicole was greeted by the charming manager of the hotel.

'I'll be back, Mr Diab,' she said. 'This is one of the few places in the world where I've been able to find peace within my soul.'

'Certainly, Your Highness. You are most welcome any time. Have a pleasant trip,' he replied.

'Au revoir.'

Nicole winked at him for addressing her so. She giggled to herself. Maybe I was an Egyptian princess in a past life. Qui sait? Who knows?

Aida

When Nicole arrived in Cairo, she went directly to Mouna's house, which was located on a little island on the Nile. Mouna had gathered many family members and friends to greet Nicole. They had a nice lunch together in the garden overlooking the river. The rest of the afternoon was spent socializing until it was time for Nicole to change and meet Lily.

Once at the Mena House, Nicole walked through the lobby of the hotel, up the grand staircase and turned towards the Moorish-styled bar where she could see Lily with a few friends.

Lily had seen Nicole first and called out, 'Nicole, we're over here.' She introduced Nicole to her friends from London, one of them a well-known actor. Nicole was bedazzled by Lily's entourage.

They drank mango fruit cocktails and munched on salty peanuts. Soon after, it was time to leave for the opera. Lily had arranged for a minibus to take them to the base of the Pyramids. They were six in all and she wanted everyone to be together.

They entered the venue on the traditional oriental carpets that lined the entrance to the makeshift outdoor opera house. Champagne was served. Everyone greeted their friends and acquaintances. The bells chimed. Lily escorted her party to their seats. Nicole was very excited to be seeing *Aida* underneath the starlit skies. She adored opera and read in her programme that it had been written by Verdi for the Viceroy of Egypt to inaugurate the Suez Canal in 1870; however, Verdi didn't finish it on time, and the opera premiered at the Cairo Opera House in 1871.

The audience became silent. The Ethiopian soldiers marched onto the scene. There was to be a war between the Ethiopians and the Egyptians. Radames, an Egyptian warrior, would be the one chosen to lead the battle against the Ethiopians. His goal was to be victorious and come home a hero, so that he could openly proclaim his love for Aida, the servant of the Pharoah's daughter, Amneris. Aida was torn between her love for Radames and her loyalty to her father, the King of Ethiopia. Amneris, also in love with Radames, had found out through a devious ploy that Radames and Aida were in love.

Radames returns victorious with Aida's father, King Amonasro, as one of his prisoners. He makes a deal with the Pharoah to free the prisoners but to keep Aida and her father as hostages. In Act III, the act that most intrigued Nicole, Amneris goes to the temple of Isis to pray. What a coincidence! Amneris seeks guidance on her love for Radames. Moments later, Radames and Aida meet secretly at the same temple, not knowing that Amneris has just been there. They declare their love for one another. Filled with love for Aida, Radames unwittingly reveals the route that the Egyptians will take to conquer the Ethiopians once and for all. Aida's father, who has been hiding in the shadows of the temple, rejoices because his people will, hopefully, defeat the Egyptians. The opera finishes on a tragic note, with the lovers awaiting a cruel death and Amneris lamenting her love for Radames.

The ending triggered deep emotion within Nicole's heart and she silently wept. The stars and a full moon glowed over the entire cast taking their bows, while the fabulously lit up Pyramids formed a majestic backdrop. The audience applauded and whistled with grand approval of the performance.

'What a thrilling love story!' Nicole said to Lily.

'You're a poet in your heart, darling. I knew you'd love it. That's why I was so insistent, even though you told me you had plans to meet John's friends in Sharm el-Sheikh.'

'True, but I rearranged my trip to see *Aida* with you, and I'm so glad I did,' said Nicole, while giving Lily a big hug.

They left the Pyramids in the minibus and returned to the Mena House. Nicole said farewell to Lily and her entourage as she was collected by Mouna's driver in front of the hotel.

Once in bed, Nicole listened to the sounds of the Nile floating by and drifted off into a deep happy sleep. The next morning, she woke up naturally from the early sunlight streaking through the wooden shutters. She'd leave this morning to fly to Sharm el-Sheikh. After breakfast, she thanked Mouna for her gracious hospitality.

'No need to thank family,' Mouna said, 'you're welcome any time. Please let me know when you are coming again.'

'I will,' said Nicole, and they kissed each other goodbye.

* * *

Nicole was finally off to meet an old school friend of her brother's. Before her trip, John had phoned and said, 'Do call Michel. He's now living in Jordan, married to a Palestinian woman called Zeinab. She's a beautiful and kind person, you'll like her very much. You know Michel, he's crazy but fun. They'll take good care of you like you're part of the family. It's all part of Arab hospitality.'

Nicole loved her brother and appreciated the way he looked out for her on her sometimes sudden and spontaneous trips. Once, someone asked her name and she had replied, 'Nicole Wanderer.' Sometimes, wanderers wandered with a purpose in life.

While in Cairo, Nicole called Michel to confirm their rendezvous in Sharm el-Sheikh for the day following the opera. She looked forward to seeing him again and meeting Zeinab for the first time. On her flight there, she reflected how wonderful it was that Michel, a Lebanese Maronite Christian, had the courage to marry a Palestinian Muslim woman. Both families must have been extremely tolerant and open-minded. This proved people could get along with each other. Things only went wrong because of those egotistical and maniacal leaders who used religion as a tool to gain political power for themselves.

As Nicole gazed out of the small window of Lily's private jet, she saw the Red Sea dotted with colourful fishing boats. White sandy beaches lined the coast. Sharm el-Sheikh must be approaching. It was a relatively short flight with no turbulence but Nicole's heart thumped wildly and her palms sweated profusely. Noticing Nicole's anxiety, the cabin attendant sat next to her and guided her to take deep breaths until the aircraft landed. Lily had let Nicole borrow her husband's jet for the morning. It had worked out well because Lily wanted to pick up her younger sister who was vacationing with her lover in Sharm el-Sheikh. Apparently, they had phoned Lily and wished to return to London. Nicole was just grateful that she had so many wonderful, generous, loving friends.

She met Michel and Zeinab at the airport in Sharm el-Sheikh. Michel made the introductions with warm greetings. The plan was to snorkel for a few hours in the Red Sea near the coral reef, where an array of spectacular coloured fish could be seen. Afterwards, they would trek up Mount Sinai, all in one day.

In the chauffeur-driven Mercedes, Zeinab said, 'When you have more time, come and visit us in Jordan. It's a very spiritual country with many historical sites to visit.'

'I'd love to.'

Nicole felt the warmth and love of Zeinab. John was right about her. He always had an uncanny insight into people's characters.

After frolicking in the sea, the caravan departed for the base of Mount Sinai near St Catherine's monastery. Once the car was parked, Michel and Zeinab unloaded the boot. Michel attached a huge backpack to Nicole's shoulders, and she literally toppled over backwards from the weight. She felt pinned to the ground and couldn't lift herself up. She must have looked like a turtle flipped over on its back, its four legs flailing in every direction. Michel and Zeinab laughed until tears rolled out of their eyes. Since the trek up the mountain lasted about three and a half hours, Michel negotiated with a Bedouin who had two camels to transport all of their belongings as far up the trail as possible. In a single line, Michel led the way, followed by Zeinab, Nicole, the Bedouin and his two camels. The further Nicole climbed up the mountain, the more she felt this trek was one of penitence and transition. A time of transition from pain, anger and guilt to one of forgiveness, freedom and adventure.

When night descended upon them, the Bedouin, guided by the stars, now led the way. Michel didn't want to lose Nicole so he put her in the middle. As they climbed in the dark, the ascent became steeper. Nicole could hardly see anything and tripped a few times on the loose stones that sprinkled the path. She paused and looked up at the billions of stars shining in the sky and satellites spinning in the cosmos. Zeinab urged her forward. No longer able to talk, Nicole was afraid she was experiencing a heart attack; the pain in her chest increased and her heart pounded loudly. At last, there was a rest stop. Michel paid the Bedouin for his services, and he quietly disappeared back down the trail with his two camels.

Out of nowhere, a couple of other Bedouins appeared, and offered mint tea. Michel accepted. The hot sweet tea warmed them from the chill of the desert night. One of the Bedouins started singing and strumming on his oud. Michel and Zeinab sang along in Arabic. Nicole was entranced by the magic of the evening. Michel offered to pay for the tea, but the Bedouins refused and wished the trio farewell, 'Maca salaama.'

Collecting their possessions, Michel and Zeinab took the heaviest backpacks and gave Nicole the lightest. The last part of their journey arrived – only a thousand steps more to climb to the summit. This was the narrowest and steepest part of the path. The steps had been built by monks from another century, using big rectangular stones. In some places there was a distance of two feet between each one, and Nicole had to stretch her legs as far as she could to climb them. The struggle continued but she was determined to climb to the top. After all, she must have come all this way for a reason.

One thousand steps later, they arrived. For three hours, Nicole sat in silence while Michel and Zeinab slept. Gazing at the stars, the universe spoke to her soul, and she felt temporarily purged from her pain and suffering. Slowly, the stars faded and the sun rose over the mountainous rocky desert. Nicole woke up her friends to see the sun rise. An orange-reddish hue hugged the ground while the deep blue sky disappeared over the horizon. The three of them clapped in unison, and then stood up and danced arm-in-arm in a circle. It was the most beautiful sunrise Nicole had ever seen, the image of a crescent moon descending behind the sun as it rose as though it were an optical illusion. This was a sign from the universe for her to move on with her life. She received the message loud and clear.

Unbeknownst to Nicole, her guardian angel, Michel, rejoiced because she was learning to follow her heart.

Part Two

Magic and Adventure

Chapter 7
Astrological Predictions

Dinner in Manhattan, Winter 1999

Nicole had been invited to a dinner on the Upper East Side by Kerala and Rajiv Misra. They were hard people to connect with because of their busy performance schedule. Their apartment was on the forty-second storey with ten-foot floor-to-ceiling grey-tinted windows. The front view was of Central Park and the Hudson River. To the left, one could see the Empire State Building lit up in red and green to celebrate the Christmas season, and to the right, the Carlyle Tower stood majestically with its green dome bathed in golden light. Manhattan at night with all of its scintillating lights was spectacular, especially during the holidays. Nicole was glad she had chosen to fly back there rather than to Paris from Cairo. She enjoyed New York from Thanksgiving to Christmas; however, for New Year's Eve, she often ventured to exotic or tropical places, such as Phuket or the Mauritius Islands.

They would be five altogether at dinner. Kerala and Rajiv hosted the intimate party. Nicole arrived first. Kerala was busy organizing a buffet of sushi, sashimi, cooked rice, noodles and a variety of vegetables. Nicole was amused as she had expected an authentic Indian meal. She looked around their spacious home. The Misras had an aesthetic sense, and made their guests feel comfortable. Whenever Nicole entered their home she felt cheerful, because the interior design evoked a colourful atmosphere for living. The furnishings were modern with cranberry, emerald, gold and indigo colours. The living room was dominated by two eight-foot wooden, sculpted ladders crafted by the Dogon people of Mali. Kerala and Rajiv often brought back art from their travels around the world.

Nicole looked at Kerala. 'Oh, you're so beautifully dressed in your sari. Such striking shades of orange and fuchsia! I hope you don't mind that I didn't wear Indian garb.'

'Not at all, my dear. I wish I could slip into those chic pantsuits that you wear but I'm afraid I'm a bit too plump,' chuckled Kerala.

Before the other guests arrived, Kerala escorted Nicole to their soundproof recording studio where Rajiv was working on a new song. Kerala and Rajiv composed folk music with the sitar, the santor – a zither of Persian origin – and the shahnai, an instrument like the oboe. Kerala left the two together so that she could get back to the kitchen.

'Would you like to listen to the new song?' Rajiv asked Nicole.

'I'd love to.' Then an instant later, 'What's this? You won a Grammy? For what?'

Rajiv smiled and said in a humble tone, 'Kerala and I won the award for the *Best Traditional Folk Album* a year ago.'

'That's so exciting. I didn't know.'

'Listen.'

Rajiv played the recording of his new song. After the song ended, he handed an invitation to Nicole. 'I'll be playing at Carnegie Hall next month. Please, come with a friend.'

'Thank you, you're very kind.'

Kerala came in and announced that the other guests had arrived. They left the recording studio and went to the living room. Nicole hugged Mohan Singh, whom she hadn't seen since her birthday celebration in Cannes. The other guest, Sushil Khan, was a shy man. He was a professor of mathematics at New York University by day and an astrologer by night. As Kerala introduced him to Nicole, she mentioned that Sushil's close friends nicknamed him Deep, because he was mostly submerged in never-ending calculations.

Astrological Predictions

Sushil said to Nicole, 'You can call me Sushil or Deep, whatever you prefer.'

Deep wanted one day to become a full-time astrologer. New York was full of talented people who lived there temporarily, permanently or were just passing through. It was a city of constant movement. Everything happened in New York. Nicole loved the cultural, active side of New York but preferred the quality of life in Paris. These two great cities inhabited a part of her soul. She felt at home in both places.

Kerala was happy that Nicole had met Deep. Since he was an astrologer, she thought he might be able to give her some insight about her life. Nicole was curious as to what an astrologer might predict about her future and allowed him to try. Deep sat next to her on one of the couches in the living room while Kerala, Rajiv and Mohan talked about the latest Bollywood film, *Kaho Naa . . . Pyaar Hai, Believe in Love*, that had become a hit at the box office. Mohan, who was also a writer and lyricist, had composed five of the songs for the soundtrack, one of which had reached number one in the charts in India. The song described how love blooms like a flower.

Deep asked Nicole, 'What's your birth date? Where were you born?'

'June 2 1966, in Paris, France.'

'It's December 1999. That makes you thirty-three years old.'

'Yes.'

He went into deep thought while quickly making many calculations and drawings on a piece of paper.

Kerala said, 'He's the best. Listen to what he says to you.'

When Deep finished his brief astrological study for Nicole, he said in a guttural voice, his eyes closed in a trance-like state, 'You've travelled all of your life, lived mostly between Paris and New York. Your apartment in New York is on a dead-end street. I see you moving from there. You've been married but it ended recently. Am I right? You're not saying anything.' His eyes twitched, and his hands fidgeted with the paper that he had scribbled on.

Nicole said with disbelief, 'Kerala, you told him about my life.'

'No, I didn't.'

'No, she didn't. I need to know if what I'm saying is true.'

'Yes, for the most part, except about moving from my New York home. I have no plans to move.'

'You'll see. You'll be moving soon. And your husband?'

Nicole felt uncomfortable with Deep. Even though she was amongst her dear, loving friends she didn't want to discuss Marc-Antoine and reopen a chapter of her life that was filled with painful memories – a chapter that she had thought closed. Her shoulders twitched up and down as she looked first at Mohan, then at Kerala for reassurance.

Kerala empathized with Nicole's uneasiness. 'You're amongst old friends, my dear. We know everything about you, the good and the bad. Don't worry. Anything that has been said here will not go outside our home. Right Mohan? Right Rajiv?'

Mohan nodded his head in agreement while Rajiv had no comment. He wasn't listening to Nicole and the astrologer because he neither believed in soothsayers nor astrological predictions, and he happened to be watching an Indian movie produced and directed by Mohan.

In a shaky voice Nicole said, 'OK. This past summer my husband got killed in the crossfire of a rebel uprising in the Congo. Are you satisfied?'

Deep apologized for his insistence, 'I'm sorry. I didn't realize . . .' Then he blurted out, 'Have you ever been to India?'

'I've planned to go there many times but it never worked out. But this year, Mohan and his wife, Cherry, have invited me to spend New Year's Eve with them so that I'm not alone.'

Mohan smiled and dipped his handsome head.

Deep said, 'You're going to meet your soulmate. It'll be on this trip to India that you've mentioned – at a special event. Someone new. You'll go back to India many times.'

Nicole looked at Deep and asked incredulously, 'Many times?'

'At least two or three times.'

Nicole looked at Mohan with a funny expression on her face.

Mohan quipped, 'I wish I were the lucky man! You need a knight – someone who will treat you like a princess.'

Nicole's porcelain-white cheeks turned bright red.

Deep said, 'That's right. This guy has been dreaming of you. He's confused. He doesn't know if you're an angel or a ghost. When he meets you, he'll know in his heart that you're the one.'

'Am I going to recognize him?'

'You'll see. He's going to be the most important man in your life for the rest of your days. He's a foreigner, from the Middle East, and can't stay in one place for a long time. It seems as though he's been wrongly accused of something, and this makes him run from country to country. I see that justice will occur in his lifetime, and he'll want to settle down with you.'

'How can you see or know these things?'

'It's a vision that comes into my mind. It's like watching a movie filled with symbols and metaphors. Spirits put these images into my brain when I'm supposed to relay an important message from the other side.'

Kerala said to Nicole, 'Almost everything he has said to me has been true or come true.'

'We'll see,' Nicole said, in a sceptical tone.

All of a sudden, Deep poured out these messages: 'You've been together in many lifetimes with this man – a couple in pharaonic Egypt, father and daughter in the royal kingdom of Siam, many times as his wife in Greece, Italy and southern France. You liked being reincarnated in the Mediterranean region. You were monks together in Kathmandu. You can communicate with each other through mental telepathy. Your bond is strong and powerful. It'll be a love for both of you unlike anything either of you have ever experienced before – in this lifetime.'

Nicole, her eyes wide open in astonishment, asked Deep, 'Are you a psychic or an astrologer?'

There was no reply.

She politely smiled and said, 'Thank you for your insight. I appreciate how you've illustrated my future as a colourful canvas full of hope.'

Deep acknowledged her gratitude and then sat in silence.

Nicole sighed and asked her Hindu friends, 'How do you believe in astrology and reincarnation without any doubt. How do you do it?'

Mohan replied, 'It's a science.'

Rajiv interjected, 'I'm a Hindu, but I don't believe in astrology, and I have a hard time believing in reincarnation.'

Nicole said, 'I've read that astrology *is* a science and has been around for thousands of years, but I have to agree with Rajiv about reincarnation. It hasn't yet been scientifically proven. At least, not to my knowledge.'

Mohan retorted, 'Reincarnation exists. When you come to India, I'll have you meet Dorab Doran. He's an astrophysicist based in Delhi who can explain reincarnation to you in a scientific way.' During dinner, Mohan asked Nicole, 'Could you come a week earlier to India so I can show you the places where I'm shooting my next film? The scenes will be in my home town, Jaipur; then onwards to Bikaner; and then, Jaisalmer, near the Pakistani border in the Thar Desert for the heroin trade scene; and finally Udaipur for the marriage ceremony at the Taj Lake Palace Hotel on Lake Pichola.'

'Wow! I'd love to go. But you're crazy to shoot near the Pakistani border where there's all that guerilla warfare.'

Mohan chuckled, 'We'll be miles away from Kashmir, my dear.'

'Is it true that Kashmir was the most beautiful area in India until its peace was destroyed by the Pakistani and Indian armies?'

'Yes. But you'll see that India has many other captivating places to visit. Rajasthan is the most beautiful.'

There was a moment's stillness as Mohan dreamed of one of the scenes from his new film and then he said, 'The Lake Palace bubbles with romance and magic.'

'That's why you're having the wedding scene in Udaipur!'

Mohan smiled.

Nicole responded to his first question, 'Let me look at my diary and I'll let you know before we leave tonight.'

Kerala and Rajiv ended the evening on a musical note by playing the sitar and the santor. Mohan sang poetic verses in harmony with the music. Deep was in his own reverie, far, far away on another planet. Nicole listened with her eyes closed while her body swayed to the gentle sounds. It was a lovely way to end the evening.

Nicole wished her friends well, in advance, 'Happy holidays and a wonderful Millennium 2000!' She told Mohan she could arrive on December 27 and that although it wasn't a week, she hoped three days would be sufficient.

Mohan said in a sarcastic tone, 'Three days to see Rajasthan! Three days is enough to see Mumbai and Bollywood.' He teased, 'You'll have to see the rest of India with your new mate.'

Kerala exclaimed, 'That would be the most beautiful present the new millennium could offer you.'

'Now, I have something to look forward to in my life,' Nicole replied. 'I hope Deep's predictions come true.'

Kerala kissed Nicole goodbye and murmured into her ear, 'Why not, my dear? Have hope of a beautiful future. Think positive. Be optimistic.'

These words reassured Nicole. For the first time in a long time she felt peace reign in her soul, but the thought of embarking on another voyage to an exotic land created butterflies in her stomach. In Egypt, she had sought Enlightenment and was forced to face her pain, climbing up Mount Sinai, to be mercifully redeemed at the summit. This time, she decided to go with the spirit of adventure and discover India through the eyes of Mohan and Cherry. Magic and romance danced through Nicole's head as she left the Misras' home.

Chapter 8
Meaningful Coincidences

Mumbai, December 1999

Nicole arrived at around one in the morning at Sahar airport in Mumbai and couldn't find Mohan and Cherry amongst the masses of Indian faces. She felt lost in the commotion of so many people. Manhattan buzzed but this felt like a swarm of bees. Indians and tourists shoved and pushed their way out of the airport looking for taxis, hired cars, friends and family.

Nicole called Mohan on his cell phone, 'Where are you?'

'We're waiting for you past the exit. Come out through the sliding glass doors and you'll see us.'

'I see you,' said Nicole as she closed her phone.

She embraced Mohan and Cherry. They were so kind to pick her up at the airport so late at night – or rather, early in the morning.

They drove her to their home in Malabar Hill, known for its film stars' mansions and businessmen's apartment buildings. Nicole could just discern the grimy makeshift cardboard and tin houses for the poor that lined both sides of the road along the highway. The underprivileged bustled at this hour. It looked like an open-air market at night that reminded her of another city that didn't sleep. When they finally arrived at the Singhs' residence, the maid greeted them and served them chamomile tea with homemade cookies. The friends chatted, then kissed each other goodnight. The next morning, Nicole would discover Bollywood.

After breakfast, Mohan took Nicole to his film studio in a high-rise building with a huge terrace overlooking a section of Mumbai. Beautiful actors and actresses came in and out of the director's door, along with his famous Bollywood friends, producers, directors and a renowned cinematographer. It was an exciting new world for Nicole but one where Mohan was at ease.

Afterwards, Mohan brought her to a recording studio to see a musician record her song. It was a cool atmosphere to be in. The technicians were serious about getting the song recorded as perfectly as technology would allow, but at the same time very friendly and accommodating to their recently arrived guests. Nicole enjoyed watching the team work together to produce a pop song. Next on the agenda was a film shooting at a prestigious jewellery store, D. Popli & Sons. This was not far from the Central Cottage Industries Emporium known for its Indian arts and handicrafts, in a district behind the Taj Mahal Palace and Tower, a luxurious hotel located on the waterfront overlooking the Arabian Sea. It was an ideal location. The male actor of the moment played the leading role in this love story. The scene depicted him buying jewellery for his girlfriend. Many Indian films were based on love, dance and music. To see a film being shot live with the hottest and sexiest actor in Bollywood was pure entertainment.

They had a rendezvous at three in the afternoon to meet Cherry for lunch at Tiger Moon. The fashionable and chic restaurant was a place to be seen where the food was delicious. Cherry was Parsi, of Persian origin. The Parsis were followers of the prophet Zoroaster, who during the sixth century BC, preached about good and evil, was against the concept of polytheism and spoke of the afterlife. During the fifteenth century, many Parsis migrated to India and practised Zoroaster's tenet: 'Happiness to him that brings happiness to others.' Over the centuries, this successful minority enriched the Indian economy while blending in with the fabric of society. Cherry was proud to be Parsi and also happy with her profession as an actress.

Her beauty stunned audiences. She had big, wide, dark green eyes, with long, wavy, black hair. She was tall and slender and looked fabulous whether she was wearing a sari or a tight pair of fashionable jeans. The

Bollywood film industry equated her with the image of both Cleopatra and Elizabeth Taylor combined into one. Cherry's love affair with Mohan was publicized in India as much as the Taylor/Burton romance had been exposed to the world in a previous era.

Mohan and Cherry were vegetarians. Mohan spoke in Hindi to the waiter, and asked for plain basmati rice, naan bread, and an assortment of vegetable dishes. The waiter brought potato patties with a spicy chickpea filling called aloo tikki, curried lentils with bell peppers known as sambar, okra spiced with hot red pepper flakes and eggplant in sweet and sour sauce. They drank Indian beer to accompany their meal. Nicole thought everything was delicious.

At the end of the lunch, Mohan told Nicole he'd be inviting about thirty people over for a buffet dinner. As promised, he had also invited his friend from Delhi, the astrophysicist Dorab Doran, to explain reincarnation to her. Nicole was thrilled.

'Maybe Mr Doran will make a true believer out of me,' said Nicole.

'You love to please our friends,' teased Cherry.

'Darling, I'd like to have her understand our culture better and its belief in karma and reincarnation,' said Mohan.

Nicole mimicked the charming Indian accent that she loved and did so well to her friends delight. 'I shall become an enlightened person in the process. This has been a never-ending goal of mine.'

The couple giggled and thought Dorab would have a tough time convincing her about the afterlife. They didn't want to change Nicole, only to broaden her mind a little more to include another culture and civilization.

* * *

At the dinner party, Mohan immediately introduced Dorab to Nicole, and she took her opportunity to ask him about his theories.

'Reincarnation has been part of our culture and our civilization for the past five thousand years,' he said. 'We believe in the cycle of birth, death and rebirth. The physical body is considered a temporary vehicle for the soul. The soul is eternal and lives for ever.'

Nicole replied, 'The idea that the soul is eternal is beautiful, and I'd like to believe that reincarnation exists but it hasn't yet been proven by scientists. Although I have read that some scientists in the UK and the States have conducted experiments to see if our consciousness survives after death. I've been to psychics, clairvoyants and energy healers. They were the ones who introduced me to the theory of karma and reincarnation because they discussed my past lives and how some of them were linked to the present. It seems to make sense but I'm still sceptical. Sometimes I see my own future through dreams. How does one explain that? Does it mean we have prewritten our destiny? I'm not so sure.'

'Let me try and explain. Consider this analogy with a sword. Place a sword in water. Why do some particles dissolve? Some turn into crystals? The rest remains as solid mass?'

'I don't understand your line of thought.'

'OK. Think of it like this – matter can operate at different frequencies like radio waves . . .'

'Please, different frequencies, altered states of consciousness . . . I've heard of all this before but it doesn't explain the theory of reincarnation. Where does the spark of life come from?'

'I think I'll have to try to explain this at another time. My head is spinning from Mohan's whisky. He was right – you're a tough nut to crack. I must go now because I have to fly back to Delhi tomorrow morning to start working on a new government project.'

Dorab stood up, shook Nicole's hand and said, 'It was a pleasure meeting you.'

'It was nice meeting you, too. Have a safe journey home.'

Nicole, jetlagged, discreetly left the party, slowly climbed a flight of stairs, opened the door to her bedroom, flopped onto the bed and instantly fell asleep.

The next day, Mohan, Cherry and Nicole flew from Mumbai to Udaipur on Jet Airways, a relatively new regional jet airline, considered the best for service and food. Aboard the plane, Mohan met Mala, an old girlfriend from Jaipur from his schooldays, who was flying to Udaipur to meet some friends to celebrate the New Year. She asked Mohan if he was invited to the same Millennium party at the Taj Lake Palace Hotel.

He nodded his head and said, 'Mala, I'd like you to meet Nicole. She's a friend of mine from Paris who I met in New York. She's sitting in front of me and she'll be coming with us to the party.' Mala first kissed Cherry on the cheeks, then leaned over the seat to say hello to Nicole.

'I look forward to seeing you at the party,' Mala said.

Surprised, Nicole replied, 'It'll be a pleasure to see you too.' She didn't know who the woman was because she hadn't overheard Mohan's conversation. Though slightly confused by this impromptu encounter, Nicole found this pretty woman to be beautifully dressed in a fine silk traditional sari in the most striking colours of green and gold with jewels to match. She felt an uncanny affinity for this woman who had just greeted her, it was as though they were old friends.

Before going back to her seat Mala addressed Nicole once more, 'I'd like you to meet some friends of mine from London who'll be attending the New Year's Eve party. Come with Mohan and Cherry to the courtyard of the Taj Lake Palace Hotel to have a drink, and meet them around 7 o'clock.'

'I'd be delighted,' nodded Nicole.

Turning to Mohan and Cherry, Mala said, 'See you tonight, my friends.'

The pilot announced that everyone should return to their seats. They were going to land in Udaipur in seven minutes.

Udaipur

Before going to the hotel, Mohan, Cherry and Nicole made a good-will call to a hospital that specialized in treating polio. Mohan and Cherry supported this medical facility with their time and donations. The hospital had been built with the support of doctors from American and Indian patrons. With hospital administrators and a couple of doctors, the three walked through the corridors, viewed the operating rooms, then visited the polio victims who had been recently treated. The hospital had run out of painkillers, so the sufferers acutely felt the post-operative effects. Sadly, many were children; often, three patients occupied one bed.

Mohan held the children's hands. They knew who he was and looked up at him and smiled. Those with more energy asked him for his autograph. Cherry signed autographs, too, held the children's hands, and told them stories. Some of the little ones wanted Nicole's autograph as well. She hesitated, and looked over to Mohan.

'Do it,' he said. 'It'll make them happy.'

Nicole had thought that polio had been eradicated from most countries in the world but apparently not yet in India. She couldn't help it; tears welled up in her eyes underneath her dark glasses. Never had she seen such decrepit conditions. The poor children moaned and groaned in pain. Visits like these from famous film directors, actors and actresses lifted their spirits. The hospital director remarked to Nicole that the patients were intrigued by 'the foreigner'.

She smiled and thought, if our presence brought happiness to these polio-stricken patients, then this goodwill trip was certainly meaningful.

The director escorted them out of the hospital to plant a tree in the front garden. Mohan dug a hole with a shovel, Cherry and Nicole placed the young tree – symbolizing new life – into the hole. Mohan covered the roots with earth. The three of them received garlands of pink roses round their necks. Hospital administrators and locals clapped when this benevolent deed had been accomplished; paparazzi from local and national newspapers covered the event. Nicole discovered how caring her friends were and how she herself felt humbled by this experience. This emotional occasion was soon to be followed by a magical evening, dining aboard a boat on Lake Pichola.

* * *

The Taj Lake Palace Hotel was situated on an island in the middle of the lake. Mohan had done the sweetest thing: he had reserved the Khush Mahal suite for Nicole. The name translates as the Palace of Happiness. Nicole was delighted with her room, although she was sad she couldn't share it with someone she loved. She told Mohan to take the suite since it would be better suited for a couple.

'No, we want it for you,' he replied. 'We want you to experience India in a memorable way. This way, you'll come back again and again and tell your friends to come here.'

Nicole was impressed and flattered by her friends' kind hospitality. The suite, with its lavish and colourful decorations, reflected the splendour of India in a bygone era. A wooden swing hung from the ceiling in the centre of the bedroom. The brass ropes holding the swing were decorated with elephants and birds, which reminded Nicole of her safari trip in Africa. She wondered what the Indians used such swings for?

The windows were decorated with mosaic glass. The light streaming in reflected a rainbow of colours that warmed the room and made the atmosphere very romantic. Painted walls in vibrant shades depicted scenes of nature composed of lotuses, birds, tigers and luscious green tropical plants. Through her windows Nicole could see the calm lake and the walled city of Udaipur.

New Year's Eve

It was time to meet everyone at the hotel bar. Indian dancers and acrobats entertained the guests in the courtyard, which led through a series of arched doorways to the bar. You could simultaneously sip your drink and watch the traditional festivities. At the bar, Nicole sat down next to Mohan and Cherry. They were due to meet Mohan's niece who was from Udaipur. She was a young woman in her first year of college studying mechanical engineering. Both her parents were medical doctors. She was sweet and shy and loved talking to Nicole about France and the States because one day she wanted to visit both of those countries. Throughout the whole evening, she never left Nicole's side. Nicole didn't mind, it felt as though the girl were her little sister, and she had to look out for her during the New Year's celebrations. By entrusting her to Nicole, Mohan and Cherry could also enjoy themselves without having to worrying about their niece.

Mala finally arrived at the bar with three of her guests, and introduced everyone. Mounir didn't know why Mala was introducing him to these people but something compelled him to walk straight over to Nicole in long, bold strides. He wore a white silk scarf around his neck that flowed with his steps. He offered his hand and she graciously shook it.

'Why are we meeting one another when we're not going to be together tonight?' he asked.

Nicole was a little surprised by his question and remarked, 'But we are going to be together on the boat.'

Mounir smiled and went back to talk to Mala and two other women.

Later, they all boarded the boat and slowly they sailed around the lake. The sun had already set. One could see the city lights, the many palaces lit up on the shores of Lake Pichola and the white palace in the middle of the lake from where the Millennium Party guests had embarked. The city lights dancing on the water made Nicole feel happy. All night long, Indian stringed music was played, the musicians strumming on sitars and singing softly. At the stern of the boat, there were comfortable cushions for about a dozen people. Nicole sat between Mohan's niece and a French–American woman named Jeanne. Opposite them were Mala, Mounir and his girlfriend, Mohan and Cherry and a young man who happened to be an admirer of Mohan. There was always someone who wanted to be near the director to talk about his films.

Everyone had to take their shoes off to sit on these large cushions, which made the area feel cosy and friendly. For some reason, on Mohan's side of the boat everyone was being attacked by little flying bugs. Nicole's side seemed to be immune from the nasty little biting mites. The skipper brought special candles and placed them in strategic areas. Moments later, the pests disappeared. Music wafted through the air. Champagne and hors d'oeuvres were served by candlelight that magically created a romantic ambience and put all the guests into a merry mood.

Nicole's life seemed to be filled with more and more meaningful encounters and coincidences. As she chatted with Jeanne, she occasionally looked at Mounir cuddling with his companion underneath a big, creamy-coloured pashmina. He seemed to catch Nicole's glances and smiled back each time.

After a couple of sips of white wine, Nicole turned her head towards Jeanne, and remarked, 'Isn't it rather extraordinary to have two French–Americans aboard this boat in the middle of India?'

'Oui, oui!' Jeanne replied and then asked, 'Where do you live now?'

'Between Paris and New York. Although, I'm finding myself more and more in New York . . . How do you know Mounir?'

'His girlfriend is my best friend. She didn't want to go to India with him alone because he often abandons her on a moment's notice, so she asked me to come along. I've always wanted to come here, it's a dream come true.'

Nicole remembered that in New York an inner voice had told her to take a risk and go on a trip. It would replenish her soul. It was almost as if she had been guided by the stars to celebrate this evening with these people. Even her brother, John, had encouraged her to take this trip. Her grief, sadness and guilt faded into history. The past was the past and now she was enjoying the present moment. Once again, she gazed at Mounir and thought, what a handsome man! He seems so loving and cuddly. But why is he with that woman? He could be with someone prettier.

As usual, Mohan was jovial and had the musicians come and sit with everyone at the stern of the boat and sing some of his popular film tunes with him. The Indians knew the songs, and sang the words or hummed the tune with him. The foreigners listened with delight. For one of the songs, Nicole sang two lines in Hindi that Mohan had previously taught her and hummed the rest, swaying her body to the rhythm of the music.

As conversation started up again, Nicole reflected under the moonlight, Mounir's the kind of man I'd like to have in my life, someone who's full of love and affection.

Until that precise moment she hadn't known that what she needed more than anything else in this world was love and affection. She'd have to learn how to love a man again because Marc-Antoine had weakened her confidence in the opposite sex, both with his many casual affairs and his secret gambling. It was the Casanova side of his character that most bothered her because she believed in fidelity. She had suspected these activities but, like so many women, didn't want to believe it. Betrayal hurt the most. In her next relationship, she knew she'd have to overcome suspicion and think judiciously, innocent until proven guilty.

Out of the blue, Mounir asked Nicole, 'Would you take a picture of my friend and me? And then, with Mala, Mohan and Cherry?'

'Of course,' said Nicole.

He handed her his camera and she took a few pictures and gave it back.

'May I take a picture of you and Jeanne?' asked Mounir.

Nicole blushed. 'Yes.'

Afterwards, Nicole asked Mounir to use her camera to take some photos of her with Jeanne and Mohan's niece, as well as with Mohan and Cherry because she too wanted a souvenir of this bewitching evening.

As she handed over her camera, Mounir's companion remarked, 'She has the same camera as you. We'd better not mix them up.'

Another coincidence, Nicole thought. Is this a sign from heaven telling me that I'm in the right place at the right time? But for what reason? Sometimes people meet and cross paths and never know why. I hope I find out why.

After the impromptu photo shoot, Mounir's girlfriend and Jeanne went back to the hotel to use the restroom facilities because the ones on the boat had broken down. The captain radioed to the hotel and the concierge sent a little speedboat to pick up those in need. It was only a five minute boat ride each way. Throughout the evening, the guests were transported to the hotel based on their needs. Imperfection amidst perfection characterized one of the ways of experiencing life in India.

There was a brilliant orange full moon dominating the night sky, the biggest moon Nicole had ever seen. It shone majestically over the lake. Mohan, a poet, began reciting a lyrical poem about the moon.

Nicole said, 'My dream is to go to the moon.'

Mounir, eyebrows raised, said, 'I've always wanted to go to the moon too.'

Mohan continued, 'I can help both of you go to the moon. Listen to my words and I'll send you to the moon.'

It was a beautiful and mystical experience.

Jeanne and her friend returned and resumed their places. Suddenly, Mounir jumped up from his companion and sat Indian style directly in front of Nicole.

He said, 'I've been talking to the director and he says you're going to help him finance a film based on reincarnation. He told me that you believed in this concept, even though the other night you enjoyed trying to make a friend of his prove it to you in a scientific way. All in vain.'

Nicole laughed, 'Yes, he's asked me to get involved with his new film. And I believe in reincarnation ninety-nine per cent of the time with a healthy one per cent scepticism.'

'How do you define reincarnation?'

His question took Nicole off guard. How to answer this briefly? First she looked at both Mounir and his companion. Then she felt compelled to look deeply into his eyes. They flashed a bright white light that lasted for a second and showed her briefly a glimpse of his soul.

After a few moments of silence, Nicole replied, 'It's when you meet someone for the first time and you feel that you've known them for centuries without even knowing why.'

Mounir was speechless. His companion just looked at Nicole blankly; Jeanne was talking with Mohan's niece; and the others were grouped around Mohan.

Meaningful Coincidences

What Nicole said even astounded herself because she had just met Mounir and this was exactly how she felt about him – as if she had known him from somewhere before. But where? It certainly was the first time they had met one another. She'd have remembered him if she had met him on a previous occasion.

Mounir drifted off for a couple of seconds. He remembered his recurring dream of a beautiful woman who would come to comfort him while he was constantly running away from his enemies.

He looked at Nicole again and thought, 'she's the one in my dreams! I was born to love her.'

The magical evening was full of surprises for both Nicole and Mounir.

After many glasses of wine and appetizers, dinner was served at a table near the bow of the sailboat. The orange light of the full moon shimmered across the lake. Nicole sat next to Mohan and across from Jeanne. Mohan flirted in a friendly way with her. Mounir sat at the other end of the table. The night turned dark. Only the moonlight and the candlelight illuminated the outline of each person at the table. Nicole couldn't even see Mounir at the far end.

The waiters served individual rimmed dinner plates, called thali, with several tiny bowls, katori, filled with a variety of curries and side dishes of dal. Lentils were Nicole's favourite dal but her stomach fluttered with butterflies. She reasoned that no one could see what she did or didn't eat, so she drank champagne.

Mounir didn't realize that Mohan was married to Cherry, and thought Nicole might be his girlfriend. He frowned and muttered under his breath, 'How could she be with that man?'

Although he conversed with Mala and his girlfriend throughout the dinner, he was obsessed with finding out whether Nicole was with Mohan. He would get both their telephone numbers after dinner. Luckily, the dinner didn't last too long.

The musicians started playing again. Midnight struck. Everyone hugged and kissed each other. Mounir found Nicole amidst the millennium cheer and kissed her gently on both cheeks. He loved the warmth of her soft, rosy skin. He decided, with all the happiness in the air, to kiss her again. He brushed his lips very close to her lips this time. He longed to feel her skin next to his.

Nicole noticed that he kissed her a second time. No one else did that. Who is this man? she thought.

Mounir asked her, 'May I have your number? I would like to invite you to dinner.'

'You don't even know where I live.'

'I overheard you say that you live between Paris and New York. My business takes me all over the world.'

'Are you a spy?'

Mounir smiled and replied, 'I'm a trained observer by profession, and the process has made me become highly sensitive to my surroundings, especially when there's a lovely lady nearby.'

Flattered, Nicole gave him her personal card and said, 'I'll be back in New York next week.'

'You'll have a fax waiting for you when you get home.'

Nicole smiled and thought, is this going to be another man with empty promises? If I receive a fax then he's a man of his word. I'll know the answer when I get home.

The fireworks that marked the beginning of the end to this enchanting evening boomed overhead. Mohan called Cherry, Nicole and his niece over to his side and hugged all three of them in joy. Mounir took this as a sign to leave and went back to his friends.

When the festivities wound down, everyone was brought back to the hotel by the little speedboat. Nicole ended up on the same ride as Mounir and his girlfriend, Jeanne and Mala. As they departed at the dock, Mounir kissed Nicole goodbye on the cheeks, followed by his cheerful companions, who also kissed her, saying, 'Happy New Year!' Mounir couldn't control his excitement and went back to kiss Nicole and wish her happiness and love for many years to come. It was really an excuse for him to feel the warmth of her soft cheeks, look into her beautiful eyes and see her smile, one more time. He loved her smile.

She noticed his kisses. She liked it when he kissed her again. His kisses were soft and caressed her cheeks gentle as rose petals. She liked his presence and had felt an uncanny connection with him. It had been as though she were reciting a message from the universe: 'It's when you meet someone for the first time, and you feel that you've known them for centuries without even knowing why.' In her imagination, she acted out the verses of Mohan's poem and flew to the moon not understanding the whirling emotions stirring within her heart.

When Mounir entered his suite with his girlfriend, he said abruptly, 'Go and sleep in Jeanne's room. I want to be alone tonight.'

This upset her very much. They argued, then she stormed out of the room to spend the night with Jeanne.

That night Mounir dreamed of Nicole.

Before he dozed off, these thoughts romanced through his head: I want to get to know her better, explore her body and feel the warmth of her skin next to mine. She believes in reincarnation just like my mother and is the first woman I've met to discuss this subject with an open mind. I know she'll become a very important person in my life.

On the ceiling above his bed was a small, square mirror. Mounir whispered, 'One day, I'm going to bring Nicole back here and admire her under this mirror. And we'll swing together on that antique swing hanging in front of my bed! I'll sit Indian style and she'll sit on my lap with her legs wrapped around my waist, and her arms holding me tightly. We'll kiss each other for hours.'

It was love at first sight for Mounir. He gazed at the mirror on the ceiling reflecting a white sheet covering the lower half of his body and he could see a tent pointing upwards. He hadn't seen his penis stand so proud and strong in such a long time. His body shivered with expectation.

He concluded, 'She's the love of my life.'

Nicole retired to her suite. She looked at the glistening lake, the city lights that lined the shore and felt joy bubbling inside her heart. That night, Nicole dreamed of making love to Mounir in positions she had never seen before, not even in the books about Kama Sutra. The creators of Kama Sutra hadn't yet imagined these positions. In one of the dreams, Mounir was sitting on the antique swing that was in front of her bed and she was sitting on top of him. They were making love in this position, and kissing each other passionately. She had her legs wrapped tightly around his waist, and he kept the swing in motion with his strong arms. Backwards and forwards. Backwards and forwards.

When she woke up and remembered this dream it embarrassed her, because she was making love to a man she hardly knew.

Confused by her emotions, she thought rationally, we'll see if he follows up on his word to fax me.

From that moment onwards, Nicole decided to read everything about Kama Sutra, Koka Shastra and tantric sex because she wanted to explore the next man she fell in love with, discover all his erogenous zones, learn to tantalize him in intimate and loving ways, and in return, he would intuitively do the same for her. She wanted to love him completely on all levels of existence: physical, mental and spiritual.

Secretly, she hoped it would be Mounir.

Chapter 9
Mythical Love

The Taj Mahal, 2000

From Udaipur, Mohan, Cherry and Nicole flew to Delhi. They met Dorab Doran again. He was with his girlfriend, a professional photographer. They decided to take two chauffeur-driven Mercedes and drive the two-and-a-half-hour trip to Agra, the site of the Taj Mahal. Mohan told Nicole that she couldn't leave India without seeing the Taj Mahal. She agreed, although she would have preferred to have taken a forty-five-minute plane flight, but as she was their guest she diplomatically compromised and rationalized that driving would be a good way to observe the secrets of India.

Chaos reigned along the journey. Masses of people walked alongside the roads and highways. Buses and trucks, filled to capacity, were used as a means of public transportation. On the back of delivery trucks, signs read 'Blow Horn' or 'Horn Please' because they didn't have rear-view mirrors. The vibrant orange, lime green, yellow and purple painted designs on these trucks were reminiscent of the way the elephants were dyed with floral patterns and adorned with jewels. The Indians took pride in their trucks and elephants. Taxis, mopeds, scooters, bicycles, push carts and wagons pulled by camels wove in and out of the cars. Big black cows with horns grazed by the edge of the highway or meandered amidst the traffic. Occasionally, a dead dog lay in the middle of the road. The chauffeur proved to be an expert driver who dodged all the people, caravans, cars, trucks and animals. Somehow the cows on the main road knew how to walk and stop with the flow of traffic. They knew when they could take a right or left turn and seemed to follow the red and green lights. They rarely caused traffic jams.

Indian cows may be considered sacred, thought Nicole, but they're also smart. They know how to keep up with the daily hustle and bustle of Indian life. Where else in the world could one find cows that adapted so well to modern society?

Lost in her observations, she silently chuckled. A few moments later, Mohan announced their arrival at the Taj Mahal.

Nicole swung open the door and jumped out of the car. The caravan of friends gathered together and entered through the main gate to see the breathtaking view of the Taj Mahal. Their eyes followed the two long canals that led up to the Taj Mahal, surrounded by oriental gardens designed to reflect paradise. Nicole stood quietly mesmerized by this architectural masterpiece of translucent white marble shimmering in the sun, its reflection dancing on the still waters of the shallow, oblong pools. Her Indian friends, who had visited this memorial tomb many times before, emitted an awe-filled sigh. It was one of the Seven Wonders of the World and, once seen, its image and presence remained in one's soul for ever.

Mohan hired a tour guide named Raja, who greeted everyone and then explained the history of the mausoleum, 'The Taj Mahal was built by Shah Jahan for his beloved and favourite wife, Mumtaz Mahal, who died while giving birth to their fourteenth child at the age of thirty-nine. The emperor was heartbroken and decided to build this stupendous memorial tomb in her honour. He employed twenty thousand craftsmen and labourers over a span of twenty-two years. The structure was completed in 1653.'

The story of Shah Jahan fascinated Nicole. While at the Taj Lake Palace Hotel, she had read that before Shah Jahan became emperor, he sought refuge from his father in Udaipur at the seventeenth-century Jag Mandir Palace, not far from the Palace of the Maharanis on Lake Pichola. It was this latter palace that was transformed into the Taj Lake

Palace Hotel during the twentieth century. Nicole felt she was following in the ancient footsteps of Shah Jahan from Udaipur to Agra. She also noted that family rivalry had existed in the past as it did in the present, and concluded that it would be a long road to peace since people changed their attitudes and behaviour slowly.

The guide interrupted Nicole's thoughts and said, 'Come, let's visit the gardens and the tombs.'

While they walked, Mohan addressed Nicole, 'Shah Jahan was a Muslim and part of the Mughal dynasty. He had been married to other royals but his love and affection for Mumtaz was the strongest. She was beautiful, intelligent and wise. Shah Jahan consulted with her on the most confidential, administrative matters. In those days to seek advice from a woman was rare. Shah Jahan ended up loving only her. She was his *grand amour*.'

The guide overheard Mohan and added, 'It's true. When she died, the whole empire lamented her loss. Shah Jahan was devastated, and erected this grandiose mausoleum to show his eternal love for Mumtaz.'

Nicole hoped to have a beautiful love story of her own one day.

The Taj Mahal was created by the best craftsmen, with angelic hands. The white marble was embellished with precious and semi-precious stones in floral patterns. The marble of Jodhpur and gems from Asia were transported to Agra by elephant. The mausoleum was built on a square platform flanked by four slender 130-foot minarets in each corner that slightly leaned away to prevent any damage to the memorial in the event of an earthquake. The main building had four small domes surrounding the major dome – called the pearl – that dominated the skyline. At sunset, the pearl floated up to the heavens, emitting a warm, blue misty glow.

Mumtaz's tomb was in the interior of the main building, inscribed with a couplet from the Holy Koran. Emperor Shah Jahan was placed next to her when he died in 1666. His tombstone was beautified with precious gems. His dream had been completed. He was considered the most magnificent builder of the Mughal dynasty. The Taj Mahal was a monument to love in its purest form, expressed by largeness of scale, elegance and lavish ornamentation. Shah Jahan created on Earth his concept of paradise, to be for ever with his beloved.

Mohan, Cherry, Dorab and his girlfriend, and Nicole entered the Taj Mahal by the central staircase, where they had to take off their shoes.

They visited the tomb barefoot, according to Muslim custom. Nicole admired the beauty of the room housing the remains of Mumtaz and Shah Jahan. Silence permeated this sacred sanctuary. After fifteen minutes, they left the tomb and visited the gardens. Dorab's girlfriend took Nicole's photo with the Taj Mahal as the backdrop. Nicole felt honoured; it would be a great souvenir for her to treasure for the rest of her life.

* * *

Days flew by as Nicole immersed herself in the culture of India. The process of discovering this exotic country intrigued all her senses. Her life in France and the States had been all but forgotten until her last night, after a fantastic farewell party, Mohan's chauffeur drove Nicole to the airport. Before the flight's departure, Nicole had contacted Celeste, who would pick her up at Charles de Gaulle Airport and then have lunch with her in Paris. Nicole left mystical India a renewed woman, and her heart reopened like a budding rose to breathe in the wonder and beauty of life.

On the plane, she dreamed of walking arm in arm with Mounir beside the Seine in Paris, their legs walking in the same rhythm. It would be around dusk at the time the Eiffel Tower lit up like a Christmas tree. Their footsteps would stop. They'd hug and kiss, unaware of passers-by. Her dream continued. It would be a summer evening, a winter's night, an autumn afternoon, a spring morning. Their kisses would last many seasons, many years. They would sing with the birds as the buds blossomed on the trees lining the riverbank. They would dance the waltz through the piles of leaves that accumulated along the quay. They would be in many places together. In New York, they would make angels in the virgin snow in Central Park after a blizzard. Near Portofino in northern Italy, they would swim nude in the aquamarine sea off the coast of paradise, to cool their sun-drenched bodies. Nicole felt her soul merge with Mounir's during this dream. She woke up smiling and very happy. Her dream was powerful, and hopefully, prophetic of what her future could be like with him. She was in search of divine love that would come closest to her secret wishes. How she loved to dream.

Paris

Celeste welcomed Nicole at the airport with a big hug. Afterwards, they went to eat at Café Costes at Hotel Costes on rue St Honoré, one of Nicole's favourite restaurants. The chic café was both a relaxing place to be with one's friends and a romantic location to be with one's lover. The two women often met there for lunch.

Nicole looked at Celeste, who was now always adorned with jewels and dressed in the latest mode with fashionable accessories. Celeste had been truly transformed but retained her big heart and remained a loyal friend. The two women always had fun together. Nicole recounted her trips to Egypt and India and showed Celeste some photos. They had a lot of news to tell one another.

Celeste commented with dreamy eyes, 'I'd love to go to India. You're so lucky. The pictures of India are like stepping into a dream or another world. It's wonderful that you live a life where travel and friendship flourish.'

'Come with me the next time I go.'

Celeste smiled, perhaps transported to another place by the exotic images in her mind.

Their lunch lasted three hours and they were the last to leave the restaurant. They were both glad to see each other again. Nicole felt happy. Now, she had something to hope for – romance, love and affection with Mounir. She hoped he wouldn't let her down like Marc-Antoine had done. As Mohan had assured her in New York, she deserved to be with someone who'd treat her like a princess.

Celeste interrupted Nicole's daydreaming and said, 'When you feel the need to relax and get away from your hectic life, come and visit me. It's winter now and the mountains are peaceful. Or, come in the summer to Ramatuelle. You're always welcome. I have to go now, I have an appointment. Je t'embrasse.' They kissed each other goodbye.

It's always wonderful being with friends, thought Nicole with a big smile. She went home, although just for one night as she was travelling to New York the following afternoon. Business obliged.

New York

Back to the city that never slept. Nicole arrived at night, and saw all the skyscrapers lit up from the Triborough Bridge. Her favourites were the Empire State Building and the iconic art deco crystallized sculpture capping the Chrysler Building that gleamed for miles. The dazzling lights of the Big Apple greeted Nicole but she felt the winds of change blowing.

When she got home, she noticed there was a fax waiting in the tray. She didn't want to look, because if it wasn't from Mounir she'd be disappointed. With some courage, she walked over to the machine and picked up a couple of pages. It was a letter from Mounir. She decided to read it sitting down comfortably on her creamy beige sofa. In anticipation, her hands trembled with excitement.

His letter was polite and charming. He said he'd soon be in New York. She checked the dates that he mentioned in her red crocodile Hermès diary. As she continued reading the letter, many thoughts ran through her mind. He's coming in February and he's invited me to dinner, a restaurant of my choice. Mon Dieu! He's also invited me to a very important black tie event. The Sheikh of Dubai and his wife, Princess Jamilah, are the guests of honour, and Princess Jamilah will be the keynote speaker. Wow! His invitation makes me feel honoured and special. He says that the speech will address how education can increase geo-political knowledge, broaden cultural understanding and promote religious tolerance under the umbrella of globalization. Inherent in this paradigm shift is that each nation and nation-state respects international law and each respective country's customary laws, along with cultivating pragmatic cooperation for the betterment of the world as a whole. What an intellectual. How interesting!

He had signed the letter, 'With Love, Mounir.'

Nicole's heart sang. She couldn't move and gazed off into space, oblivious to the sounds of yellow cabs screeching to a halt, sirens from ambulances and the base, thumping noises from her rap-star neighbour. She heard nothing except the symphony conducted by her soul.

Nicole was woken the next morning by the sound of her phone. It was Gordon Stanton the President of the Hayaté Foundation, where she had ten per cent ownership and a seat on the board. After Marc-Antoine's death, Nicole had sold her private equity interests in the companies that they had invested in together. She preferred now to focus only on the Hayaté Foundation, because she wanted to help make the world a better place to live in. The foundation acted like an umbrella company for a venture capital firm, a bank and a hedge fund. From the profits, the board would decide what percentage to keep for themselves in the form of dividends and what percentage to donate to philanthropic societies. Nicole managed the donations to humanitarian organizations for projects throughout the world that focused on community development through finance and asset building. This was her contribution enabling continued advancement for people in the educational, cultural and commercial fields. Nicole found organizations in need through her travels and through her friends. Philanthropic projects enriched her life.

Nicole had developed a friendly working relationship with Gordon, who was a long-time friend of her father.

'How was your trip to India?' Gordon asked. 'I hope you were able to relax.'

'It was beautiful and full of interesting people and places. I discovered certain truths about the meaning and purpose of life.'

'Sounds deep. You sound happy. Like one chapter of your life has peacefully ended allowing a new one to begin.'

'Now you sound like the philosopher. I didn't know you had it in you,' chuckled Nicole.

'By the way, this is a reminder to attend our year-end board meeting. We haven't fixed a date yet,' said Gordon in a more serious tone.

'I'd like to bring up something at one of the working sessions before the board meeting – the idea of allocating some funds to a hospital that treats children with polio in India. Mohan, Cherry and I visited it and found it in a terrible condition. The children are suffering because of a lack of funds,' said Nicole, getting her point across in direct, professional tones.

'We'll put it on the agenda. In the meantime, take care of yourself.'

'You too and kindest regards to your family.'

Click. Nicole let out a big sigh.

Mounir, Mounir. She kept thinking about Mounir. Was he thinking about her? She couldn't get him out of her mind. Did the universe have some kind of plan for her, more surprises? She loved surprises. The events in her life took a form and shape of their own, leading her down a new path, a path not yet charted on the destiny map – or was it? Nicole decided it was time to go with the flow, ride on the wave of life and see where it would lead her. She would try to listen to her inner voice and follow her dreams. On the other hand, the logical side of her brain would help in the decision-making process so that she could remain balanced yet flexible, in case she needed to change course and try another path, perhaps less travelled. In any event, Nicole liked change. If life were perfect it wouldn't be as enriching or interesting, or so she thought.

Tribeca Grill

Mounir arrived in New York as scheduled and called Nicole.

'Did you reserve a place for dinner?' he asked.

'Yes, I reserved a table at Tribeca Grill for nine o'clock this evening. Or if you'd prefer, we can go somewhere else.'

'No. I like Tribeca Grill. It's fun and casual. Can you come to my hotel first, then we can go together?'

'Sure, I'll come by at half past eight,' said Nicole, trying to contain her excitement.

When she arrived at the hotel located on Central Park South, she saw him standing there waiting for her at the entrance. She waved to him, happy that she recognized him. As she opened the door to get out, he jumped in.

'At this time it's difficult getting a cab,' he said.

'That's New York,' replied Nicole.

They kissed each other on the cheeks to say hello and she moved over to the other side of the cab to keep a space between them.

During the taxi ride they engaged in small talk and tried to figure out where the cab driver was from, based on his name plate posted on the window shield that separated the driver from his passengers. Mounir guessed Pakistan and Nicole thought the guy was from India. Mounir was right. Apparently, Mounir liked to find out everyone's country of origin; especially, in America, the land of immigrants. Nicole would later adopt this interest in wanting to discover more about the different nationalities and ethnicities that exist in the world.

They jumped out of the cab and entered the restaurant. It was filled to capacity due to a film screening event taking place on the second floor. The evening had a festive spirit with the occasional cameo appearance of a Hollywood movie star. The couple followed the hostess to their table. Nicole, already floating in the clouds, meandered in the wrong direction and had to be redirected back to her table by the gentle embrace of

Mounir's hand on her arm. The hostess seated them in one of the booths at the back of the restaurant behind the bar to ensure their privacy, because they looked like two doves that had just fallen in love with one another. For both Nicole and Mounir, it felt as if they were the only two that existed in that time and space. They discussed everything under the sun, from their New Year's Eve together in Udaipur to her travels with the Indian director and his wife, from his business and philanthropic pursuits to philosophical concerns about religion and politics around the world. Mounir never mentioned his past revolutionary activities or the assassins still chasing him. He was afraid to tell her the truth right away because he thought this might scare her and she would run away from him. Deep down in his heart he prayed for her love.

Between the appetizer and the main course, Nicole produced a poem that she had written for Mounir. She said shyly, 'I've written a poem about our mystical encounter in India. Here's a copy for you. May I recite it to you?'

Mounir was overcome with joy and said, 'I'd love to hear it with your voice. Please, go ahead.'

'It's entitled "Udaipur".' And then she read the poem:

UDAIPUR
Friends of friends,
Meeting one another,
From faraway lands.

Mood is magical,
Moon encircles the lake,
Overpowers us,
With its mysterious, orange glow.

The poet sings,
Sails flap gently,
Candles flicker,
Rhythmically to Indian instrumental music.

Boat moves at a snail's pace,
Wine, *hors d'oeuvres*, chit chat,
Friendship and romance.

> Wings of desire,
> Fly to the moon.
>
> Is it a Dream
> Or
> Destiny?

Mounir loosened his tie and told Nicole, 'It's beautiful.' He chuckled, 'And so true, that the boat did move at a snail's pace.' In a more serious tone he added, 'It's destiny. Our encounter was prewritten in the heavens.'

Nicole smiled and looked deeply into Mounir's beautiful, round, hazel eyes. She was speechless.

Changing the subject, Mounir asked Nicole if she knew about the Sumerian myths of Inanna. As a scholar, he loved to delve into the different mythologies that existed across civilizations and decipher them.

She had to dig into her brain for a moment and then said, 'From the vivid stories my brother recounted to me, I remember that the Sumerians had myths of origin, creation, resurrection and of a great flood that predated the stories found in the Old Testament in the Bible and the Torah.'

'You must have grown up in an intellectual household! You're right. What you've said has been scientifically proven by various anthropologists who have done extensive research on the Sumerian civilization. However, I'm interested in Inanna because she was the Queen of Heaven, the Goddess of Love, Fertility and Procreation. Her Semitic name was Ishtar. She was the tutelary deity of Erech in Sumer. Sumer is present-day Iraq.'

'Isn't there a myth about the quest for eternal life related to Inanna's descent into the nether world?' Nicole asked.

Mounir nodded his head.

Nicole, who always loved to embellish myths, fairytales and stories with her own imagination, suggested, 'Why don't we create our own story based on Inanna's quest for eternity?'

Challenged by this idea, Mounir said, 'OK, you start.'

'Once upon a time, Inanna, the Goddess of Heaven was bored. She decided that immortality for the gods wasn't enough. She wanted eternal life for man.'

Mounir continued. 'Ah! It was her revolutionary spirit that moved her to invade the nether world, to raise the dead and eliminate death completely. She was in love with a mortal named Damuzi who had been a shepherd. They married in a sacred marriage rite with the blessing of the gods. Damuzi became the shepherd-king of Erech. He was later punished for abusing his power, and the gods sent him to the nether world. His sister pleaded on his behalf, and they agreed that she could take his place for six months but that he had to stay the other six months. Inanna was heartbroken for he was the love of her life.'

Nicole took over the narrative, 'Inanna set her heart on saving Damuzi from his fate. She put on her golden crown, her lapis lazuli necklace with matching ringed earrings and a beautiful white linen robe with golden leather sandals. She brought a cedar box filled with treasures for her older sister, Ereshkigal, the Goddess of the Nether World. She told her faithful servant, Ninshuber, that if she had not ascended after three days, to plead with her father, Enki, the God of Wisdom, to free her from death. She, the goddess of love, light and life, descended into this dark world to free her husband from the grip of death.'

Mounir interrupted to comment on how well Nicole knew the original myth. She looked bashfully down at her plate of uneaten food.

Mounir went on, 'Ereshkigal despised Inanna. She knew Inanna's ambitions to destroy the nether world and give immortality to mankind. Inanna knocked at the door of the nether world. The gatekeeper, Neti, opened the rite of passage, on the command of Ereshkigal. Inanna had to pass through several gates and each time had to take off a piece of clothing and some jewellery, until she was left with nothing and stood stark naked. She pleaded to see Damuzi. Ereshkigal was cruel and had Inanna judged before the seven Anunnaki, the dreaded judges of the nether world. They made her kneel in front of them and sentenced her to death. They hung her on a stake next to her beloved Damuzi.'

'How horrible!' exclaimed Nicole and she continued with their story, 'Three days and three nights passed. Inanna's servant went to Enki and told him what had happened. He took pity on his daughter, Inanna, and created two creatures, composed of the mud of the Earth, to descend into the nether world. Enki made them promise that when they met Ereshkigal they would ask her for the corpses of Inanna and Damuzi. Once the dead bodies were brought back from the nether world, the two creatures had to sprinkle water and the food of life on the corpses to bring them back to life. Once reborn, Inanna and Damuzi were told to return to Erech.'

Mounir added, 'They succeeded but because Damuzi was a mortal man, he still had to abide by the conditions that had been previously agreed upon with his sister. Inanna was heartbroken but at least she could see her beloved six months out of the year. She tried to bring light to the nether world and abolish death but was unable to achieve immortality for the mortals. That's it! The End.'

'We make a good team!' said Nicole excitedly.

They were so caught up in their storytelling that the waitress wanted to take away their main meal. They looked at each other and laughed. They ate a small portion of their cold dishes quickly and silently. It was already midnight. Mounir had an early morning business meeting and wanted to get back to his hotel soon. He ordered two espressos and the bill. He asked Nicole what she was doing for the weekend. He was going to New Orleans and wanted her to come along with him.

After a moment's reflection she said, 'I'd love to but I've already promised to meet my brother in Marrakech. We're driving through the Atlas Mountains.'

Mounir hid his unhappiness because he really wanted to get to know Nicole better. Every day was precious to him. He never knew if tomorrow would come, although he had taken the necessary precautions to feel secure. Since Greece, there had been no more attempts on his life. Mounir wanted to open up his heart and reveal his past to Nicole because he felt he could trust her. But she might become frightened and he didn't want to lose her. He would tell her at a more appropriate time. The waitress came back with the bill interrupting Mounir's reverie. Mounir paid by credit card. Afterwards, he nervously tightened his tie around his neck.

'Are you still coming tomorrow night?' he asked.

'Of course, it will be an honour to go with you.'

In the future, Mounir thought, I'll have to ask her in advance to meet me or go somewhere. It's only fair. I shouldn't have expected her to be free to come along with me.

He didn't say anything further except, 'Shall we go?'

They both got up from the table, retrieved their coats from the cloakroom and left the restaurant in a state of bliss.

Mounir hailed a taxi to take Nicole home. As soon as they got into the cab, he put his arm around her to draw her closer to him. She looked up at him and gazed into his eyes. He put his soft moist lips on hers. Her lips parted. Love songs were whispered into her soul. It was as though they were making love to one another through a deep engaging kiss. Mounir merged with Nicole as though they became one being. A magnetic force held them together for the entire taxi ride from Tribeca to the Upper West Side.

They didn't even realize that they had arrived at Nicole's apartment building. The taxi driver had to interrupt them, 'Hey, you two.'

They blushed. Mounir asked the taxi driver to wait a couple of minutes.

'Yeah, OK,' said the driver in a grouchy tone.

Mounir escorted Nicole to her building and kissed her goodbye on both her cheeks. 'Remember to be on time tomorrow night. It's a very important event,' he said.

'I'll be on time. My parents sent me to summer camp in Switzerland when I was a child, and the Swiss taught me how to arrive either five minutes early or exactly on time.'

He smiled at her and jumped back into the cab. She winked at him and waved. A kiss of fire branded their hearts for ever.

Gala Event

Nicole met Mounir at the New York Historical Society. He introduced her to some of the people who would be sitting at his table. He was one of the sponsors of this symposium on 'How Education Bridges the Gap Amongst Nations'. After the last assassination attempt on his life, Mounir's philosophy of life had changed. He had decided to not live in fear, but to enjoy life, and contribute some of his resources to proactive, educational causes that would enlighten society, such as this one in New York. There were about twenty sponsors. Some were private individuals and the rest were prestigious non-profit institutions, banks and corporations. As Mounir greeted guests, Nicole walked around the Great Hall through white granite fifty-foot arches. It was a splendid reception area. She picked up a brochure on the history of the building. The society was founded over two hundred years ago for the purpose of preserving the records of America's struggle for independence. Its modern day responsibility was collecting and documenting New York City's history.

She felt Mounir's hand on her elbow. She instinctively let him guide her to the theatre where the symposium would be held. It was a grand and modern lecture hall seating about three hundred people. He introduced her to two more of his friends – a couple from Manhattan. Apparently the man was a Nobel Prize winner for his scientific research at the Rockefeller Institute. They ended up sitting together in the lecture hall.

The debate commenced. Five distinguished people were on the panel: a columnist from *The New York Times*; a professor from the School of Foreign Service at Georgetown University; a former politician from Carter's White House administration who was now a senior adviser to the Center for Strategic and International Studies; a Senior Fellow from the Council on Foreign Relations; and, the only woman, a foreign correspondent who represented both *An-Nahar*, an Arabic newspaper, and MSNBC, covering events in the Middle East. Their views were mostly in harmony with one another.

Nicole empathized with what the woman journalist said: 'In order to change as a nation, we must change from within. We need to educate our own people first. Education is the catalyst for productive problem-solving, a bridge across cultural barriers and a means to enlighten our society. We do not need to wait around for Big Brother to help us or give us aid and then blame him if our government and public institutions can not organize themselves to promote an educational infrastructure that is needed for the advancement of the country. Knowledge and wisdom keep a nation strong. Ignorance is plentiful and is the cause of so many of our problems such as nationalism, racism, protectionism and isolationism. Education can serve as a means to better understand the world. It's important to deal with problems on both national and international levels with learned diplomacy.'

She was the last to speak. A question and answer session followed the speeches and debate, then the host of the symposium made his closing remarks and the audience applauded. The host announced that cocktails would be served in the Great Hall and thereafter everyone should proceed to the second floor, to Luman Reed Hall, for the dinner.

Nicole's bladder was bursting. Once everyone exited the theatre, she left Mounir and went in search of the ladies room. Along the way, she noticed many journalists from ABC, BBC, TV5 (a French television station), NEW TV (a Lebanese television station) and CNN roaming around in anticipation of the arrival of the Sheikh of Dubai and Princess

Jamilah. As Nicole stood in line, she noticed how beautifully dressed most of the women were. The wait seemed to last for hours. She missed the cocktail reception but was in time for the dinner.

When she returned to the Great Hall, she spotted the first man that Mounir had introduced her to that evening. She walked up to him and said, 'Hello.'

He seemed a bit upset with her and said, with a reprimanding tone in his voice, 'You'd better find Mounir. He's been looking all over for you. He thought you'd left.'

'Where can I find him?' There were masses of people in the Great Hall.

'Look up on the staircase.'

She looked up and there he was standing in the middle tier of the grand staircase with a couple of women. At the same time, he was surveying the hall. Nicole caught his eye by waving her hand to him. He acknowledged her with a big, beautiful, magnificent smile.

He's so handsome, she thought, but why would he ever think that I would leave an event that he has invited me to without even saying thank you or goodbye? Did something happen to him once that now makes him jumpy and insecure? Whoever hurt him must have made an indelible mark on his soul. I'll have to remember in the future to reassure him of my presence.

Nicole climbed the stairs. She whispered into his ear that she had had to go and wash her hands. He understood and felt better. He kissed her on the cheeks and introduced her to a Druze woman from Syria.

He said to her, 'You have a lot in common with one of my dearest friends, Dr Nuha Zahreddine. You both believe in reincarnation. The Druze faith has believed in reincarnation for thousands of years.'

Nicole smiled and Dr Zahreddine started to tell her about a documented case of reincarnation that occurred in her own village. 'A young girl fell into a well and drowned. That same day, she was reborn into another family. When she was five years old, she told her family that she had another family in the same village. She brought them to this family and told them that she was their daughter who drowned in the well. The family confirmed the story. The two families had a big celebration, and the little girl remained with her new family with permission to visit her previous family. This type of story surfaces from time to time. It sounds unbelievable but it's true.'

Nicole mentioned how she had seen TV documentaries about similar stories in India. Reincarnation proved to be a long-lasting subject. Mounir, a courteous and sociable host, told the ladies that they were being summoned to dinner.

Everyone took their seats at their appointed tables. Nicole loved the dining room set up in Luman Reed Hall. Oil paintings from the Historical Society's renowned collection covered the walls from floor to ceiling. There was also a beautiful big fireplace. Nicole felt as though she were sitting in the dining-room of a nineteenth-century Victorian home. Suddenly, there was a commotion near the entrance.

The sheikh and princess had arrived. Everyone stood up to greet them. As they walked past Mounir's table, Princess Jamilah acknowledged Mounir by tilting her head towards him with a smile. He greeted her in Arabic. During last night's dinner at Tribeca Grill, Mounir had mentioned to Nicole that his brother, Naji, was a close friend of Princess Jamilah and that they had worked together on projects to help educate poor children around the world. Nicole noticed that the table of honour was right next to theirs. Her Highness was considered to be one of the most beautiful women in the world. 'Jamilah', in Arabic, meant beautiful, graceful and lovely. When Princess Jamilah delivered the keynote address, Nicole thought she was poised, elegant, intelligent, humble and humorous. After the main course, Mounir introduced Nicole to her. They exchanged a few words and Nicole felt honoured to have met her. Soon after, the sheikh and princess left while dessert and coffee were being served. Nicole thought Mounir's timing was impeccable and was truly appreciative of his royal introduction.

While at the dinner table, she mostly talked to the people who sat closest to her. It was hard to hear those at the opposite end. Mounir sat directly across from her. He had planned the seating arrangement that way so he could look at her throughout the dinner. The lady sitting next to Mounir was talking about marriage. Nicole's ears pricked up when she heard the word.

Mounir captivated her with his sparkling eyes and asked her silently with his heart, 'Do you want to get married?'

Nicole got scared, and replied with her eyes, 'I'm not ready yet.'

Her strong reaction surprised her – she thought she was ready to get remarried.

She let this brief moment of mental telepathy dissipate into space. They both turned their heads and resumed their conversations with those nearest to them.

Another woman at the table, an entertaining Brazilian, Mrs Priscila Salim, now living in La Jolla, California, recounted an incredible story about her father who she characterized as the heroic type. She commenced, 'Arto Bahia, my father, was an avid pilot and he was crazy. At the time, we were living in Mexico City. One day, he received a parachute from a friend of his for his adventures. He happened to put on this parachute for his next flight over the jungles outside Mexico City. His fuel ran out but, thanks to the parachute, he was able to jump from the plane. He landed in the trees and was knocked unconscious, dangling by the ropes of his parachute. Native Indians found him but they were from a tribe known to shrink heads. He tried to negotiate for his life and his safe return to Mexico City. He promised to give them anything they wanted as long as they brought him to Mexico City first.

'Incredible but true – a strange coincidence occurred. A Brazilian man who knew my father was part of the tribe. Heaven only knows how he ended up with them. Consequently, my father was able to negotiate his way back to Mexico City. He was a very lucky man. This all took place during one week. Meanwhile, my family had been searching for him, and finding only the remains of his plane, we thought he was dead.

'When my father came back home, he witnessed a funeral procession and asked a bystander, "Who's this for?"

'The man looked in astonishment at Arto, and exclaimed, "It's for you!"'

Everyone at the table laughed and thought her father was truly an adventurer.

Mounir loved to hear Nicole's laugh. He thought she was beautiful. He excused himself from the table and asked Nicole if she would mind leaving now. They said their farewells and wished everyone a safe journey home.

Mounir asked Nicole if she would like to have a drink. 'Is it necessary to go to a bar?' he asked. 'Would you like to come up to my room with me so we can talk?'

'I'd love to.'

They reached the room, and sat on the sofa in the salon of his suite.

Mounir got up and said, 'I brought you something from India.'

Nicole opened up an ivory silk pouch that contained a beautiful antique silver bracelet. She kissed him to thank him. Although they were consumed with the kiss of fire the night before, they were shy about what to do next.

Nicole didn't know what to do or say, and nervously blurted out, 'Shall we take our clothes off?' . . . then thought to herself, what a dumb thing to say!

Mounir stepped forward and hugged her, then kissed her warmly on the lips. Slowly, they undressed each other, discovering with their gentle, poetic hands, silky, soft sensuous skin. Soon, consumed with one another, orgasmic delight shivered throughout their entire beings. A dark room, nothingness, preceded bright morning sunshine. Nicole and Mounir woke up and both smiled to find themselves intertwined in the most loving embrace.

Chapter 10

Rugged Adventure

Morocco, 2000

At Casablanca Airport, Nicole could see neither her brother nor the others who had been invited to trek the Atlas Mountains. She paced up and down the arrivals area and wondered if John had arranged for someone to meet her. The terminal slowly emptied until only a few passengers remained. She stood alone with her luggage. Should she book a hotel in Casablanca or continue to wait? It was hot and dusty. Her cell phone rang, it was her brother.

'We're stuck in Paris. We can only get the next flight out tomorrow morning. We'll all be arriving at the villa around two or three in the afternoon.'

'What happened?'

'There was a huge storm that swept through Europe, closing down all the airports. Mum called, and told me that fallen trees had cut off electrical lines in their neighbourhood, 160,000 trees have been knocked over, and there's been over a hundred deaths in and around Paris.'

'I'm glad everyone's all right. I had no idea. My trip was so uneventful, and it's so sunny here. What a contrast!'

John continued, 'I hired three drivers for three Pajero turbos. The chief guide's name is Youssef. I've already told him what happened and he's looking for you. He's tall, dark and handsome. I'll give you his number. Tell him to leave two Pajeros in Casablanca and we'll pick them up tomorrow and drive ourselves to Marrakech. You take the other one. Have Youssef drive, accompanied by the two other drivers.'

'Will I be safe with three strange men all the way from Casa to Marrakech?'

'I wouldn't have suggested this if I didn't think you'd be in trustworthy hands. Youssef has usually been my driver when I go to Morocco and he's a responsible young man. They all want to keep their jobs, you know. The unemployment rate is very high.'

'Does Youssef know where the villa is? I have no idea how to get there.'

'Yeah, he knows. He's been there before. It's at the foothills of the Atlas Mountains, about twenty minutes south-east of Marrakech. By the way, visit the mosque in Casa. You'll have plenty of time. Take care and a big hug from all of us,' he said.

'Thanks for arranging everything. See you tomorrow.'

'One more thing, invite a friend to come over if you want. We have one extra room. Nicolas and his wife decided to cancel at the last minute because of the storm.'

'That's really sweet of you. Ciao, ciao,' said Nicole as she closed the line.

At that moment Youssef arrived. They introduced themselves. Nicole relayed John's arrangement. Youssef was a polite young man and interpreted from French to Arabic for the other two drivers. Nicole conversed with them in French throughout her journey because she couldn't speak Arabic well enough to sustain an in-depth conversation. She considered becoming fluent one day, because it seemed that life pulled her towards the Middle East and northern Africa, however most of the Arabs she met spoke English or French as a second language. Thus, for the moment, she decided to get by with what she knew, and perhaps there were more important lessons to be learned at this moment in time.

'Would you like to take a brief tour of Casa?' Youssef asked.

'That would be lovely and I'd love to see the mosque,' replied Nicole.

'I can take you to the mosque but it's Ramadan so I regret you will not be allowed to enter.'

They set off in their black Pajero turbo, a sports utility vehicle that was made to traverse difficult routes through the desert, rivers and mountainous terrain. However, on this day, they travelled on well-paved highways until they reached their destination early in the evening.

On the way, Youssef explained that the Grand Mosque of Casablanca was named Mosque Hassan II after a previous sovereign. A French architect built its foundation on a seabed near the shoreline, surrounded on three sides by the Atlantic Ocean. Youssef told Nicole there was a Koranic saying: 'Allah has His throne on the water.'

It was a beautiful metaphor. As they approached the mosque, she saw a towering minaret made from white marble.

Youssef continued his guided tour with enthusiasm, 'It is the tallest minaret in the world but the mosque itself is smaller than those of Medina or Mecca.'

It was a sight to behold, with misty spray as a backdrop, surfing on waves of a sapphire-coloured ocean that enveloped the mosque and its surrounding esplanade. Nicole strolled around the site and admired it from a distance. She was disappointed that she could not see the inside but she respected the traditions of Islam. She walked around the immense courtyard and breathed in the invigorating salty air to help rejuvenate her tired, jetlagged body. Near the sea wall, she leaned over, and gazed dreamily into the aquamarine horizon. She remembered what John had said about inviting a friend and decided to call Mounir while she had this private moment to herself.

'Mounir? Hello? May I speak to Mounir, please?' asked Nicole.

Mounir instantly recognized Nicole's voice and said, 'I was dialling your number when my phone rang and it was you.'

'We're thinking about each other at the same time,' said Nicole.

Mounir was so excited to hear from her that he garrulously gave her every detail about his day in New Orleans. He told her how he went from jazz bar to jazz bar and how he dreamed of her by his side listening to the music.

After a moment's pause, Nicole said, 'Would you like to come and spend a few days in Marrakech with me? My brother John said I could invite someone. There's plenty of room. We'll be here for a couple of weeks.'

She could hear his voice tremble, 'I'd love to come. Could you meet me at the airport? I can be there within forty-eight hours.'

Nicole's heart thumped rapidly. 'I'll have one of the drivers take me to Marrakech Airport, and I'll be there to welcome you to Morocco. Just let me know your flight times.'

'Will do, my love. I've been day-dreaming about you. You are the most beautiful woman in the world. Je t'aime,' declared Mounir.

Nicole thought he was romantic and charming and said, 'Me too. I've got to go now. A big hug and a kiss. Au revoir.'

Nicole floated upwards towards heaven, like the pearl dome of the Taj Mahal that ascended at dusk to meet the stars and the moon, emitting an ethereal, misty blue light. She returned in happy spirits to the car where the three boys stood and chatted with one another.

'What did you think?' Youssef asked.

'It's a shame I couldn't see the inside but the outside is breathtaking.'

They jumped into the jeep. Youssef took them to an old colonial square and called it 'Pigeon Square'. It looked like a scene right out of Alfred Hitchcock's *The Birds*.

'Do you want to get out and walk around, madame?'

'I'm not having all those bird droppings on my head!' Nicole replied. 'Could you show me Rick's bar from the legendary film *Casablanca* instead?'

Youssef and the other two men laughed, and in unison said, 'There's no such place, madame.'

'Are there any other places of interest to see or historical monuments to visit?' asked Nicole as she replayed the scenes of Humphrey Bogart and the piano man at Rick's bar in her mind.

Youssef replied, 'No, madame. Marrakech is more beautiful. That's where we're from.'

It took about three and a half hours to get to Marrakech. At sunset, the boys stopped at a makeshift café along the road to eat the traditional Ramadan snack. The snack would keep them going until dinner at ten or eleven at night until the month of Ramadan was over. Between sunrise and sunset, the Muslims could not drink, eat, smoke or have sex. It was their way of fasting according to the Koran. The snack consisted of a hearty chickpea soup called harira, Moroccan crepes that were salty in flavour, a hard-boiled egg, fresh dates, and a couple of sweet cakes – shebbakia – that were deep-fried pastries dipped in honey. They drank tea, water or coffee, but no alcohol. Nicole tasted and shared the food with them at their insistence and experienced the Muslim culture and tradition of their country.

These simple restaurants lined the roads about every fifty miles during Ramadan and at dusk the masses stopped and ate their snacks. Hundreds of cars, bicycles and donkeys filled the temporary parking lots near these cafés. It all took place in about fifteen minutes. Those who practised the religion had to pray towards Mecca unless they were working or travelling on a long journey. This exempted Youssef and his two colleagues. The atmosphere became festive during this traditional breaking of the fast. Afterwards, the religious practitioners resumed their daily activities until dinner. When Nicole and her companions had finished drinking their tea they left the roadside café.

A deep orange skyline ran parallel to the highway towards Marrakech until the sun disappeared. When they arrived before the ramparts of Marrakech it was already night time. The city was lit up with orange lights that looked like an ocean of twinkling ships. Above, the stars sparkled brightly. Nicole noticed three stars shining in a distinct line but didn't know what constellation they represented. Like a little girl, she wished upon the first star that she had seen and hoped her wish would come true. Youssef, who Nicole nicknamed 'Chef' because he was always in charge, dropped off the other two boys in the city because they were not needed for a day or so. He was the one who knew how to get to Villa Fiori, which was located somewhere in a small village called Ourika.

Half an hour later, they arrived before two huge wooden doors that formed the entrance gate to the grounds of the villa. There was a guard who mysteriously opened the gates just as they arrived. He was better than the electric gate openers one found in the Westernized world. Dressed in a traditional djellaba, he greeted the visitors with a big smile dotted with a few black holes. In another five minutes, they arrived at the house. The household staff of two men and three women stood with a plump little girl in front of the house and greeted Nicole and the driver. Youssef told the butler that Nicole spoke French. She should ask him for anything she needed and speak to the others in sign language.

The terracotta-tiled entrance hall, lined artistically with fragments of antique Roman pillars, led to the main living room with a fire lit in a white adobe hearth. Although it was late, almost midnight, the cook had prepared dinner. Nicole thanked Youssef for bringing her to the villa and invited him to stay for dinner.

Youssef said, as his body twitched nervously, 'Thank you, madame, but I feel like I'm in prison here with all of these guards and servants. I'm newly married, madame, and I want to go back home to my wife.'

Nicole understood and bid him farewell. She, herself, felt a bit ridiculous sitting at an enormous, wooden, round dining table that could easily fit fourteen, being served by four or five household helpers. She experienced, once again, the gracious Arab hospitality for which she was most appreciative in her exhausted physical and mental state. In essence, her situation – a beautiful woman, all alone, for one night in a splendid Italianate villa – resembled the first act of an absurd comedy.

After dinner, Nicole sat in front of the warm fireplace, and dreamed about Mounir. The household staff suggested she stay in the master bedroom for one night, until the others arrived the following day. Normally, it was for John but according to Hani, the butler, he wouldn't mind if Nicole used the empty room. The name Hani meant 'happy' in Arabic and he was hospitable and courteous. Hani escorted Nicole through the villa to view all of the rooms so she could choose a guest suite for her and Mounir for the rest of the stay. Since she was the first to arrive, she should have first choice. He made her feel at home. The bedrooms were built around a courtyard two storeys high. She chose a duplex apartment. The entrance opened onto a living room that had a stairway leading up to the main bedroom with a huge adjoining bathroom. From the bedroom, double French doors opened onto a large, terracotta-tiled terrace with a ladder.

'What's the ladder for?' Nicole asked.

Hani replied, 'Madame, it's to climb up onto the roof of the villa and look at the spectacular views of the valley and the mountains by day and gaze at the stars at night.'

Nicole thought about the possibility of nude sunbathing in total privacy on this sun deck and at dusk she and Mounir could climb the ladder and watch the stars being born one by one. The other rooms were smaller and didn't have these options. After she had made her decision, they went back to the master bedroom upon Hani's insistence.

Hani unlocked the door to the master bedroom and guided Nicole through three huge rooms. The first was the bedroom, the second the dressing-room and the third an Italian-marbled bathroom. Arched doorways separated the rooms. Nicole fell in love with the dressing-room. In the middle was a divan, where one could sit and look up and see the sun or the stars through a pyramid-shaped window pointing upwards to the heavens. She imagined making love to Mounir on the divan. She kept having erotic dreams about this enigmatic man whom she had recently encountered in Udaipur and united with for the first time in New York. What was happening to her emotionally? She tried to focus her attention on what Hani was saying. He was giving her a history of the artefacts found in the bedroom. The three zebra rugs had been brought back by the owner of the villa as trophies of big game hunting in the wilds of Africa. Nicole was glad that Hani had finally persuaded her to enjoy the exquisite master bedroom for the night and thanked him for everything. He left the room and she locked the door. Before going to bed, she bathed herself in the immense, marble bath tub overflowing with bubbles. She sculpted funny animals out of the foam and giggled. At last, she cuddled under the covers and out of sheer exhaustion slept for twelve straight hours.

Singing birds and warm sunshine woke her up the next morning, or rather midday. Breakfast was served next to the pool and Nicole soaked in the rays of the noonday sunshine and peered at the mauve mountains in the distance. She spotted a falcon in search of his prey. Honey bees buzzed nearby, gathering nectar from the pale pink roses. Palm trees lined the garden around the pool. From the tops of the trees, her gaze went to the mountains that were almost as high as the Alps in Europe, with the highest summit measuring around 4600 metres. After the leisurely breakfast, Nicole brought her things to her new room and waited for John and his entourage.

They were scheduled to arrive in late afternoon and then, the festivities would begin. It was to be a group of nine. Tomorrow, Mounir would make it ten. They were all John's friends so Nicole was happy that Mounir would be joining them. Nicole knew one couple: Stephen and Nadine Murat from Paris. John had raced the Paris–Dakar Rally in the motorcycle category with Stephen last year, both as amateurs. This rally was classified as the toughest and most gruelling off-road race in the world, about ten thousand kilometres long, starting in Europe and ending somewhere in Africa, depending on the politics of the African region. During the race, John and Stephen had become friends with an

Italian from Rome, Enrico Murano, who had also been in the motorcycle class. They had all agreed to go four-wheel driving through the mountains in Morocco together with their families. Nicole hadn't yet met the Murano family. Enrico would bring his wife and their three young boys, aged six to twelve. Rugged adventure excited this crowd.

John and Stephen were great friends and did many things together. At times, they hunted big game in Africa; during the open season in France and Scotland, they shot pheasants and ducks. Two years ago, the two men jumped out of a helicopter and skied down one of the Canadian mountains through virgin powder. They had often been together to Morocco and participated in 4-x-4 excursions through the Sahara desert, including, on one occasion, a trip all the way to Timbuktu. John knew Africa the best, a result of both his anthropological studies and his adventurous spirit. Nicole loved the risk-taker in her brother and wished she could be more like him. That was one of the reasons she had agreed to come on this trip – to experience true outdoor adventure.

John had mentioned to Nicole that he had organized excursions to the south and south-east of Marrakech through the valleys of oases and kasbahs. In particular, he would have them drive through the Draa Valley, the Dadès Valley and the Todra Gorge. She couldn't wait to visit a small town near Ouarzazate on their itinerary where the Kasbah Aït Ben Haddou was located, known as the most elaborate kasbah in Morocco.

Nicole treasured time spent with John because he knew how to communicate with her and push her beyond her self-imposed limits. They were from the same family, yet he was a free spirit while she remained more reserved. Real adventure awaited her. Up until this point in her life, the photo safari in South Africa was the extent of her wild escapades. Although she had travelled, she had instead explored ancient civilizations and immersed herself in the culture of exotic lands, as in Spain, Egypt and India. Admittedly, she also enjoyed sunbathing on a pristine beach with the sweet, murmuring sea telling her mysterious stories about the universe. Culture was indigenous to her nature; she loved the arts and the history of civilizations – a passion she shared with Mounir. Soon, Nicole would also learn that Mounir had many things in common with John and Stephen. Together, new roads were to be discovered.

At dusk, John and his friends finally arrived in time for an aperitif. Stephen was smart and had brought a couple of champagne bottles with him from France. Alcohol, let alone champagne, would have been hard to find during Ramadan. Hani chilled the two bottles on ice. Hani's wife, Fousiya, who was also the cook, prepared little bowls filled with almonds, black olives and freshly roasted chickpeas. Meanwhile, Nadine introduced Enrico and his wife, Isabella, to Nicole. Enrico called his three boys, who had already found the ping-pong table by the pool, to come and meet her. They were adorable. All had dark brown hair with blue eyes, and were dressed in Ralph Lauren polo shirts and Bermuda shorts. From eldest to youngest, they presented themselves as Sergio, Thierry and Jean-Luigi. Once the introductions were made, the boys quietly disappeared while the adults sipped champagne. While they were all chatting, Nicole told John that she had invited Mounir, the man she had met in Udaipur on New Year's Eve and with whom she had attended the gala in New York. When Stephen and Nadine overheard this juicy piece of news, they were thrilled for Nicole and toasted the safe arrival of Mounir. Nicole's cheeks turned hot pink.

That night there would be nine at the big, round, wooden table. Nicole felt more at home tonight with family and new friends to dine with, rather than being the solitary woman of the night before. What a difference a day made! During dinner, the men spoke about road races and the women talked of trying to fit in some time to go shopping in the colourful souks of Marrakech. The boys traded jokes with one other and giggled to themselves until they caught the attention of Stephen, who egged them on to tell the rest of the group at the table at least one joke.

Jean-Luigi, the youngest, recounted a joke in English, 'What do you call an alien surfing the Internet?'

No answer.

'ET.'

His brothers bellowed with laughter while the adults rolled their eyes and chuckled.

The appetizer was served. It was the famous Moroccan pigeon pie called pastilla. It looked like a *mille feuille* with wafer-thin layers of pastry but in between each layer was a mixture of pigeon and almonds. The crust was dusted with powdery white icing sugar. Tajine followed, John's favourite dish. It was chicken stewed with preserved lemons and green olives in an earthenware dish topped with a conical lid. The household help served the dishes with the lids on, to preserve the beauty of the presentation, and then lifted all the lids in unison. Their actions were well-synchronized. This was a wonderful dinner to celebrate the meeting of old and new friends. Cookies and fresh dates made up the dessert platter. Mint tea was served after the meal.

The Murano family excused themselves first because they wanted to tuck the boys into bed for a good night's sleep. Stephen and Nadine decided to go for a romantic walk through the moonlit gardens. Nicole and John drank tea in front of the roaring fire.

'Who's this guy Mounir?' John asked.

'I told you. We met in Udaipur and then he invited me out a few times in New York. In many ways, he's just like you . . .'

John interrupted, 'What's his last name?'

'A bit unusual, Munir . . . I never met anyone before whose first name rhymed with his surname.'

John's teacup crashed onto the floor, 'Damn it! Why do you always have to get mixed up with crazy guys?'

'I don't know what you're talking about? What's bothering you?'

'I just don't want you to get hurt again,' said John.

'You'll think he's terrific.'

'I've already met him. He's a good man but a revolutionary. Years ago he stayed with me in the African jungle, which saved his life,' said John as he gazed at the fire.

Nicole didn't want to believe what she had just heard but John never lied to her. Also, when he told her how Mounir's life had been saved, a warm, tingling sensation rushed up and down her spine. Someone once told her that when the body shivers in reaction to a statement, the truth has been spoken.

She looked at her brother with misty eyes and said, 'Tell me more.'

'Tomorrow. I'm tired now, we'll talk more then,' as he kissed his sister on her cheek and left the room.

Nicole sat alone in silence and watched the flames dance, until she herself grew tired and turned in for the evening. Once in bed, the tango of love with Mounir whisked her off into dreamland.

* * *

Mounir arrived the next morning. Nicole met him at the airport as promised. She felt a warm, shivering feeling traverse her body from head to toe when he kissed her. Their public display of affection was minimal, out of respect for Ramadan. Although born a Muslim, Mounir was agnostic, due to his belief that if one behaved towards others with good intentions then that was what was important. Nicole was in full agreement with his philosophy. While Youssef drove them towards the villa in the Ourika Valley, she told Mounir that the others had gone to Essaouira for the day and wouldn't be back until late that evening. She was happy to be reunited with Mounir and as he held her hand tightly she dreamed of making love to him. He had the same dreams of making love to her all day long and well into the night, until they fell asleep in each other's arms to awaken to the warm sunshine the following morning. Their dreams came true.

The next day, the adventure started with an excursion in the SUVs. Nicole introduced Mounir to everyone as they walked out of the house towards the Pajeros. Meanwhile, John was busy organizing the drivers, showing them the maps with the charted course and telling them that he would be the leader of the pack for the day. When Mounir saw John, he started coughing and clearing his throat.

'Are you all right?' Nicole asked.

'I'll be fine . . . I didn't know your brother was John Townsend. He saved my life. There's something I need to tell you.'

John, who had been preoccupied with managing the logistics of the four-wheel-drive trek, looked up and saw Nicole with Mounir. He walked over and shook Mounir's hand, then they embraced each other.

John said, 'It's been a long time and I'm happy to see you alive and well. You're better looking without that big, bushy beard.'

Mounir chuckled. Nicole was moved by this display of friendship. She would ask Mounir later about what had happened earlier in his life.

It was time to start the adventure. Nicole and Mounir jumped in the back of John's vehicle as asked. John, the expert, drove the whole time. While he drove, Mounir held Nicole's hand. Their caravan of three black Pajero turbos followed the Tizi-n-Tichka route from Ourika Valley to the final destination of Kasbah Aït Ben Haddou about eighteen kilometres before Ouarzazate. The group travelled through the valley of ksars and kasbahs dating from the nineteenth century.

They looked like sandcastles and were made out of mud and rubble called pisé. Ksars were palaces while the kasbah was a fortified village. In the High Atlas region, Berber architecture prevailed. The Berbers were known to be amongst the earliest inhabitants of north-west Africa. When the Romans reigned from 25 BC until the arrival of Islam in AD 682 they gave the name of 'Barbarus' to these wild tribes, which evolved into the name Berber. The Berber communities were constructed like fortresses to protect the people, animals and food supplies against invasion. The architecture resembled Ancient Egyptian and Sumerian layouts of villages, farms and granaries. As Nicole peered out of her window, she viewed her first mud-built castle, sitting in a valley, nestled amongst ochre-coloured rolling hills, with snow-covered mountains towering in the distance.

Amazing, she thought.

Moments later, the group pulled up at Dar Glaoui, the splendid Kasbah of Telouet, built in the nineteenth century on the bank of the Oued Imare. Unfortunately, many of the buildings were in ruins as the site had been abandoned by the Pasha of Marrakech about fifty years ago. As they explored and walked through a couple of the preserved rooms of the palace, Nicole noticed how the interior decoration mirrored the Moorish design that she had seen at the Alhambra Castle in Grenada. It was almost as if she was meant to see Alhambra first, in order to appreciate more deeply her journey through the slopes of the High Atlas.

Mounir interrupted Nicole's thoughts, took her hand and guided her to a former harem, one of the preserved rooms. Nobody was looking so he kissed her under one of the off-white stucco arches that had been finely carved with floral motifs. When Nicole opened her eyes and looked up, she observed a painted ceiling in honeycomb patterns of wood. Mounir brought her closer to the walls to view the geometric patterns of the blue, white, green, yellow and red tiles.

'All of these tiles were hand made and placed one by one by the artisans who designed these walls. It took hours of work,' he said.

Nicole was dazzled by the craftsmanship. She remarked, 'These palaces were built for princes. Yet today, all you see are the locals who live nearby, with their cows, goats, cats and sheep running around in freedom.'

When they left the main building, a goat nudged Nicole's knee. She jumped, looked down at the goat and squealed, 'What do you want?'

Mounir grinned and shooed the goat away. He batted his eyes and said, 'My dear, it's a good thing I came along to protect you from these savage beasts.'

Nicole chuckled gleefully. 'You love teasing me.'

Mounir sang to the tune of 'Ya Mustafa' to Nicole, '*Chérie, je t'aime – comme les bonbons de la Shocolata.*'

Nicole couldn't believe what she was hearing. It was a play on words from one of her favourite songs, the one that the chubby Nubian man had sung for her at the Old Cataract Hotel in Aswan.

She sang back to Mounir, '*Ya Mounir, Ana Bahibbak! Je t'adore – comme la Shocolata, aussi.*'

They giggled and embraced each other one more time before walking back to the Pajero.

Once the others arrived, they got back into their vehicles and continued on their journey. John led the way, veering off onto a rocky trail that ascended a mountain. Halfway to the top, he stopped at a small Berber village where one could see stone houses near cultivated terraced fields. The group got out of their jeeps and went to have lunch under a low awning made out of goat and camel hair. John had prearranged for Tajine to be made for everyone, including the hired drivers. If needed, Youssef and the other two were to trade places with John, Stephen and Enrico. Youssef also acted as a guide; as a native he knew the region even better than John.

As a compliment from the restaurant owner, the lunch was accompanied by traditional Berber song and dance. The Berber men sat on the ground, playing drums and flutes, while their women stood behind them, clapping their hands to the lyrics. Shortly afterwards, the women danced a circle around their men and they all sang together. Next, the women jumped up and down energetically, towards the men sitting at the front at low copper tables and pulled them up from their stools to dance. John and Mounir were the bravest and moved up and down to the music with the Berbers, while the onlookers clapped in rhythm. Nicole thought John and Mounir were moving more like those who danced techno or house music at the nightclubs in Paris and New York. She couldn't help but laugh at this weird scene of be-bopping around in the High Atlas. Soon the whole gang joined in the entertainment. When the music stopped, they went back to their tables and drank mint tea.

Nicole was pleased that Mounir fitted in easily and was impressed that he could speak Arabic with the locals. The Moroccan dialect was very different from the Arab language spoken in Egypt, Jordan or Syria.

John was the only other person fluent in Arabic and he also knew the Moroccan dialect. Otherwise, French was the dominant language. Nicole began to observe that when any of the Moroccans addressed Mounir, they did so with respect and admiration, as if he were someone very important. All she knew from what he had told her was that he was an anthropologist educated at Stanford just like her brother, who lived in London and travelled extensively to research ancient civilizations. Perhaps he had studied the Berbers and they remembered him. Or was she reading too much into these friendly exchanges with the locals?

As thoughts raced through her head, Nicole reminded herself to stop thinking and analysing too much as K had suggested in Egypt. She imagined huge yellow and orange flames leaping from her head and laughed inwardly. At that moment, her thoughts returned to the love she felt for Mounir and how he made her feel deeply loved and desired. Mounir read Nicole's mind, took her hand in his and squeezed it. He had refined hands with sensuous long fingers. Her body temperature rose ten degrees. Their eyes danced with love.

The group thanked their generous hosts, and descended back down the mountain to the main road that led to the fortified village of Aït Ben Haddou, one of the most beautiful villages in Morocco. This was the kasbah that Nicole had most wanted to visit. Since it was a UNESCO World Heritage site, many tourist shops and local artists lined the road near the entrance. The site was on a small hill and was still inhabited by a few families. The others preferred to explore the local arts and crafts and view the kasbah from a distance. Meanwhile, Nicole and Mounir traversed a shallow river by donkey to get there. She sat in front of him on the same animal. He held her tight around the waist with one arm, and with the other he looked through his binoculars and spotted a stork's nest high up on top of one of the crenellated towers.

He gave Nicole the binoculars to look. 'Storks are good luck. Maybe it'll bring you a baby.'

She leaned backwards and kissed him on the cheek. As they hopped off the donkey, an eager local boy ran up and offered to give them a tour of the ancient village. '*The Jewel of the Nile* with Michael Douglas was filmed here,' he said proudly.

They walked down narrow streets. The young lad told them that the kasbah was one big village that contained many little villages, built out of the deep red earth found in the nearby mountains. At a distance, the fortified village blended harmoniously with the hills in the background. Mounir tipped the young boy, who bowed and said thank you many times. Nicole and Mounir went back to the river and waded knee deep through it, rather than ride again on the dusty donkey. They walked up the hill towards the parked car and looked back at Aït Ben Haddou and decided it was more spectacular seen from afar.

Along the way, they met some children who were clever and sweet. They asked in French for one dirham, one pen and one notebook. Money was always useful but the kids seemed to be in short supply of writing materials for school. King Mohammed VI, the son of the late Mohammed V, had vowed to turn his country from a sixty per cent illiteracy rate into ninety per cent literacy. As the group toured the remote villages of the Atlas Mountains, children appeared out of nowhere and demanded over and over: one dirham, a pen, or a notebook. This was a sign that the king's educational policy was beginning to work in areas far away from the more affluent modernized cities. Nicole and Mounir felt bad because they didn't have any school supplies with them. They shrugged their shoulders and said in unison, 'Sorry, no pens, no notebooks.' The children became distracted and asked some other tourists the same question.

The convoy of friends made one last trek for the day, this time on some treacherous roads through the mountains to experience the thrill of switchback rides. These steep trails terrified Nicole. The roads were blasted from the sheer earth-toned cliffs. One false move by John and they could slip off piste and dive a thousand metres into a gorge. Up and down the mountain were hairpin bends. The views were of ravines and vertiginous drops into the gorges. Nicole thought she was crazy to participate in these four-wheel-drive raids, as though life itself was not difficult enough. She looked over at Mounir who had put on his seatbelt. A flash streaked through Nicole's mind that this was Morocco's Grand Canyon.

Eventually, everyone took turns driving, according to ability. Sometimes it was necessary to cross shallow rivers at the base of the mountains, the easiest part of the route, and that was where John let Nicole drive. The riverbeds were called oueds. Each time they traversed the abundantly flowing streams, John yelled out in glee, 'Oued!' that sounded like 'wed' until the others caught on and participated with him in his game. John was a kid at heart and this brought out the playful child within Nicole, to her soul's delight. Mounir also enjoyed the childish game for it relieved him of any worries that he might have had stirring in his mind.

Most of the trails were only wide enough for one car. Occasionally, a truck would drive by with food to sell to the villagers who lived in these mountains. It was frightening when the truck driver came from the opposite direction. John always took control of the wheel when they met another car head on. He'd shift the gears of the SUV into reverse and backtrack along the path that they had just driven along, until he found a relatively safe place to park, so that the other vehicle could pass by. Nicole would look back at the other two Pajeros and, invariably, Stephen and Enrico were the designated drivers during these times of mini-crises. Every time this type of encounter occurred, Mounir helped John navigate while Nicole closed her eyes and prayed for their safe passage. Luckily, everything worked out fine each time.

On their route through the mountains, there was really only one part that was truly difficult. Only John and Stephen were skilled enough to manipulate the SUVs under a large boulder, with only a few centimetres between the roof and the underside of the boulder. The driver had to make a sharp turn under the boulder. The turn involved backing up because the jeep was too big to make it in one fell swoop. It was a bit like a city parking manoeuvre but the difference here was that if anyone of them didn't make it, the SUV would literally fly over the cliff and plunge into the depths of the rocky ravine.

Since John thought this turn in the road was so dangerous, he had the passengers jump out of the Pajeros and watch the feat of driving dexterity. John and Stephen manoeuvred the three SUVs through the tight hairpin bend sandwiched between huge boulders; Mounir, Enrico and Youssef helped them navigate from the path so that they didn't go too far forwards or backwards. Nicole felt helpless and watched in admiration. The men triumphed, though John teased Stephen because he scraped the black paint off one of the doors during the three-point-turn. Stephen laughed at John's competitiveness. Nadine, Isabella and Nicole clapped, and Isabella's three boys cheered and pumped their fists in the air. Nicole marvelled at the men's teamwork, at how they loved to solve problems and challenges and overcome nature. Afterwards, Youssef parked the cars while Nadine had everyone congregate at a man-made lookout point to observe the surrounding landscape.

Nicole said to Mounir, 'Apart from the colours, this looks like the surface of the moon.'

Mounir replied, 'We always wanted to go to the moon.'

As the others walked back to the parked cars, Mounir drew Nicole close to him and hugged her gently. Nicole's body tingled with warmth as she felt his growing erection.

* * *

After they returned to Villa Fiori, Mounir received a call and walked into the library for privacy. Nicole waited for him in front of the crackling fire burning in the adobe hearth. While in the library, Mounir spoke to his cousin Salim.

Salim said, 'I'm calling you from your mother's home in Damascus. Where are you? I've been trying to reach you all day. Your phone has been switched off.'

Mounir replied, 'I'm in Marrakech with Nicole and her brother. We were trekking through remote villages in the mountains. There probably was no network.'

Salim couldn't wait anymore, 'You've been given amnesty. The president himself issued a decree saying there is a pardon for Mr Samir Shami for a crime that he never committed. The sentence has been lifted. You're a free man and you can return to Syria with no fear.'

Mounir said, 'I can't wait to go home and see everyone.'

Salim responded, 'Talk to your mother. Meanwhile, I'll prepare my private jet to send to you to bring you home. All you will have to do is arrange for transportation to Casablanca tomorrow morning.'

Seconds later, Mounir heard his mother on the phone crying softly and speaking at the same time. She said, 'My dear, this is the day we've all been hoping for. My soul and body have been lifeless during all of these years. Finally, the light has come back into my eyes. The whole family has felt deep sorrow. Now, for the first time, we feel joy.'

Tears trickled down Mounir's face as his emotions started to overwhelm him. His mother heard him sniffling over the phone as he said, 'I can't wait to see you and hug you, Mama. I'm organizing my things to come home, immediately.' Then, the line disconnected.

After he spoke to his mother, he strolled out of the library and went back to sit next to Nicole in front of the fireplace. Their thighs touched and Nicole could feel Mounir's legs trembling. She looked into his eyes and saw a bright light shining from within. She leaned forward and kissed his moist, salty cheeks.

'Is everything alright?' she asked.

'I don't know where to start. I've been meaning to tell you since I first met you.' Mounir cleared his throat. 'Nine years ago, I was falsely accused of being involved with a failed coup d'état in Syria. The government wanted me dead or alive with a bounty on my head as a reward for capturing me. I should have already been dead twice but my guardian angels kept me alive.'

Nicole asked, 'Why would they accuse you?'

'I was considered a revolutionary in my student days because I believed in the values of freedom and democracy. These rights still aren't granted under the Syrian authoritarian, military-dominated regime,' replied Mounir.

'Why are you telling me this now?'

'That was my cousin, Salim. He just told me that the president himself pardoned me. I can now truly live my life as a free and safe man.'

Instinctively, Nicole held Mounir in her arms as a mother would comfort her child and caressed his soft hair with her fingers. Sensing her unconditional love, Mounir buried his head in Nicole's chest and wept tears of happiness.

At that moment, John walked into the salon, carrying the Arabic newspaper Al Hayat, and fixed himself a whisky on the rocks at the bar. It was around midnight. He noticed Nicole cradling Mounir like a baby and admired her motherly instinct. Mounir must have been already informed about his proclaimed innocence and had confided in Nicole. John walked over and greeted them. They hadn't noticed and jumped in a startled fashion.

John sat down next to them and showed them the front page of Al Hayat. Mounir looked at an old photo of him next to the leading story.

John translated the headline to Nicole, 'Samir Shami's Sentence Has Been Lifted.'

Mounir kissed Nicole on the lips before she could utter a word. John placed the newspaper on the coffee table in front of the fireplace and sipped his whisky.

Mounir lifted his head and said, 'Now, that the truth's out, call me Sami. Samir Shami is my real name.' He sighed out of relief.

John, who already knew Mounir's real name, nodded his head in agreement. Nicole, on the other hand, was confused and overwhelmed with all of this news.

She responded, 'But I met you as Mounir. It might take me a while to get used to calling you Sami.'

Mounir pleaded, 'Please call me Sami. That's what my family and friends called me at home before the death sentence.'

From now on, everyone addressed Mounir as Sami.

Sami changed the subject and said, 'My cousin, Salim, is sending a private plane to pick me up at Casablanca Airport. I just need transport from here to Casa and I noticed there's a helipad on the property.'

John knew what Sami was alluding to and said, 'I'll ask Hani to hire a helicopter for you. When do you need it?'

'Tomorrow morning,' replied Sami.

Nicole asked, 'Where are you going?'

Sami tenderly said, 'Ma chèrie, I'm going home to see my mother whom I haven't seen in years.'

'Where's home, darling?'

'Damascus,' replied Sami realizing Nicole didn't even know his true origins.

John stopped Nicole's interrogation of Sami with a question of his own, 'Can I help you in any other way?'

Sami looked into John's eyes and said, 'You're like a brother to me, always there when I need you the most.'

'Yeah, seems like it's my destiny.'

After a moment's reflection, Sami said, 'Please take care of your adorable sister while I'm gone.'

John stood up, kicked his heels together, saluted and said, 'Will do, Captain.'

He always knew how to make people lighten up and remember the playful side of life.

Sami put his arm around Nicole's shoulders and squeezed her tightly next to him.

'It's nice to see you two love birds smiling,' said John as he walked away.

That night Sami made love to Nicole like never before in front of the smouldering fireplace. Passion consumed their hearts. It was as close to paradise as one could get on Earth.

The next morning, Nicole couldn't hide her emotions from Sami and tears ran down her face. It was the first time she had openly cried in front of anyone, as her beloved kissed her and said, 'Until we meet again.'

The helicopter ascended into the sky. Sami cried inside his heart as he watched Nicole become smaller and smaller on the ground. He too never let anyone see his true emotional state but something new had happened to him in Marrakech. Nicole had opened up his heart to experience true love.

Sami thought, my home is in her heart and hers in mine. She sways with happiness on the antique swing from India as she resides in my heart.

As Nicole shook her head back and forth, and massaged her forehead, she asked, 'Why can't my life ever run smoothly? My head's spinning. Again, I feel deep pain in my heart.' She reminded herself to try and look on the bright side of life, and hummed one of her favourite tunes, 'Don't Worry, Be Happy!' that she had been introduced to by her mother, who always sang it at the family's country home in Sologne. Nicole spent the rest of the day relaxing by the pool with the ladies and the three active boys. The men wanted to chat and have tea at Hotel La Mamounia in Marrakech.

At the Villa Fiori in Ourika, Hani, the butler of the household received a visit from the police. The police had traced the rental of a helicopter to Mr John Townsend at this address. Hani told the authorities that it was for one of the guests and he was on his way to Casablanca. That's all he knew. The police asked for Mr Townsend. Hani told them that they would find him at La Mamounia. Thirty minutes later, the police found Mr Townsend having tea with two friends. They spoke to John in Arabic and told him that the helicopter he had rented that morning had been shot down from the ground. John choked on his tea. He stood up and told his friends he would meet them back at the villa and not to mention this encounter to anyone.

As the police escorted John out of the hotel, they told him that he was needed to identify the pilot and the passenger at the scene of the murder. John consented. He had no other choice. Once they arrived at the site, John told the police he couldn't confirm the pilot's identity but he could verify the passenger as Samir Shami. Sami's body had been badly burned but his face was still recognizable. John turned his head away and threw up. Minutes later, he cried out, 'What a cruel fate. Those thugs, damn them.' The police helped John back to the car. While one officer was filling out a report, the other told John how they had captured a man whom they believed to be the murderer. The man had confessed he was angry at Samir Shami's pardon and he had been tipped off by a Syrian agent who had had Mrs Shami's telephone tapped in Damascus. John put his head in his hands and wept. He thought, how am I going to tell Nicole? This will devastate her.

The police drove John back to Villa Fiori. Hani rushed out to help John to his room to freshen up, and then John recounted everything to Hani.

Hani said, 'He was such a kind man. What about Madame Nicole? She was so in love with him.'

'I know. Merde, I need a double whisky on the rocks,' said John.

'I'll bring one up, sir,' said Hani as he left John alone to recuperate from this tragic ordeal and for John to figure out how to break this horrific news to his beloved sister.

Hours later, around cocktail hour, John asked Nicole to meet him in the garden. Hani served John another double whisky and Nicole a flute of champagne. The others hadn't yet come down for drinks, for which John was grateful. He needed to have a few private moments with his sister. He started with small talk.

'You asked me the other day to tell you more about your boyfriend but I was too tired. You know most of Sami's story because he already told you but I want you to know that we met nine years ago when he fled Syria after being falsely accused of the failed coup d'état. He stayed with me when I was studying the tribe in Sierra Leone for my thesis. We became very close to one another, like brothers. Remember the mask I gave you? He was with me when the tribal member offered it to me. When it was safe for him to leave, I thought I'd never see him again. Who would have thought that you of all the people on this planet would have met and fallen in love with him?'

Nicole sipped her champagne and stated, 'That's why he said you saved his life and you're always there for him.'

John leaned forward and held Nicole's hands with compassion, and then said in a grave voice, 'Not this time.'

'What do you mean not this time?' asked Nicole.

John looked at the ground and said, 'I don't understand life. Just as Sami was proclaimed innocent, some thug . . .'

Suddenly, Nicole pulled her hands away from John and ran to sit under a palm tree in the garden. She sat Indian-style on the grass, her head in her hands, and screamed. She shook violently and tears flowed down like thundering waterfalls. John ran off to the kitchen and brought back a glass of water with some Valium. He told Nicole to take it to calm her down as he took one himself. He couldn't bear watching his sister being hurt again but he remained strong to help her through this tragic event.

After she swallowed the Valium, John escorted Nicole to her room to rest. She collapsed onto the sofa and buried her head into a pillow to shut out the world. Words seeped into her mind from Deep the astrologist, whom she had met at Kerala and Rajiv's dinner in Manhattan.

'. . . a man from the Middle East, can't stay in one place for very long, wrongly accused of something but justice will occur in his lifetime.'

His remarks had been uncannily accurate but mentioned nothing about death. Curled up in a foetal position, she cried herself into a long profound sleep that lasted until the following morning.

Damascus

The next morning John informed Nicole that they had been invited to attend Sami's funeral in Damascus. The pilot who was supposed to take Sami to Damascus from Casablanca had phoned Sami's cousin Salim and had told him of the devastating news. Salim called his aunt and she requested that the pilot invite Nicole and a friend or a loved one to come and mourn the death of Sami with the family. Sami's body would be aboard the same flight out of Marrakech to Damascus.

A few hours later, Youssef tooted the car horn. As John positioned himself in the front passenger seat, Nicole jumped in the back, rolled down her window and waved goodbye to the Murats, the Muranos and the same household staff that had greeted her upon her arrival.

On the way to the airport, Nicole's heart felt as if it was being squeezed by a boa constrictor. She was mystified about Mounir who was really Sami, a man proclaimed innocent and then brutally murdered. Love and the meaning of life eluded her. What was her purpose on Earth? To experience unconsummated love or love relationships that ended in tragic deaths, both by gunfire? If karma and reincarnation existed, what had she done in past lives to deserve this? Or was it all about learning and practising compassion, unconditional love and forgiveness, as stated in the tenets of Buddhism? Perhaps it was all the above and more that she couldn't quite yet fathom in her foggy mind. Once aboard the private aircraft, she slept from emotional exhaustion all the way from Marrakech to Damascus.

Upon arrival, Sami's body was transported to the hospital, and Nicole and John were escorted by Mrs Shami's private chauffeur to the Sheraton Hotel that was located near her home on Abu Roummaneh Street. The chauffeur told them in Arabic that he would pick them up around eleven in the morning and bring them to the hospital. Nicole and John walked a little around the hotel for fresh air, noticed how many policemen patrolled the streets and then returned to the hotel to eat a light dinner before retiring to their rooms to try and get some sleep.

The next morning at the hospital, in preparation for the burial, the family washed Sami's body with clean scented water and wrapped his body with sheets of clean white cloth. Although Sami was killed as a martyr, since his body was badly burned, the family decided to follow this procedure rather than bury him in the clothes he died in. Mrs Shami, Sami's brother, Naji, and his two sisters took one last look before covering his face. All of them prayed and wept quietly. When they were ready, Sami was placed in the coffin and the coffin was closed. The extended family and friends gathered at the hospital around eleven in the morning as scheduled. Naji, Salim and Sami's closest friends carried the coffin to Omayad Mosque for the midday prayers.

Nicole noted hundreds of people mourning on the streets, following the procession towards the mosque. Hundreds were at the mosque and prayed silently while the imam prayed in front of the deceased, facing away from the crowd. No one bowed or prostrated themselves, everyone stood in prayer.

After the funeral prayers, the family took him in a hearse to the cemetery. Again, hundreds of cars followed the hearse. Nicole realized that Sami must have been an important person. Salim volunteered to be in the same car as Nicole and John because he knew of Sami's love for Nicole. En route, Salim told them that all these people were Sami's friends and members of the underground party for freedom and justice that he had founded before going off to study in the States.

At the cemetery, in a break with the traditional Islamic burial procedure, both men and women accompanied the coffin to the gravesite. The sheikh said a prayer while the coffin was lowered into the ground, facing Mecca. Sami's family, extended family, Nicole and John, friends and party members placed carnations and lilies on the grave. Afterwards, they were all invited to Mrs Shami's home for a buffet luncheon. No one talked very much because everyone was very emotional. Nicole observed that the Sheikh of Dubai and Princess Jamilah were there, together with some of the other people from the New York symposium. There were other notable figures from the Middle East, including artists and poets. They all conversed with one another, and paid their condolences, not only to Mrs Shami, but also to Nicole.

Meanwhile, Salim introduced John to Mikis and Captain Theo from Greece and they told him of how they had protected Sami from the assassins while sailing through the Greek Isles. Recognizing Mikis, Sofia Capucilli walked over to them and reintroduced herself as an old classmate of Sami's during their high school days in Beirut. Looking at John, Sofia added that she was a recent divorcee, twirling her r's with emphasis. John's heart fluttered as he succumbed to her voluptuous beauty and her sexy voice.

Finally, there was a moment when Nicole was able to offer her condolences to Mrs Shami.

Mrs Shami replied in French, 'I understood you were very close friends and he loved you. Who knows? We might all meet again in heaven.'

Tears welled up in Nicole's eyes as she hugged Mrs Shami. Eyeing all the people who still wanted to give their condolences, Nicole let go and allowed Mrs Shami to continue receiving the visitors.

As Nicole found herself alone amidst the masses of people, Salim came to her rescue and offered her a plate filled with lamb and rice. She accepted his kind gesture graciously and ate the food for physical strength. John joined them and told her about Sami's adventure in

Greece while on the run. Nicole's eyes bulged out of her head listening to this incredible story. John and Salim chuckled at her reaction.

In a more serious tone, Salim said, 'We all lost a great friend. And he is a loss to the nation. He left behind a legacy. He was a fighter for freedom and justice in a peaceful way. His call to arms was through the power of the pen. We need more enlightened people like him in the region. He'll be missed. People will remember him.'

Nicole's appetite faltered and she put her dish on a nearby table. She thanked Salim for his hospitality and walked away with John towards Mrs Shami. They gave their respects one more time, and also to Naji and Sami's two sisters, who all asked Nicole to stay in touch. She agreed and thought Sami had a very loving family. Mrs Shami's chauffeur brought them back to the hotel.

The next day, Nicole and John flew back to Paris. During the flight, John confided in Nicole about his newfound love who was a former classmate of Sami's.

Nicole said, 'Do you remember the film *Four Weddings and a Funeral?*'

John replied, 'Stop the joking. I think she's the one.'

'Is she an actress?' asked Nicole.

'No, but she looks like a blonde Sophia Loren,' he said, with a smile on his face.

Nicole smiled. 'I hope this time you've found your soulmate.' She paused, 'I appreciate your being with me in Damascus. I couldn't have done it without you.'

'Like I tell all my friends, you're my favourite sister.'

Nicole laughed, 'Yeah, I'm your only one.'

At Charles de Gaulle Airport, they hugged each other goodbye. John stayed in Paris and Nicole took a connecting flight, direct to New York. She mourned the death of Sami as if she were his widow and decided to create a scholarship in his name at New York University to help young men and women in his region through education.

Chapter 11
Mystical Encounter

New York, August 2001

Throughout many lonely months in Manhattan, Nicole couldn't get rid of that feeling that Sami's spirit was alive. She had a vision that he galloped on a black stallion in the depths of the Arabian Desert and his soul beckoned to her across the vast Mediterranean Sea and immense Atlantic Ocean. At night, he visited her in her dreams. Romantically, he would wrap his arms around her, pull her closer to him and kiss her neck, cheeks and lips. He felt alive under her skin. Sami's death had broken her heart.

After drowning in despair and feeling sorry for herself, Nicole volunteered her bilingual skills at St Jude's Research Hospital for children in Memphis, Tennessee. St Jude's had patients coming in from all over the world. Since some of the foreigners weren't fluent in English, the hospital depended on staff and volunteers to translate documents and information from the doctors to the patient's family. For over a year, she commuted back and forth, and worked out of a virtual office in her home in New York. Back in New York, on a hot, sticky, humid day in August, the phone rang. It was Celeste. She asked Nicole if she'd like to go to Sedona.

Nicole replied with a question, 'Is Sedona the Red Rock Country in Arizona you see photographed all the time?'

'Yes. I thought Sedona would be good for you because it is a spiritual power centre due to its vortex energy. I've been going once a year since you know what.'

'You never told me. Forgive me for my ignorance but what's a vortex?'

'I'm not really sure except that it's a place of increased energy. When you go there, whatever issues are going on in your life become amplified. You tune into the beautiful and healthy surroundings of the canyons and ask for your prayers to be answered. Many people return home positively uplifted and find solutions to problems they might have been having with their relationships, career or health.'

'That sounds too good to be true,' said Nicole with scepticism.

'It doesn't matter if you believe or not. Do you want to go?'

'I do and I'm ready for positive changes to occur in my life. You're my angel.'

'I'll meet you in Sedona since I'll be flying from Geneva via Los Angeles. I'll email you all the details.'

'OK. See you soon,' said Nicole.

Sedona was a spiritual place filled with positive energy and Celeste had asked her to stay there a while for physical, mental and spiritual rejuvenation. There was no doubt she needed it. She'd call St Jude's and tell them she'd be taking a month's leave of absence for her own wellbeing. The staff would understand. Nicole realized that her life worked in curious ways as long as she remained patient.

En Route to Sedona

As she stepped outside the terminal at Phoenix Airport, the heat hit her like a ton of bricks. Shortly afterwards, a chauffeur-driven car picked her up and she was grateful for the air conditioning. Celeste was to arrive later and rent a Land Rover for their stay in Sedona. The two women were scheduled to meet at the ranch. The ranch owner was a friend of Celeste and Eduoard, who had said they could have it for the month of August and the beginning of September, since he preferred to stay at his summer residence on the Amalfi coast of Italy at this time of the year. Nicole thought he was smart to leave Arizona during the hottest month of the year and enjoy the cool sea breezes off the Mediterranean. Suddenly a guilty thought flickered through her brain: perhaps she should have gone back to see her parents and John – but she reasoned she could see them in September, one of her favourite times of the year in Paris.

While riding in the back seat of the black sedan, Gary the chauffeur, talked non-stop and entertained Nicole. He claimed to have been abducted by a UFO during the Seventies when he was camping with a buddy in the southern Arizona desert near the Mexican border. 'There were these flying saucers hovering above us. And then our bodies were bathed in blue light as if we were being scanned. Seconds later, we were mysteriously transported into the alien ship and given medical examinations. We communicated through mental telepathy at lightning fast speeds. The extraterrestrials told us about the upcoming Aids epidemic, the threat of bioterrorism and other catastrophes that would occur in the future.'

Nicole asked incredulously, 'This happened in the Seventies?'

'Yeah!'

'But why would they tell you these things if you couldn't do anything about it or you wouldn't go public with the information? It doesn't make sense. We're in the year 2001. Everything you've said has already happened,' she said, thinking that he had fabricated this fantastic story.

'I'm sure they implanted a chip into my body.'

'Have you ever taken an MRI? Surely that would find a chip in your body. Or if you've flown recently, maybe the chip would have set off the security alarm at the checkpoints.'

She didn't mean to be rude, the words just came out that way. Gary stopped talking about UFOs.

Nicole believed in the existence of extraterrestrials and UFOs, but she wasn't sure about people being abducted by aliens, although anything was possible. Rather, she had the utopian idea that beings from other planets were peaceful and friendly towards the Earth, not enemies as depicted by Hollywood. There was also that famous scandal of the US Government's shocking UFO cover-up at Roswell, New Mexico, in 1947. Apparently, former Pentagon officials and retired Air Force and

Army personnel had concurred that the government keep this information classified, so as to not cause worldwide panic about a supposed alien invasion.

Nicole thought, who are we to think that we're the only ones who exist in this boundless universe?

Gary chipped in with one last piece of information, 'Sedona is full of hippies, artists and new-agers.'

Red Rock Country

Entry into Sedona at sunset was magnificent. The Red Rock Country was aglow from the fiery bright yellow sun setting in a cloudless blue sky. The colour of the red rocks deepened at dusk. Gary and Nicole arrived at the ranch; Nicole wished Gary well and gave him a nice tip. The woman who took care of the house while the owner was away greeted Nicole and introduced herself as Rebecca. They chatted on the porch, which faced the magnificent red rock formations. The view was of Courthouse Butte, Bell Rock and Cathedral Rock. Cathedral Rock didn't look like a cathedral, but Rebecca pointed out that they were looking at the back view and suggested that she and Celeste go to Oak Creek on the other side to see the real shape.

Celeste arrived about an hour later. She agreed that the rock didn't look like a cathedral. Where were the gothic spires? The gargoyles? The two women laughed and caught up with each other's stories over a light dinner on the patio under the stars. Dining outdoors was pleasant. A crescent-shaped moon appeared and the planet Venus came forth. The stellar formations were fabulous to look at; one could even see the Milky Way. It was a stargazer's paradise.

While Nicole sipped some of her favourite chardonnay, she wished upon the first star that she saw, as she had always done. It was a silly but comforting ritual she liked to perform. This time her wish was for Sami's soul to rest in peace. Instantly, she mysteriously felt Sami's presence. He held her tightly from behind, his arms looped around her waist. She looked behind her but saw no one. Maybe a bug brushed against her back to make her feel a tingling sensation or perhaps it was her bountiful imagination. Celeste was tired after her flight and they both went to bed early.

Mystical Encounter

At breakfast, they decided to hike through Boynton Canyon with a hired guide since they didn't know the territory. Celeste said that Boynton Canyon was in the middle of a vortex and a good place to start their journey.

They drove there and parked on the side of a dusty road at the foot of crimson cliffs. Their guide was from Ireland of all places, and named Kelly. She informed the two women that this was the longest hiking trail to be found within a vortex site. Each leg of the trek was about an hour and a half and approximately two and a half miles each way. Nicole and Celeste were eager to discover the energies of this vortex.

First, Kelly said, 'We have to ask the canyon if it would like our presence here today.'

The three women stood and silently asked Boynton Canyon if they could walk on its trails. An incredible wind came from the east and the answer was a resounding yes. Go forth and feel the energy. The women started hiking along thirty minutes of sandy trail. To the right they could see the Kachina Woman, a tall, red rock spire with what looked like a hat, or possibly more like the hairdo that Native American brides styled for themselves. As part of their marriage custom, the hair was spun on both sides of the head. Celeste amusingly described it as looking like Mickey Mouse ears; Nicole with her erotic mind thought the red rock spire looked more like Sami's sexy organ. She kept these sensual thoughts to herself.

To the relief of both Nicole and Celeste, after walking the sandy trail under intense sun and heat, a shady trail commenced. Twisted juniper trees, pine trees and redwoods lined the trodden path. Lizards and geckos scurried along the ground. Hummingbirds gathered nectar from the flowers – this was Nicole's favourite bird, along with the eagle. Celeste noticed the hummingbirds first and pointed them out to Nicole and Kelly. Kelly, an animal totem expert, described the symbolic meaning of all the creatures they encountered. Lizards and geckos represented a good omen and helped one to be more optimistic and adaptable.

She added, 'The Father Sun is shining warmly upon you two.'

The two women considered it a kind comment but didn't understand the message.

Kelly went on to talk about the meaning of hummingbirds. 'In general, birds are considered messengers, but the hummingbird teaches clear sight, grace, healing, the drawing out of the old and the drawing together of the pieces of your life so that it makes sense. Maybe this is something you both need to learn since we're seeing so many hummingbirds.'

The three continued hiking, Kelly repeatedly reminding them to drink lots of water. Celeste picked up her pace and led the way, while the other two lagged behind and chatted with one another.

Nicole told Kelly how she had seen a golden eagle and kept seeing red-tailed hawks since her arrival in the Southwest.

With great interest, Kelly reflected, 'You're probably meant to become a messenger of some sort to the world.'

'What's the meaning of a golden eagle? It's the most regal winged bird I've ever seen. Early this morning I saw him flying majestically through the valley. I ran to get my binoculars and he disappeared as suddenly as he appeared. The wing span must have been ten or twelve feet.'

Kelly said, 'The Native Americans are inspired by the golden eagle. Eagles represent clarity, vision, greatness, inspiration, healing and new beginnings. They are considered spiritual messengers. It's the eagle that flies the highest and sees the most clearly.'

'And red-tailed hawks?'

'The red-tailed hawk is also very special for the Native American. They're magnificent flyers and engage in exotic mating dances in the air. Hawks teach us insight, truth, adaptability, optimism, openness and foresight. This bird can lead you to your life purpose. It's also a messenger bird. Pay attention when the red-tailed hawk shows up; it means a message is coming.'

In the future, Nicole thought, she'd try to learn and understand the symbolism of these wild animals and birds. The girls walked on in silence up to the end of the trail. The last part was the hardest because they had to climb up rocks. Once at the top the view of Boynton Canyon was spectacular. It was worth the hike. A bit further up beyond the end of the trail, a natural cave formed under some trees. Kelly offered to do psychic readings; it was part of the guided tour. While Nicole looked at the trees, flowers and rock formations, Kelly gave Celeste a private ten-minute reading up in the cave. After the tragic events that occurred in her life and the insights gained from both K and Deep, Nicole decided she would rather be surprised and treat her life more like a mystery to be solved. Circumstances had forced her to live day by day and to stay focused on the present moment. Admittedly, she would never stop dreaming. Dreaming gave her hope and helped her cope with her life on Earth.

Celeste and Kelly came down from the cave, and called out for Nicole. She stood up and walked over to the wooden sign marking the end of the trail. She found the girls chatting. Celeste confided in Nicole about most things but not this time. Nicole respected this uncommunicative gesture; whatever was said it must have been highly personal. After a little break munching salty nuts and drinking more water, they retraced their steps to the beginning of the trail, at a much faster pace since most of it was downhill. At the end, Kelly asked Nicole and Celeste to pay tribute and give thanks to Boynton Canyon for allowing them to walk in this healthy and beautiful environment. They replied that though they didn't feel any special energy they were happy with the hike, and gave their blessings of gratitude.

Kelly said, 'You'll feel the effects of the subtle vortex energy later. This vortex balances your yin and yang, or your masculine and feminine sides. It should help make your relationships work better.'

'In what way?' asked Celeste.

Kelly answered, 'Intimacy, commitment, honesty, openness and trust.'

Nicole asked, 'What about a loved one who has had his life tragically taken away, but you still feel in your heart that his spirit is alive, and he's with you at all times?'

'Whoa! I'm not sure. Maybe your prayers have helped strengthen your relationship on the spiritual level, and you feel connected to him through the heart,' Kelly replied in a thoughtful and caring manner.

Nicole rarely divulged her innermost thoughts to the outside world and managed to keep a smile on her face. Celeste, who knew Nicole too well, gave her a big hug. Slowly, Kelly walked away and Nicole and Celeste followed.

After the successful completion of their hike through the vortex, Nicole invited Celeste and Kelly for a drink on the terrace at Enchantment Resort which was located right in the middle of Boynton Canyon. Nicole ordered a banana and strawberry fruit smoothie; Kelly, a freshly squeezed lemonade, and Celeste, the more adventurous of the three, ordered a prickly pear margarita, the signature drink of the resort. Prickly pear was a red fruit found on cacti in the Southwest. The beverage was a hot pink colour served in a navy blue fluted glass and tasted delicious. Nicole and Kelly wished they had ordered it too.

Celeste was interested in learning more about Sedona's history and Native American traditions and asked Kelly to share her knowledge.

Kelly recommended, 'If you have time, drive up Schnebly Trail. There's a panoramic view from the top; in the past, it was used for transporting goods to Flagstaff.'

Nicole interjected, 'I read something about the Schnebly family. Their home was at the end of the trail and used as an inn for travellers. Mr Schnebly saw the need for a post office – but the town had no name.'

'That's right and he named the little town Sedona, after his wife,' said Kelly.

'Oh! How interesting! Sedona was named after a woman,' said Celeste.

Kelly suggested other vortex sites to visit and things to do: watch the spectacular sunset at the Airport Mesa; climb up Bell Rock and meditate; go to Cathedral Rock, the most photographed of all the Red Rocks. Nicole and Celeste were pleased with their tour and Kelly's insights and wished her the best.

During the next few days, the two hiked around the vortex sites, explored the region and felt good, positive energy. They combined their physical exercise with relaxation at the pool and spa. This experience rejuvenated both of them. One of the places the girls visited was the Chapel of the Holy Cross that was built to blend into the austere and serene sandstone cliffs. The heiress and sculptor Marguerite Brunswig Staude built this chapel in 1956 to be open to all, regardless of creed. Two red rock pillars to the right of the church, known as the Twin Nuns, inspired her to use this location. Marguerite thought that the red rock sculpted formation behind the Nuns looked like Mary holding the baby Jesus. That confirmed her belief that this was the right site, and she dedicated her chapel to her parents.

Nicole and Celeste lit a candle inside the chapel for their loved ones and prayed for those who had passed on to the other side. Spiritual peace emanated from this holy sanctuary. Celeste continued to pray, as Nicole walked to the end of the chapel behind the altar and looked through massive glass windows at the panoramic view of Red Rock Country. Walking back past Celeste, Nicole noticed tears rolling down her cheeks and thought maybe Celeste was going through the process of forgiving her former husband, Arnauld, and finally letting him go. Back outside, Nicole expanded her lungs and breathed in the fresh air. She liked the spiritual vibration of this place, and deeply inhaled the surrounding natural beauty until Celeste was finally ready to leave the sacred grounds.

Flight to the Grand Canyon

The next morning, Nicole had planned a tour to visit the Grand Canyon by plane, helicopter and boat, all in one day. Celeste wanted to be back home for when her children began the new school year. She had already been to the Grand Canyon, so she decided to leave for Geneva on the day that Nicole was to make her trip.

There were five people on Nicole's tour, plus the pilot. They boarded a Cessna at Sedona Airport. Nicole marvelled at the view of Red Rock Country from the aircraft. In the distance, the pilot pointed out a former mining town, Jerome, that later became a ghost town. Today, hippies and artists lived there. Indian reservations could be seen, as well as the once-secret places where outlaws used to hide. The pilot said that this was still a young and rustic state and had only been incorporated into the United States in 1908. After about forty minutes, the plane approached the South Rim of the Grand Canyon, which was on a lower level plate than the North Rim. The group's final destination would be the West Rim. The Havasupai Indians inhabited this region and lived at the bottom of the canyon near the Colorado river. The flight was smooth and the landing successful. The favourable weather conditions, the pilot's entertaining information and the view of the Grand Canyon distracted Nicole to the point that for once she actually enjoyed her trip in the small plane.

Once at the tiny airport, a guide escorted everyone to the helipad. The helicopter was named Sundance and was piloted by a handsome young man. The thrill ride commenced. The lady next to Nicole shook with fear and held onto her son as they flew through the narrow ravines of the West Rim to reach a landing spot near the Colorado river. Nicole felt as though she was in a video game as the helicopter turned left and right and on its side to manoeuvre around the canyon walls. One nick of the propeller on the rocks could send the flying machine into a tailspin; or if the engine stopped running, everyone aboard could plunge a mile to their death. The ride took three minutes. Short, terrifying and thrilling, all at once.

A Havasupai Indian man greeted them and they hopped onto a platoon boat to raft down the gentle part of the Colorado river. The Native American guide pointed out the various species of plants near the river's edge, a beavers' dam and the red-tailed hawks and ravens. What looked like a massive black kite flying towards them turned out to be a black vulture. It disappeared as suddenly as it had appeared, just like the golden eagle Nicole had seen days ago. In the Southwest, black vultures looked more like eagles but with a shorter wingspan, not at all like the hideous ones found in Africa. The ravens played in the air, almost as if they were putting on an acrobatic show for the tourists. This was the first time Nicole had seen the playful side of birds in the air. They stopped in a remote area to have a barbecue lunch prepared by the Havasupai Indians.

Nicole toyed with her barbecue chicken and corn on the cob. She wasn't hungry. She excused herself and walked along a dirt trail. Two white butterflies caught her attention and seemed to lead her to a flat rock overlooking a waterfall that flowed gently into the icy cold Colorado river.

She thought silently to herself, what's the meaning of a butterfly? Metamorphosis, life and hope. They spread joy wherever they float and flutter in the wind.

On the rock, she meditated, prayed for her loved ones and focused on peace and love. In her mind, she saw an array of vibrant colours – violet, pink, blue, yellow and orange. The rainbow of colours changed into a white wavy pattern. Her spirit soared over the Grand Canyon with a golden eagle. Wisdom whispered to her that each moment is a new beginning. Freedom of flight gripped her soul. Her body felt as light as a feather. She achieved an inner state of harmony with nature.

When she opened her eyes, she looked at her watch. It was exactly twenty-two minutes later. She stood up, stretched her muscles and decided to walk down an overgrown path to the river. The bushes scratched her legs but her inner voice told her to continue and not be afraid. High in the sky she heard the screech of an eagle. She followed the eagle with her eyes across the calm river, not a ripple to be seen.

Nicole rubbed her eyes, blinked twice and screamed, 'Sami, Sami is that you?'

Her echo reverberated back.

She yelled once again, hoping it wasn't a mirage, 'Sami, Sami.' His name echoed in the canyon.

Mystical Encounter

'Nicole, Nicole, I love you, I love you, I love you,' trailed an echo.

Sami disappeared. Nicole's heart stopped. She knelt by the river and wept.

Another eagle soared above her and let out a cry.

Sami reappeared and cried out from his heart, 'Hold onto your dreams, dreams, dreams . . .' and disappeared once again.

Her tears turned into laughter. She remembered how he loved to tease her. But was this a dream or a vision, or was he really over there?

Nicole's heart softly spoke to her and revealed a clue: 'The eagle is the answer.'

She was awakened by the echo of her laughter in the canyon and it touched a chord in her soul.

A Havasupai Indian guide found her by the river weeping and laughing. He thought the Great Spirit must have brought her a message. He tapped her on the shoulder and indicated it was time to leave. The platoon boat brought them back to the helipad. Nicole's group stepped into the Sundance helicopter and ascended the mile-high canyon wall within a brief ten minutes.

The pilot commented, 'If you look to your left, you'll see two bald eagles flying side by side.' A golden light streaked past the eagles, and then they flew out of sight.

Waiting at the airport was a big white school bus driven by a friendly Havasupai Indian woman. She drove them to Eagle Rock, which was an eagle sculpted by nature into the canyon cliffs. The eagle stood proud with its wings outstretched. Each wing must have been hundreds of feet long.

Eagles, eagles everywhere pondered Nicole.

The sun was bright and lit up the sandy colour of the canyon. Down below, the Colorado river glimmered a jade green. The Grand Canyon was immense, no surprise since it was considered one of the natural wonders of the world. There was no noise. Peace reigned. Spontaneously, Nicole laughed out loud and heard again the echo of her laughter. This time her companions followed suit but hollered out 'hello'.

'Hello, Hello, Hello, Hello, Hello,' the Grand Canyon replied.

Their playfulness delighted the Havasupai Indian guide.

It was mid-afternoon and the heat was intense. The tour was over and they took off for Sedona. The cabin of the Cessna had no air conditioning and the pilot tried to cool the plane down by climbing slightly higher in the sunny blue sky. The rising heat from the canyon was causing moderate turbulence. Nicole was nervous not only about the plane bouncing up and down but also about the difficulty of breathing in oxygen at 8500 feet. Nicole remembered John telling her that these planes shouldn't go higher than 8000 feet, which was the standard for the average person to be able to fly comfortably without an oxygen mask. She was the only one in the cabin who suffered. The heat, low oxygen levels and her low blood pressure almost made her pass out. Her head bobbed weakly against the window pane. When the Cessna finally landed, she could barely walk. Her arms tingled, her legs wobbled and she had a headache. While the pilot talked to the other passengers and said goodbye, Nicole went off by herself to sit on a couch until she felt better. At least she had survived the incident.

Luckily for Nicole, the chauffeur arrived an hour late, which gave her enough time to recuperate from the flight. Before going back to New York, she hooked up with a friend from Phoenix. They hadn't seen each other since the end of their schooldays, about ten years ago. Her friend, Myrna Khoury, was of Lebanese origin. She had grown up in Paris with Nicole and then married an American, who brought her first to San Francisco and then, after the big earthquake, to tranquil Phoenix.

Nicole met Myrna at the bar at the Hermosa Inn. With bubbly champagne, they raised their fluted glasses and toasted one another, 'Long live friendship!'

It was good to catch up with each other's news. Myrna spoke enthusiastically about her six-month-old baby girl who had completely changed her life and of her recent trip to Lebanon to meet some relatives for the first time since it was safe to travel there again. Both the French and American consulates issued statements declaring that the travel warnings for its citizens to visit Lebanon had been lifted. She described how certain sections of Beirut had been completely destroyed by the civil war and left that way, while other parts of the city had been beautifully rebuilt. Nicole recounted the past few years of her life to Myrna. They chatted for hours and finally hugged each other goodbye.

Nicole didn't want to go back to New York the next day but nothing more kept her in Arizona. During the flight she admitted she was confused about life and love but these past few days of hiking and meditating around Red Rock Country, renowned for its positive spiritual energy, had renewed her inner strength to move forward in life.

She decided she'd start a new life back in Paris where her family and dearest friends lived. She'd collect a few things in New York and then return to her home city. The foundation of her life had already been laid down in that city of lights. Nicole realized that she had endured a painful cycle in her life and was now ready to deepen her roots in Europe and blossom into a new person.

New York

She arrived at home a little before midnight. Tomorrow, she'd arrange her business and domestic affairs, and call a few friends to have them over for a farewell dinner party before going back to Paris. The following morning, Nicole overslept, stretched, got up and wandered into the living room to watch *The Today Show*. She was sipping her piping-hot coffee when all of a sudden breaking news interrupted the show. It was 8.45 am. A camera zoomed in on a smoking tower at the World Trade Center. Nicole thought it must have been a little plane that had lost its way and crashed into the tower by accident. Eighteen minutes later, the second tower was up in flames and she received a phone call from Celeste.

'Are you all right? Did you see what happened?' asked Celeste nervously.

'I'm OK. I can see the clouds of smoke from my apartment.' The line went down.

Nicole received calls all day long from her parents, John, family members and friends when they were able to get through, whether on the land line or the cell phone.

'Hello, Hello?' answered Nicole to a static line.

'Are you all right? Can you hear me?' echoed a worried male voice through what sounded like a metal tunnel.

'Hello, Hello,' repeated Nicole. The line went dead.

This sequence of telephone calls continued over the next few days and, invariably, the line became disconnected. No one could leave Manhattan. During the weeks that followed, Nicole volunteered her services to the American Red Cross Disaster Relief in New York City as well as helped distribute rubber boots, which were in high demand, to all those men and women working on site trying to find survivors, and then the remains of those who perished from this terrorist act. Terrorism rose up once again in Nicole's life, this time on a global level rather than a personal one. Although she tried to help out in the best ways that she could, her emotions began to overwhelm her.

Scared and confused, she called Kerala who told her to call Deep. Nicole didn't want to consult an astrologer to figure out the answers to her concerns about life, yet when she spoke to him he did point her in the right direction.

Epilogue
Past-Life Regression

In a plush Fifth Avenue psychiatrist's office, Nicole underwent a past-life regression while remaining semi-conscious. The psychiatrist was world-renowned for her research and therapy and, through Deep, Nicole had been able to secure an appointment rather quickly. After the deaths of Marc-Antoine and Sami, and her fear of flying small aircraft exacerbated by the terrorism of 9/11, she thought the only recourse for understanding her life would be through her past lives. At this point in her life, she became a firm believer in the theory of karma and reincarnation. It gave her a sense of security and support.

The psychiatrist, Barbara, had Nicole lie down on a comfortable brown leather sofa and told her to take her shoes off. Before the session started, Nicole told Barbara that she wanted to know what kind of relationships she had had with her late husband, Marc-Antoine, her beloved Sami and her brother John, as well as why she became so nervous flying in small planes. Moments later, Barbara hypnotized Nicole and guided her in a semi-conscious sleep state to a beautiful garden filled with blooming flowers. Nicole sat on a wooden bench smelling the sweet aroma and listening to the bees gathering nectar. The psychiatrist asked that only goodness and love surround Nicole during her journey through time, whether in the past or present. The session would be recorded, even though Nicole would be able to remember everything. Three chimes would signal the end of the past-life regression and would prompt Nicole to return to full consciousness.

First, Barbara prodded Nicole to go to a lifetime with her brother John and to describe the scenes. It would be as though she were directing her own film, seeing images and actions. Nicole looked down and saw pointy metallic shoes. She wore a metallic suit of armour.

Nicole said, 'I have two brothers. We fought to keep each other alive. We were soldiers in Joan of Arc's army that fought for the liberation of France from English dominance.'

'Do you know who your two brothers might be in that lifetime?'

Nicole replied, 'It feels like John and Sami.'

The psychiatrist guided the process and asked Nicole to go to another lifetime. Speaking aloud, Nicole viewed herself as an aristocrat in eighteenth-century France. She was a young woman and had two younger brothers. Behind the scenes, the three of them were involved in overthrowing the regime. They supported the Revolution through espionage and money.

Nicole reflected, 'It's odd, I'm an aristocrat but I want to replace the monarchy with the masses as the dominant political force. Apparently, I had a few enemies.'

Barbara told Nicole to continue looking at the vivid images.

Nicole continued, 'I'm wearing a beautiful, creamy silk gown. There's a dinner party at my father's home. It's a castle outside Paris. I'm talking to my father on black and white tiles in the courtyard when suddenly I fall into his arms. He's holding me and weeping. I've just been assassinated by a traitor.'

'Who is your father?' Barbara asked.

Nicole said, 'It's Marc-Antoine.'

Barbara continued the past-life regression and asked Nicole to leave that life and go on to another one. Nicole smiled and saw many students at some sporting event along a river.

'I'm sitting and singing songs with my boyfriend. He proposes with a three-stone emerald ring. We're both giddy with happiness. He drives me home to announce the news to my parents.'

Barbara interrupted, 'Who is your fiancé?'

PAST-LIFE REGRESSION

'It's Sami but he has some other name that begins with an A. He seems to be from a foreign land. I see protests, violence in his country. He's fighting for justice and freedom.'

Barbara remarked, 'There's an underlying theme of revolutionary spirits and martyrdom running throughout these lifetimes that connect you to John, Marc-Antoine and Sami. All of the past-life experiences that you've mentioned have been connected to turning points in history.'

Nicole continued, 'When we arrive home, my father shows us a photo on the front page of the newspaper. I'm with my boyfriend, carrying an anti-apartheid banner at a student rally. Although my mother and father were happy with the engagement news, we had to promise to never again engage in radical demonstrations.'

'Was it a happy lifetime for you two as lovers?'

Nicole beamed a smile. 'Very happy.'

The psychiatrist asked to see one more lifetime.

Nicole said, 'I'm with my soulmate. We're in a desert. The heat from the sun is so intense it feels like we're melting. We seek refuge in a cool dark cave. At first we're groping around in the darkness, until we see each other's ring of fire. We seemed to have been transformed into two separate translucent, swirling white balls of energy. Next, we reconnect through our voices. Suddenly, an angel appears. He's funny and calls himself Michel and tells us he's our guide. We're to be reborn with some mission to fulfil. We don't understand.'

Before terminating the session, the psychiatrist asked Nicole to go to any other lifetime that might be pertinent for her today.

Nicole regressed and said, 'I see a monk sitting Indian style. He's meditating and surrounded by a bright white light. He's wearing brown clothes.'

The psychiatrist guided Nicole back to the beautiful garden and told her to wait there until she heard three chimes. The bells chimed thrice. Slowly, Nicole opened her eyes and felt beads of perspiration bubbling up on her forehead. Barbara told her to rest for a few more minutes until she reoriented herself back to the physical surroundings of the room. To further soothe and relax her client, she placed a lavender-scented cold wash cloth on Nicole's forehead.

Barbara said, 'You can have the cassette to listen to at a later date to understand more how these past lives relate to your present life. Did this session help?'

Nicole sighed, 'I believe so but it has stirred so many emotions within me.'

'What do you think is the underlying meaning of this session?' Barbara asked.

Nicole said, 'It seems that my relationships with men in this life are karmic. The Indian wisdom says that karma and reincarnation is a never-ending process until we attain Enlightenment.'

'Is there any other insight that you might have gained from your regression?'

Nicole reflected, 'I think it's not meant for me to fight for a cause in this lifetime, although it was Sami's and he fulfilled his mission. Also, after my experience in the Grand Canyon, I know now that his soul occupies a place in my heart. My heart sees the truth like the golden eagle that hovers over the Earth looking down, knowing the secrets of the universe, trying to relate it to mankind.

'On a more philosophical note, considering the past events in my life, along with 9/11, the relevant question should be how to keep an inner spirituality alive while changing constantly in order to adapt to life.'

At the end of the session, Barbara escorted Nicole to the door. Nicole walked home through Central Park to breathe in the fresh air and absorb what had happened to her during this past-life regression. A red-tailed hawk flew over her head and screeched. 'The heart sees the truth' resonated over and over in her mind. Her spiritual quest for Enlightenment had only just begun.